The Ex List

×××

GRACE PEARCE

For my best friend: you are the glue,
so halfway across the country means nothing.

1

Sunday

I AM THE serial dater.

At least, that's what my best friend Sage, the serial loner, and my other best friend Evelyn, the serial monogamist, tell me.

Supposedly, having six boyfriends in two years earns you this nickname. One roughly every four months. Back to back to back… and so on.

When I started dating boyfriend number four after breakup number three, Sage cackled and came up with these nicknames for us.

Sage is the Vice President of Media and Public Relations for a hospital in San Diego. Like me, she's competitive, rational, and self-sufficient. Unlike me, she's the confident one. All tight-lipped smiles and strong words. Her independence and self-assurance are deeply ingrained in her, and she walks through life never stumbling in her tight custom-fitted pantsuits and four-inch high heels.

Evelyn owns a clothing boutique on Prospect Street that overlooks the ocean in La Jolla, an upscale neighborhood in San Diego.

Like me, she's loyal, honest, and careful. Unlike me, she's the bubbly one. All wavy hands and bright colors. Her charm flows easily, and she walks through life in her strappy sandals able to smile her way through anything and anyone.

When I first moved to San Diego, I had no idea how to make friends. New city, new job, new life. Completely alone. I was scared shitless that I didn't have school to make automatic friendships. I'd have to actually put myself out there. So, I boldly signed myself up on Sage and Evie's team at Guava's Beach Volleyball Complex. I'm not a college volleyball star, but I played in high school, and I'm decent enough at defense. Our setter, Amy, is married with kids, so she doesn't have as much time to hang out, but we three have been inseparable ever since—and even have a few season championship T-shirts to show off.

After meeting Sage's and Evie's mothers, I understood my two best friends on a scary deep level. It was like peering into the future. Whether it's genetics or nurture—I don't care about scientific arguments—it was like seeing my friends thirty years from now. Sage will still not be taking anyone's shit, while Evie will be the head of the PTA.

And that freaked me the fuck out. I do not want to become my mother. Lord, please do not let me become my mother.

Is this an unavoidable fact of life?

My mother lives with my father in a loveless marriage back in Dallas because she settled and continues to do so. She thought it was time to get married; that she wasn't getting any younger. The right time with whomever she could reach out and grab first meant they were unhappy by their first anniversary. They thought having a child (me) would fix things. Breaking news: it didn't.

Things were okay growing up. They were civil enough for me. It's not like I can point to all of these terrible things that happened to me. I don't really have bad memories, but my memories aren't overflowing with happiness or comfort either. The house was quiet. Avoidance was better. My parents were like roommates, calling each other on the phone from separate rooms.

And now when I visit, they bicker and bicker some more. The worst part is that they've become so accustomed to it that they hardly notice their misery and how it affects everyone around them. Even though I'm not a child who has to be shielded from the realities of their lackluster marriage anymore, splitting half their 401k seems like too big a price to pay to possibly find happiness elsewhere. It's not my life, so whatever, but I think it's fucking nuts.

Well, I refuse. I will not fall victim to the whims of the universe. I am *not* my mother, and I will *not* settle.

It has to be the right time *and* the right person. So, maybe I have to date a lot to get there.

When I googled my nickname, I read that a serial dater loves "the chase." They are master manipulators. They thrive off the first date but come back for more, falling in love with the idea of love over and over. Supposedly, they get excited about the beginning of a relationship and then ghost the person once they get to know them. The power dynamic sends them on a high.

But I don't agree with my label.

I'm not afraid of commitment. I'm not chasing a thrill. I definitely don't get high off of first dates or enjoy the inevitable breakup so I can move on to the next one. Those parts all suck.

Honestly, I dread the breakup because I always know what comes after, and my two best friends didn't know me before—the before I'm chasing, the before I get high off of. The before I can't seem to replicate.

I'm only trying my best not to settle for anything less, and attending a wedding is the perfect place to remind me that love really does exist. You can't be sad at them. It's, like, a rule.

Sage slides into the seat next to me. While this plane is terrifyingly small, I'm glad we only have two seats in our row. No one has to be in the dreaded middle.

Sage motions with her head to the front of the plane. Her tiny, mousy brown ponytail bobs with it. "At least we're not the last ones to board. Thank god that will never be me."

I look up to see a woman who can't possibly be older than us with a baby girl swaddled in her arms, a two-year-old boy clutching her leg, and a four-year-old boy whining behind her. Marriage and kids are not in Sage's future. She lives up to her label, but I think it's cute. I know kids will be hard, but one day—in the future—I want them.

"Three under five. Impressive," I say.

Sage side-eyes me with a hint of green sparkle in her irises. "Lucky number seven this week?"

"It's been two weeks since six."

"Two weeks and two days," she corrects me.

"And two weddings in twenty-one days," I say.

She holds a finger to the vein in her temple like she's in pain. "Too many numbers. I need a drink."

The call button above our heads turns blue when Sage presses it with her index finger.

"I cannot look at another Dirty Shirley. For at least… a year," I say.

A little over two weeks ago, I broke up with number six (Joey), which led me to get drunk on Dirty Shirleys at our friends Caleb and Brett's wedding the next night. The memories hurt my brain.

I wince when I remember that someone put a microphone in my hands.

But no matter how hard Joey tries, we will not be getting back together. I've ignored all of his phone calls and texts. I think it's time for me to just not date. Shake off the serial dater, insert all of the obligatory *I don't need a man* comments. Because I really don't.

The real problem with dating Joey was our mutual friends. Sure, at first, it seemed great, but what about when you're going to see your ex for the foreseeable future. This weekend is case in point.

Sage laughs. Her smile is perfectly made for that professional headshot that stares at you during a Zoom meeting—while the actual person behind the computer with their camera off is still in their pajamas and their hair is in a messy bun. Actually, Sage is probably the annoying one that is always on camera, even at seven in the morning, and makes her subordinates feel obligated to reciprocate.

"Ryan, that was such a wasted opportunity to meet someone—pun intended."

I look out of my tiny rounded square window and focus on the man heaving luggage onto the conveyor belt over his shoulder like he's a child with his head buried in a toy box.

"And technically," she continues, "this one is almost like a week-long wedding."

I crane my neck back to her and hitch an eyebrow. "You're upgrading to a week-night stand?"

"Hopefully there are more people we don't know at this one."

"And more people who are sexually attracted to women," I add.

"Not entirely a deal breaker." She shrugs at my eye roll. "What? It's just sex. I'm not getting married."

"At least one of us is. I can't believe Evie is getting married," I say.

Obviously, I can believe it—Evelyn is a hopeless romantic—but it feels like the right thing to say. How did we get here? We're old enough to get *married.* That seems too grown up, too adult—like paying taxes or wondering about the school district where you live.

It came too quickly. I'm a year past a quarter of a century. Putting numbers in terms like that—decade, century—always makes them sound worse. Youth is most definitely wasted on the young, and I didn't know it, because of course, I was young.

"That's what typically comes after four years of monogamy," Sage says. "And when you're serial dating, one comes after the other."

"I *want* to find the one," I say.

Do not think about him, I think.

Dammit, when you tell yourself not to do something, you always do it anyway…

"Right. Your ever-growing list."

"It's dynamic."

Dynamic in the way that I don't realize something is on my list until it suddenly hits me out of nowhere. Like of course, I cannot marry a man that doesn't have this specific ridiculous trait. Thanks to *him*.

Coincidentally, my list has six line items.

Sage smiles. "Second chance for both of us. My money is on this Beck guy Evie keeps talking about. Painfully handsome, just out of a long-term relationship and struggling. Probably means he's looking for a casual week of fun."

"Rebound perfection," I agree. "I've never heard Elliot talk about a Beck. He's in the wedding party?"

"He's a high school friend who recently came back into his life, and Elliot invited him for the week." Sage smirks and mimics Elliot's voice. "He needs a friend right now."

"I don't think that's what he meant."

"Two birds, one stone." Sage thinks on that. "Or one bird, two stones."

"No stone left unturned."

"That's you, Ryan, not me," she laughs.

"Fine. Make sure you throw the sex stone."

"What's a sex stone?"

My smile tells Sage she walked right into that one. She narrows her eyes.

"It's just a fucking rock."

I'm so proud of myself when I don't dissolve into a fit of giggles.

"You are not funny," she lies.

"Your lips say otherwise."

Sage folds them into themselves, trying to keep them even. "What about giving Mitchell a chance?"

I shoot her a look. "No. He never laughs."

"He's hot though."

"Then you sleep with him. Laughing is not a requirement in the bedroom. Actually, that's preferable."

"Exactly," Sage says pointedly.

"I'm not going to hook up this week," I argue.

She tuts at me. "Think of him as your sex stone. Something that's not written in stone. Just a man carved from stone with something hard as stone thrust—"

"May I help you?" the flight attendant asks in a sing-song voice.

Oh, thank god. I'll forever be indebted to this random woman named Cathy with beauty pageant puffy blonde hair for interrupting Sage's tangent.

"I need a Dirty Shirley. Please," I say before Sage can answer.

Definitely knew I wouldn't last a year.

"A what?" she asks.

"You know. A Shirley Temple, but all grown up."

Cathy furrows her eyebrows, but her pearly white smile doesn't falter. I suspect she actually was a former child beauty queen.

"Vodka and Sprite and a splash of grenadine. And make it heavy on the grown up."

I detect pity in her expression before she looks at Sage.

"White wine, please. And make mine a double."

"So, like, two glasses or one big one?" she asks.

Cathy hates us already.

"Surprise me," Sage tells her.

She walks away and comes back a minute later with two glasses for each of us that look suspiciously large. I think because she wants to deal with us as little as possible.

We're one drink in by the time Sage whips her laptop out of her Louis Vuitton tote.

"Did you read this itinerary yet?" she giggles. "I didn't realize there were this many things to do in Colorado in the summer."

"Enlighten me," I say, trying to find the tiny black straw with my lips.

"Mountain biking, hiking, fly fishing, tubing, zip lining, and that's just naming a few."

I pout and roam my eyes briefly over Sage's screen. The document does look rather long. "I thought we were going to get a week of lounging by the pool."

"Elliot wouldn't dream of it."

"Too much energy, that one," I agree. "I'd have forced Evie to break up with him if I didn't love him so damn much."

Sage smiles. "And now he's going to be family."

"You think they'll adopt us?"

"Maybe if we're not too annoying this week."

I grin. "Too late. I'm already tipsy."

It's Cathy's fault really.

× × ×

BY THE TIME we've landed in Telluride, Sage has sobered up enough to drive our rental car.

Me, not so much.

I slide into the passenger seat of the black Ford Expedition. I'm glad I don't have to drive this tank because I'd probably get in a wreck even sober. The center console is so wide that I can practically extend my arm out fully to poke her.

I blabber on about my mundane work project—I know engineering is boring, especially when I geek out—until our eyes glass over (Sage's because I've bored her into a coma, mine because I've never seen Colorado in the summer).

Evie is from Denver. We've been here on ski trips the last two years I've known her, but it's always been coated in white.

I wasn't prepared for how much green and brown I see. The mountains look like they've evolved and grown. They've shaken off their snow to reveal their true inner beauty.

Downtown Telluride is more colorful, less damp. Flowers are blooming, people aren't bundled up. It feels new, like the entire town has come out of hibernation.

And I *love* to ski.

But this just hits different.

Sage pulls into the underground parking garage of the Céleste Hotel. Above us is what looks almost like an earth-toned castle with stone walls, brown wooden balconies, and a deep brownish red roof shining in the sun.

Sage and I sprung for a two-bedroom 'residence' since we're adult women with real jobs and this is a special occasion.

It's not every day your best friend gets married—unless they're the serial bride.

Actually, that would be kind of fun. And expensive.

After we check in, we don't even have to fight over a room. They are equally as gorgeous. Light wooden furniture and white linens and a balcony overlooking the Rocky Mountains for each of us.

I hang my dresses in the closet, brush my teeth, redo my

makeup, and step back into our shared living room. There is a rich brown leather couch and two chairs.

I sit. I'm not a fan of sticky, cold leather sofas but something about this one looks like it came straight out of a magazine; including the large pair of antlers in the middle of the oversized glass coffee table. I won't be sitting much apparently anyway. We have a tight schedule.

"What's first again?" I ask Sage when she appears in her bedroom doorway.

She's changed into a long navy chiffon dress, and her short brown hair is straightened and lands just below her chin.

"Welcome drinks on the terrace." Her dark hazel eyes drop to my feet and travel back up my leggings and white tee. "Are you going for airplane chic?"

I stand and flip my long strawberry blonde curls, which took me two trips to the salon a few months ago to get perfect, over my shoulder. "In vogue athleisure-wear."

"Just don't wear white!" she calls before I disappear into my room.

On the actual off-chance that there is an attractive man attending that I don't know and could have potential as a future boyfriend, I need to make a good first impression.

Wait, no. I'm supposed to be singling hard. This is for me.

I pick my best fitting dress—a peach spaghetti strap number with a sweetheart neckline and corseted top that hugs my boobs just right and shows off just enough of my back to make it the right amount of sexy—and my nude heels that make my legs look longer.

I'm five-five but around Sage and Evie heels are a must. They both played college volleyball and break five-foot-ten easily. I get lost when I have to stand around them flat-footed.

When we step into the crowded hotel bar, Evelyn sees us immediately. Her dirty blonde curls bounce with her as she makes her way to us around the rectangular bar and tall brown leather bar stools.

Everything feels earthy; warm tones and wooden accessories. Even the chandelier, hanging in the middle of the ceiling, is beautifully crafted out of sticks and twinkle lights.

All of these people must be her parents' friends. I don't recognize anyone, and they're twice our age. I guess youth is relative.

Maybe when I'm half a century old, I'll be telling quarter-of-a-century-olds how they are babies.

"I've missed you two," Evie squeals when she reaches us and loops her arms through ours.

"I dropped you off at the airport a little over twenty-four hours ago," I say. "But you didn't look this hot."

I run my hand over her white silk dress that's clinging to her perfectly. She must be pantyless and braless—with some type of magic nipple concealer.

"Likewise," she compliments me, petting my hair. "You look ten times sexier in Colorado."

Sage picks up two champagne flutes off the tray balancing on the outstretched arm of a timid college-aged girl. She hands them to us (I might as well. Otherwise, I'll just get tired) before she goes back for her own and lifts it into the air.

"To Evelyn soon-to-be Sharpe, who couldn't survive without us."

"You'll always be Evelyn Lawrence to me," I add. "And to the best week ever."

As we clink glasses, Evie mumbles, "Incoming."

"Girrrrrls," Mrs. Lawrence trills from over my shoulder.

I twist and inhale Nell Lawrence's plume of Tom Ford's Lost Cherry. Her elegance is something I've never quite gotten used to. Her short hair is a shade lighter than Evie's, but she's just as tall and thin. She's the only middle-aged mom I know that could look this stunning in her sleeveless tan jumpsuit and gold jewelry.

"Elliot must be pleased with what he sees in his crystal ball," I whisper back to Evie.

She can only make a half-second long face of disgust before she's forced to smile. "Mom."

"Nell," Sage says, "looking gorgeous as always."

"You're too sweet to me," she says slyly, wrapping her long arms around Sage. Then she pulls me into a hug. "Ryan. You both get more beautiful every time I see you. Evelyn has been counting down the seconds until you arrived."

"The rest of the wedding party won't be here until tomorrow. For now, it's just us, Elliot, and Beck."

I down the rest of my champagne. "What kind of a name is Beck anyway?"

Evie shrugs. "Boys and sports. They're always giving each other nicknames. I don't know. I'm not a male."

"I'm intrigued," Sage says lightly. "Soccer thighs? Football shoulders? Basketball height?"

"All three," Nell answers playfully.

"Mooooommm," Evie complains.

Nell feigns shock, running her fingers through her blown out hair. "What? I can still appreciate beauty at my age."

Sage nudges into me. "I'll let Ryan take first dibs."

Evie rolls her eyes and grabs me and Sage. "Come tell Elliot"— she grins—"and *Beck* hello."

The terrace is lined with glass and overlooks a sprawling green golf course. The sun is just starting to set behind a particularly tall mountain and mixing the orange sunlight with the azure blue sky into a hazy hue.

I spot Elliot's tall blond frame talking to an equally tall man with brown hair. That's all I can discern from his rather nice looking back, other than he's wearing a navy suit and those brown shoes that are dressy but have tennis shoe soles. I can just make out their conversation as we approach.

"Here they come. You have to meet Ryan."

"Is that your best man?"

Elliot laughs. "Close. One of the maids of honor." He smiles wide, which prompts Beck to slowly start to turn around.

His profile comes into view first.

I falter mid-step. My tipsy mind must be playing tricks on me.

But when he's fully facing me and our eyes connect, my feet plant themselves firmly into the floor like I've been shoved back by the force of his gaze.

Is this a practical joke? Maybe he's a body double. I didn't sign up for this shit when I agreed to be in my best friend's wedding. Why is no one laughing at the *gotcha* moment?

He chokes on the whiskey drink in his hand. I think a piece of ice is lodged in his throat.

I'm suddenly sober.

I've turned to stone.

My heart drops like one.

All of my blood is draining from my body, and I can feel myself turning white.

I never thought I would see him again.

And I haven't seen him in four years—not even a picture—but, of course, he doesn't look exactly the same. No, he looks better.

Beck is Grey Beckett.

Grey Beckett is *him*.

2

Twilight Zone

I DON'T CONSIDER Grey an ex.

Grey Beckett is boyfriend zero.

Like patient zero—he infected me.

He infected me with his charm and his laugh and his sincerity and his contagious personality and his goddamn handsome face.

That same handsome face that's still staring at me and trying to take a breath. His throat looks constricted. The muscles in his neck are straining, working to dislodge the ice cube. Is it possible to choke on ice or will it melt before you die? Maybe he's allergic to me and going into anaphylactic shock. Someone should help him— not me—and maybe perform CPR. His jaw is so tense, he could take out Elliot's eye with it.

But it is me who now has to live with the fact that every other man is not him. I'm still searching for one who is better—still comparing and failing to find a better Grey Beckett—because I'm unable to cure whatever he poisoned me with.

"Dibs," Sage hisses in my ear.

Ha. If only he wanted me.

Grey recovers quicker than I do. "Ryan."

There's no tone to his voice. It's painfully even.

Evie and Sage notice. They know something is transpiring. I can feel their brains in a whirlwind of thoughts.

Elliot is oblivious. "Ryan!" He scoops me up like he always does to bring me into a hug at his six-foot-five level.

I hug his neck, his golden waves of hair tickling my face, until Sage interrupts us. "Hey, golden retriever."

Elliot places me back on my still stunned feet and embraces Sage before he turns back to Grey and places a large hand on his shoulder.

"This is Beck. We went to high school together."

Sage peels her curious eyes off me standing there like a statue and smiles. "Beck? It's nice to meet you. I'm Sage."

Grey gently lays a hand on Sage's waist and presses his cheek against hers momentarily. "Grey Beckett."

"Sorry," Elliot laughs. "I forget his name is actually Grey." His eyes look hopeful when he slides them to me, like he thinks we could possibly hit it off. "This is Ryan."

Grey doesn't move. His deep brown eyes flash, then the one slice of light blue in his right iris goes dark. That blue streak used to make me go weak in the knees. Now, it kind of makes me mad.

"Hi, Ryan."

I think I'm smiling. Tensely. *You don't want to kiss my cheek?* I dare him with my eyes.

"Do y'all know each other?" Elliot asks incredulously.

"We've met," Grey confirms.

We've met. We've *met?* I need to flush my ears. I think Grey just said we've *met.* That can't be right.

"We used to date, actually," he adds. "In college."

Sage and Evie are quietly putting two and two together.

Elliot's eyebrows pinch deeper when he looks at me. "I thought you went to the University of Hawaii."

"I did for grad school." I look back at Grey, willing my eyes to look completely indifferent. He has zero control over me. I haven't given him a second thought. That's *exactly* what my eyes say. "I went to Texas for undergrad."

The University of Texas where I "met" Grey for two years; where I graduated from before I moved to Hawaii to get my master's degree in coastal engineering. The University of Hawaii where I'd been for about four weeks when Grey called me one night before school had even started and told me he couldn't do long distance.

And after he broke up with me, he promptly blocked my number and deleted all of his social media.

Now, fast forward four years, and we're standing on a terrace in Telluride, Colorado being introduced to each other, because let's face it, we're strangers. Strangers with one unbelievable mutual friend.

"How wild," Elliot says, cautiously this time.

God, the irony. He was setting me up with my ex-boyfriend. I knew Elliot was from Austin, but I had never bothered asking him if he knew Grey. It's a big city. What are the freaking odds?

"Wild," I repeat.

Grey runs a hand through his straight hair, which is an inch or two longer than when I knew him, nervously. His face is stoic. "Can I get you a drink?"

Who is he asking? He's not looking anyone in the eye. Everyone else's eyes are on me.

I flash a quick smile at the flash of a memory and hate myself for it. *Wipe it off your face and beg that he's turned into an asshole.*

"A Dirty Shirley, please," I say.

Grey laughs warmly, and I'm caught so off guard from the electric reaction it elicits through my body, I almost laugh with him. He holds eye contact for a beat too long.

Oh, now he has mustered the courage. I wish he'd look away. Look away, dammit. I sure can't.

"Sure. Anyone else?" He finally looks at Evie and Sage with those affectionate eyes I want to gouge out. "A blueberry lemon drop or a Cosmo or any other drink that will emasculate me when I order it?"

I could throw up he's so charming.

And he's thinking about the same thing I'm thinking about. Take that, you non-asshole.

"Now that you say it…" Evie joins in finally in a sweet voice. "A blueberry lemon drop sounds perfect."

Sage wiggles a peace sign. "Make that two."

Elliot looks at all three of us and says, "I'll help," before he turns to follow Grey.

I shake my head between Sage and Evie. "Not now," I say, walking off to the glass railing. I grip the edge so hard I could probably cut myself. I study the ground below and wonder if I'd still be able to run or if I'd break my legs if I jumped. My heels add another factor.

I can't concentrate on the calculation I'm doing in my head to figure out if the force will snap my femurs when they both sidle up next to me and lean down on their forearms. I glance over my shoulder to see Grey and Elliot at the bar laughing. It doesn't look like they're talking about me—unless Grey is revealing my most humiliating moments.

Sage's spiel on the plane hits me, and I whip my head back to Evie. "He just got out of a long-term relationship?"

She chews on her lip. "That's what Elliot said."

"How long?" I ask.

"Three… or four years," Evie replies. "I'm not sure."

"And he's sad?"

Evie's eyes dart to mine. "Elliot implied that he was."

Sage, always the pragmatic one, smiles proudly. "You look fucking hot, so at least there's that."

I turn around and rest my back on the balcony. I can't turn my back to him, or I'll be caught off guard again.

"So, that is the man that you claim you were a monogamist with? Huh," Evie remarks.

"I mean," Sage says, "two years of that looks fun. I could see it."

I lift my eyes to the sky. "I know. He doesn't disappoint. He's a whole lot of pleasant surprises until he goes radio silent from the entire world."

Sage scoffs. "He doesn't have an online presence?"

"What kind of a buzzword is that?" Evie jokes.

"You can't *not* have an online presence. Where else does the fake bullshit go? It's like personal PR," Sage replies. "You've never been able to cyber stalk him?" Her eyes trace his body. "Pity. There's not even a swimsuit photo I could find?"

"Nope," I say. "Literally, this is the first time I've seen him physically or virtually and the first time I've talked to him since he broke up with me."

"Not even a drunk text?" Sage questions me at the same time Evie snorts her disbelief.

My eyes bounce between them like they've caught me red-handed.

"I mean, well, I do this… thing," I start hesitantly before I change my mind.

I've never even told my best friends about my humiliating "thing." Like when you drive by your ex's house or cyber stalk a random girl that happens to be in a picture with him—I think every girl has some psycho-ex moments that we have never told a soul about. It's a secret club we all know we're a part of, but the secret is to never say it out loud.

Mine's more therapeutic, but it's still unhinged ex-girlfriend behavior that I did as early as two weeks ago.

"What thing?" Sage asks.

I laugh and cover my face with both of my hands.

"Tell us," Evie teases.

"Fuck," I whine. "I never thought I would see him again." I look toward the deep blue sky that is getting deeper by the minute along with my red cheeks. "He blocked my number when we broke up, okay? I know because my texts are green."

I can't believe I'm about to admit this out loud. Evie and Sage are very patiently waiting for me to finish, with blank faces and wide eyes.

"And every time I've broken up with a guy it's been because of him. It started kind of innocently, but it kept happening, and I kept texting him my updated *list*. My stupid, dynamic list that is because of him and his ability to destroy a man for me without even trying."

Sage barks out a cough. Evie bursts out laughing.

"Quite the contrast to the Ryan who dumps a guy without a second thought and never looks back," Evie teases.

"You guys suck," I deadpan.

"You are a crazy ex-girlfriend," Sage mocks me. "That list you keep is thanks to *him*?"

I cross my arms over my chest and laugh. "It was like therapy. Me yelling—well, it wasn't really yelling—at him even when I knew I couldn't. Just like a huge middle finger to him for disappearing on me. I knew he would never see it."

"I egged a guy's car once," Evie says shyly.

"*You?*" I question her. "Evelyn Renee Lawrence? That doesn't sound like you."

Evie laughs. "Freshman year of college. He slept with my sorority sister the weekend after we broke up."

"Ehhh," I agree.

We both look at Sage intently.

"Nope, I haven't done anything like that. Ever," she says. I can't tell if she's lying or not. She's good at putting on a PR face.

Grey flashes his white smile at the bartender, who looks flustered just from the attention. He hands the two blueberry lemon drops to Elliot before he turns back to the girl and says something with his pretty lips. I can hear her high-pitched, flirty laugh from here.

"Was he an asshole when he broke up with you?" Sage asks.

"No," I say angrily. "I wish he had been. It was just the way it ended so abruptly."

"Remind me," Evie says, giggling. "You've had a *lot* of break-ups."

I laugh to keep myself from getting too angry. "We said we were going to try long distance. But a month later he tells me he can't. That it's already too hard. Hawaii was so far away. It's not like we could do a weekend together. A plane ride alone took a day. We'd never see each other. Grey's love language is definitely physical touch. He's one of the touchiest people I've ever dated. He seemed just as heartbroken as I was. We *loved* each other. At least, I loved him. For me though, there was zero closure. I haven't heard from him or seen him since. I moved to San Diego. He lives in Austin. Long distance doesn't work for him, and he will never move."

"Why not?" Sage asks. "Moving is easy. Almost everything can be done remotely."

I study my nails. "Family."

"Oh," Sage breathes.

They both know I'm being vague on purpose and won't press it.

Grey's little sister, Lily, has Down syndrome. He helps his parents whenever he can, and he doesn't want to move away from home.

He loves Lily more than anything in the world, and she looks up to him more than I've ever seen another sister do. She's the happiest, most optimistic person I've ever met, and I have no doubt it's because Grey is her brother.

It's not that Grey didn't talk about her or that he didn't want to. It's that I don't feel like it's my story to share.

When I see him and Elliot leave the bar, I look down and fidget with the hem of my dress until his shoes appear in front of mine. When I raise my head, he holds a glass filled with my girly pink drink in front of me.

"One Dirty Shirley," he says.

I wrap my fingers around the cold glass. His thumb lingers briefly against mine before I yank my drink back.

I tip my chin up and thank him before Elliot drags Grey away to meet some of his family.

"I'll see you later," Grey half tells, half asks me over his shoulder.

I nod silently. That little sliver of blue in his eye slices right through me, and I feel like my heart is bleeding out onto the floor.

I can't concentrate on a single conversation I have over the next hour. They are like blips in the time continuum as I float around with no purpose, nodding and *uh huh-ing* anyone that approaches me.

Later finally comes when I'm sitting in the hallway on a greige sofa under the light from an acrylic lamp to my right.

I'm staring into my empty glass, for what feels like hours, when Grey's voice shatters the silence.

"I've been looking for you."

I spring my head up. He's standing cautiously just out of reach with his hands in his pockets. His face is soft though. He knows it's a real possibility I'm going to tell him to fuck off, but I refuse.

Instead, I narrow my eyes. "I've always been in the same place."

"Is this all right?" he asks.

"You know I'm not going to freak out, if that's what you mean."

He takes a step closer. "Are we all right?"

I lean back and cross my legs, trying to get far enough away where he doesn't fog my brain and I can't smell his soap. His eyes don't go any higher than my heels. They trace the straps around my ankles, so I wait patiently until he brings them up to meet me in the eye. I try to go for indifference in my tone and body language.

"Yep. All good," I confirm.

"How have you been?" he asks.

I scoff and try to take a sip of my empty drink. The ice rattles and falls against my lips. I sigh because I'm cringe-worthy and place it next to the lamp.

"Let's not do that," I say.

"Do what?"

"All the weird ex niceties. I'm not interested in dragging that out for a week."

He taps his hands against his thighs in his pockets. "So, do you not want me to talk to you?"

"You can do whatever you want," I say nonchalantly. Internally, anger is rising. I try to keep it off my face, but I don't think I will be able to for long. "I need another drink."

This is the only way I'm going to get past this week—drunk out of my mind and pretending like it's a dream. Classy.

I stand and brush past him. The blue fabric of his suit rustles and tickles my arm. I don't look, but I can feel him turn around, his eyes on my bare back. I hope I look really fucking sexy stalking away.

The rest of the night I know exactly where Grey is at all times. You could blindfold me, spin me around, and I'd still be able to pin a tail on his amazing ass. I see his fitted navy suit in a sea of navy suits out of my peripheral vision and instantly know it's him from the curve of his shoulders, from the way he slips his hand into his pocket, from the way he lifts his whiskey glass to his lips.

I am careful never to look directly at him. I feel like if I do, my secrets will flow out of my mouth like a waterfall. He got the closure he needed. I never did, but I don't need to make a scene during my best friend's wedding week.

I'm not that girl.

×××

WHEN SAGE AND I make it back to our house hours later, she follows me into my room. One thing I love about her is that she doesn't give up. Or I love it when it works in my favor; not when she's forcing me to face my feelings and talk.

"You want to talk about it?" she asks, leaning against the door frame.

I slip off my shoes and unzip my dress on the side. "Not really. This week isn't about me. It's about Evelyn and Elliot."

"That doesn't mean you don't have feelings about what just happened," she presses.

"I haven't sorted them out yet." I let the peach dress fall down around my feet before I step out of the heap of my clothes. "I honestly never thought I would see him again, Sage. This is weird."

"Do we need to public relations the shit out of it?"

"What does that mean?" I laugh and crawl under the covers.

Sage sits on the end of my bed and curls her legs up underneath her dress. "Putting together your game plan for a favorable public image. What's our goal?"

Sage is always droning on about S.M.A.R.T. goals: specific, measurable, achievable, relevant, time-bound.

She applies this to all aspects of her and, by extension, *our* lives—completing twelve-week beach body workouts or gunning for a promotion or trying to get a guy's attention.

I ponder at the ceiling. "I think I just want to get through this week civilly. Then we can both go back home and hopefully not see each other for another four years."

"And your list?" she questions me.

"Maybe this is what I need to get past it," I say. "We're different people now. Our relationship was a long time ago. And I shouldn't be comparing every man I meet to him anyway like he's the perfect male specimen. That's not even fair of me. He has flaws."

"They must be internal," Sage jokes.

I had him under a microscope for two years. I know he has flaws, internal and external, just like I do. Problem is, I loved him despite them, and I haven't been able to find that with anyone else since.

I haven't been able to move on.

"Closure," I say abruptly. "I need closure."

Sage smiles. "We can orchestrate one hell of a closure. I'm not a VP for nothing."

"I thought it was for the six-figure salary," I tease her.

"That's only an added bonus on top of getting to boss people around."

"Right. Boss me into how I get closure."

"R.A.C.E.," Sage says.

More acronyms. They're a jumbled mess in my mind.

"Ryan accomplishes closure effortlessly?"

Sage tsks. "So close."

I think some more. "Fire safety is also pretty relevant to my situation. Rescue, alarm, confine, extinguish? That applies perfectly to this dumpster fire."

Sage shakes her head and breaks out a condescending tone. "Research, action and planning, communication and relationships, evaluation."

"Ohhh, of course. More PR jargon," I say, rolling my eyes. "Shouldn't that be R.A.P.C.R.E?"

"I didn't make it up," she huffs. "We know the research—the who, what, why. Once we have the action figured out, we can check in and evaluate whether it worked."

"I have the smartest friends in the world," I say proudly.

"It's no math equation," she quips.

"Yeah, well, I could never talk to the media, so whatever." I give her a shrug.

"First things first, you two should talk. See where you're both at." Sage pats my leg. "Get some rest. PR campaigns take work."

When she leaves, I snuggle onto my side and pull up our text message history with his name still as Grey in my phone. Those last six humiliating green texts blare from the bright screen reminding me how unbalanced I've slowly become.

The last actual text I sent him before I started my "list" is a picture of me with a beached seal and **Got to see a seal after dinner today! I'll call you tomorrow when I wake up :) Love you!** The time difference wasn't terrible, but there was an overlap of our sleeping schedules. I kind of wish I would've deleted our text history, but I couldn't ever part with it.

What does closure look like for me and Grey? I don't know where to start. How do I open the close?

:) Hate you! That could be a fitting last text.

I probably need to brainstorm more, and I can't talk to him via this mode of communication anyway.

I quickly hit the 'A' before I can second guess myself, just to see what happens, and the little arrow that appears to the right is blue.

He's unblocked me.

I burrow deeper into my fluffy white pillow and stare at the blue send button for minutes. It's been green for years, a wall between us. There's nothing now. I could call him or text him and he would receive it. I have an open line of communication to Grey for the first time in four years.

Suddenly, three gray dots flicker.

I hold my breath, but they disappear.

I wait. They flash again and disappear again.

I imagine him lying on his side with his phone illuminating his face in the dark and debating if and what he should text me. Like one of those movie scenes where the screen is split in half and he's doing exactly what I'm doing in a mirror image.

Well, I will absolutely not be the first one to text.

Nothing comes by the time I fall asleep an hour later.

<u>3</u>

The First Ex

I'VE BEEN DATING Chase for three months, and we're celebrating my twenty-fourth birthday tonight.

There's a new fancy bar that's having its opening night around the corner from Evie's boutique, and she got invited with an open invitation to bring friends.

My two years in Hawaii were more about having fun. Living in an adventurous place. Finding the adventurous side of me. All on top of school, but it was school in paradise. Exactly where I wanted to be. There were guys after Grey over there—but we were both always in agreement that it was a temporary fling. I wasn't looking for anything serious. I wasn't going to invest my time and my heart to then find myself in another eventual long-distance situation. None of them ever made me change my mind.

Chase doesn't feel temporary. I like him. He's got cute blue eyes that make my stomach fizzle when he looks at me. His dirty blond hair is short but feels like silk. He's not overly tall, but he's fit, and we work out together at the gym where we met—cliché, I know.

He's the first guy I've decided to continue dating after the first few dates in two years. San Diego is the city I want to be in. I have a great, stable job. I'm not looking to move anywhere else because there's long-term potential for me here.

He takes me to this burger place first with string lights on the patio and mint chocolate chip shakes. One of my favorite things is a burger with an egg on it. Then we meet Sage, some guy she's hooking up with, Evie, and Elliot at Pop, the champagne bar.

I instantly fall in love with it. Everything is gold and brightly lit up. There is a glass wall behind the bar filled with water and sparkling bubbles rising to the ceiling. I feel like I'm inside of a champagne glass.

Per the invitation, Sage and Evie are wearing silver and pink sequined dresses respectively, like my gold one. Elliot and Chase have on sequined bow ties.

Who wouldn't fall for someone inside of a champagne glass? I have stars in my eyes and high hopes for this night.

I feel happy with my new group of friends. A happy I haven't felt in a long time—the kind where you feel like you're making a home.

Chase pulls me in to dance. We're both glittering under the lights until he asks me what I want to drink.

I already know what I want because I'd looked at their menu earlier.

"Strawberry Pornstar Martini," I say into his ear.

Chase pulls back and looks at me like I'm nuts. He laughs under his breath. "Yeah, I'm not ordering that."

I furrow my eyebrows. Maybe I misheard him with the music blaring. "What?"

"You'll have to come with me. I am not telling a bartender I want a strawberry whatever."

"*I* want a Strawberry Pornstar Martini," I repeat slowly. "Not you."

Chase's face looks pained just hearing me say it again. His hand travels down my arm, and he laces his hand in mine. He tugs me off the dance floor and guides me by the small of my back to the bar with him, where he makes me repeat my order to the bartender like he can't possibly bring himself to ever utter those words as long as he lives.

The chasm in my stomach splits wide open. My heart plunges down into its depths. I'm not expecting it. I can't help it.

I listen to him order his own manly beer.

He suddenly looks different to me. He sounds different. Where did the Chase I knew a second ago go?

When we make it back to my apartment at the end of the night, he kisses me and tries to come up. Instead, I break up with him while I'm still sitting in the passenger seat.

As I'm lying in bed, unable to fall asleep, I replay that brief minute at the bar a million times in my head. Everything changed in that splice of time unexpectedly, but I don't even really care.

Chase is not the one for me. And as soon as I realize it, that's it. There's no going back.

I'm confused. Two years of progress shattered just like that. I haven't had Grey overtake my thoughts like that before, and it was painful looking at someone and wishing they were someone else who I can no longer have. The only way I can think to make sense of it is to get it out. Maybe it will help if I could expel the memory, try to blow up the neuron holding it inside my brain, because I don't *want* to miss him.

I pull out my phone and make sure I am still demoted to the green send button.

Remember when we went out that night for my twenty-first birthday, and you pulled me onto your lap and asked me what I wanted to drink?

I said I wanted a blueberry lemon drop, and you laughed. I thought you were laughing at me, but you said you were laughing at yourself because you don't take yourself seriously and you would order the most girly and ridiculous thing on the menu for me as long as I got what I wanted, because I didn't deserve anything less. Then you kissed my neck.

I remember.

Fuck you.

X I cannot date a man that won't order me girly and ridiculous sounding drinks.

<u>4</u>

Monday

EVERYONE IS HERE now.

All fourteen of us—a hodgepodge of friends who know each other and don't really know each other. Also known as adulthood, where you live your life in perpetual small talk.

In a semi-quick rundown, let's start with Brett and Caleb, newly wedded as of two weeks ago in a beautiful ceremony on the beach in San Diego.

Brett, one of Elliot's groomsmen, is a lawyer who looks rigid beneath his dark brunette fade that is always parted to the left in perfection—but he gets rowdy when you peel back his exterior, and when his hair gets disheveled, I know I'm in for a good time.

Caleb is the sweet one. He's a middle school math teacher with curly blond hair and dashing good looks. There's a special place in heaven for anyone who teaches and molds—and puts up with—tweens in their most impressionable and awkward years.

Jourdan and Alana, two other bridesmaids, are Evie's best friends from high school. They both live in Denver, select fashion choices I envy but could never pull off, and I've gone skiing with them twice. They're the friends we all have who are there for you no matter what, always in your life in some capacity, even when you live halfway across the country, haven't spoken in months sometimes, and have "other" best friends.

Mitchell—the extreme stoic. Oh, Mitchell. Elliot, being the puppy dog that he is, will become anyone's friend, which makes Mitchell a friend of a friend to me. He's a financial analyst with Elliot's medical device company, crunching numbers behind his computer and making Excel spreadsheets that I'm kind of jealous of.

Hunter and Hayden I hardly know, and honestly, I get them confused. They shouldn't have befriended each other with such similar sounding names *and* faces. I don't see them often enough to remember any distinguishing features because they travel for work constantly.

Rounding out the wedding party are Andrew, Elliot's younger brother and best man, and Sadie, Evie's cousin. They definitely think we're all ancient because we pay bills and are already sticking together as the only two spry college-aged youngsters.

And now there's Grey, the shiny new object.

I turn to study the magnificent Colorado magnets on the rotating display when I see Jourdan touch her bubblegum pink fingertips against Grey's forearm and say with a smile, "Are you going to be able to fit inside that tiny tube?"

"Are you calling me fat?" he jokes, but Jourdan wasn't expecting that answer.

"No," she stumbles, fidgeting with her long coffee-brown curls.

I will not snort. I will not snort.

I cough lightly. There's nowhere in this tiny souvenir shack for me to go far enough away.

They wait for their tubes to be blown up in silence while I stare out the back window watching Elliot and Evie splashing each other on the edge of the river.

When Grey's finished, I can hear him rolling one toward me where I'm now studying the world's most interesting keychains.

"Keep calm and Colorado on," Grey says softly over my shoulder.

I shoo him away with my hand. "Rocky Mountain vibes only."

"What's wrong with my vibes?"

Everything.

You have a sleeveless workout shirt on that reveals too much of your rib cage, and I suspect you'll be taking it off soon.

Your hair is kind of shaggy, and I like it way more.

I don't like how I sense your delectable vibes from the farthest possible point I can stand away from you.

I look up over my shoulder at him and roam my eyes over as much of his upper body as I can before I give him an unimpressed look—even though I am extra impressed when I allow myself to get an eyeful.

"Hook your tube far away from me. Like all the way on the opposite end so all of our friends are in between us," I say and walk off to the front.

Ben, who looks like a teenage skateboarding badass, inflates my blue tube while I stew.

So, I'm a little angrier than I thought, but this isn't some scenario I can completely forget. My heart hurt for months on top of months. The pain seeped into my bones. I loved him, and I wanted to make it work, but he didn't.

There's not much else I can say except, yeah, I'm a little pissed off now that he's trying to talk to me like he's a normal fucking person I just *met.* Not to mention, he's sad and heartbroken over some other girl.

Ben waves the blue tube in front of my face. "Ma'am?"

A polite skateboarding badass apparently, but I snap out of it and into more anger. "Do not ma'am me. I am not old."

Ben laughs sweetly.

"How old are you, Benjamin?"

"Nineteen," he says.

I do the math in my head.

I can date as young as: $(26/2) + 7 = 20$.

Dammit.

"Good day," I say briskly before I march out the door.

The Colorado air feels crisp and dry. The sunshine feels hotter, like it's baking cracks into my skin. I assume because we're closer to the sun. Science.

I slip off my tan knit cover-up and make sure all of my body parts are tucked into my black bikini. I have a nice base tan from lying out at the beach last weekend. I put my Hawaii hat on my head and pull my ponytail through the back hole.

"Spray my back, please?" I ask Sage, waving my sunscreen in front of her face.

She takes it from me and twirls her finger for me to turn around. "This could be our lounging by the pool day. I'm thinking of taking a nap with my wine cooler."

The sunscreen coats my shoulders before Sage sprays my lower back and my body jolts from the icy droplets.

"Thanks," I say. "Whatever you want. Just hook up next to me, okay? I promise I won't talk."

Her eyes flick to Grey helping Elliot hook a tube up to float our ice chest. "Sure," she assures me. "But that's also technically not talking to him."

"I don't want to talk to him while we're hooked up to a dozen other people," I say.

Sage grumbles something behind my back—I catch the word

eventually—as I wade into the freezing water barefoot. The bottom is rougher than I expected and hurts when I take a few steps.

"Ow," I mutter under my breath when I step on a jagged rock and my knee buckles.

Grey's strong, tan arms whisk me up out of nowhere and plop me down in the middle of my tube before I can protest.

I can still feel the touch of his slick sunscreen-lathered abs lingering against my side because he definitely did take his shirt off like I suspected he would.

"I had it," I say defensively. "I didn't need your help."

He pulls my tube in by the white string and bungees me to Sage's without saying anything. She mouths *sorry* when I drop my sunglasses to my chin to give her a look, though I don't think she's sorry at all. Then Grey bungees his own to both of ours before he jumps onto his tube and rocks us all.

Sage curses as her watermelon wine cooler spills across her boobs and green striped bandeau top.

Karma.

Grey apologizes before he props himself on his elbow toward me. "Are you upset because you're too old to date that kid wearing head-to-toe Volcom?"

"No!"

He laughs. "I saw you doing the math in your head."

"I'm an engineer," I say. "I do math in my head, like, all the time. I was calculating the psi of my inner tube."

"Right." Grey pinches my tube. "Two, two and half psi?"

"Two point one seven three five," I deadpan. "And he was nineteen. I could still have sex with him. If I wanted."

"Everybody ready?" Evie calls from the front of the pack.

Grey chuckles at me and pushes off the bottom with his long legs. At the same time, Elliot walks our big blob of blue tubes into the middle of the San Miguel River before he slides on his tube and the water takes us slowly away.

I lay my head back and rest my arms on the side of the tube. My fingers dip into the cool water every few seconds as we ride the small waves. The cotton candy clouds move slowly in the opposite direction that we're drifting, and after a while, I'm on the verge of sleep.

"You're mad at me."

I pick my head up and glare at Grey behind my sunglasses. "No, I'm not."

"You were my girlfriend for two years. I'd like to think I would know when you're mad."

Interesting choice of words. I study the facial features I can see around his sunglasses. His smirk is pulled out tight to the left. I glance at Sage who looks like she's already asleep, but I can't trust that she's not purposely pretending behind her sunglasses. She's most likely looking straight at me with her head in one direction and her eyeballs in another.

I lay my head back again and cover my face with my hat. "You don't know me anymore."

Take that.

Thirty seconds pass.

"Grey," I hear Sage warn. "Don't."

Then a snap like metal on plastic. Another snap.

I lift the bill of my hat to see Sage and the rest of the group floating away.

Sage shrugs. "I tried. He's too strong." She gives me a thumbs up behind his back to pump me up for the incoming conversation I'm about to have to endure. I'm supposed to be enduring it though, so I remind myself that to accomplish R.A.C.E., I have to talk. But I don't have to be happy about it.

"Why'd you do that?" I huff.

Grey doesn't answer until the wedding party is twenty yards in front of us. "You said I don't know you anymore. So, let's talk."

"Sure," I say sweetly. "Let's start with you since you're the one who's been blocking me for years."

His bottom lip drops a centimeter because I've caught him off guard for once. I smile and bask quietly in my triumph.

When he doesn't answer, I reach for the bungee to release us from each other. I can float alone.

He gets momentarily distracted by my cleavage as I lean over. My brain smirks. I could totally have sex with Benjamin—I repeat, *if* I wanted. Just because I'm old to a nineteen-year-old doesn't mean I don't look good.

I also heard somewhere that MILF is one of the most searched porn categories, so at least we have that waiting for us as we age. Yay.

As I fumble with the bungee, Grey holds my wrist and considers his words before he goes with, "I don't know what I am trying to say."

I relent, satisfied for now. He lifts his arms to put his hands behind his head with his elbows out to the sides, and my body betrays me. If someone touches me right now, their hair will stand on end from the static electricity coursing through me.

Thank god he can't see my eyes—I think—because I can't stop looking at the lines his muscles make running along the bottom of his biceps. He probably knows though, and he's paying me back for the unintentional boobage in his face.

"Ryan, it's not like I knew you were going to be here," he continues. "I was completely blindsided."

"That makes one of us. Of course, I knew *you* would be, *Beck*," I retort sarcastically.

"We were both blindsided. Trust me, I know. I saw your face at the same time you saw mine. But now we're here for the week together. I'm trying, and you can't seethe silently for six more days.

Talk to me about why you're mad at me."

Ugh. I hate him. He's too… right… good… everything.

This is Grey. He always wanted to talk it out. He didn't want to let things fester until one of us blew up. When he was annoyed, he told me. When I got angry, he wanted to resolve it. He didn't let me brush him off with *I'm fines.*

I think Grey doesn't want to turn out like his dad either. I've met the unemotional Robert Beckett twice. Grey told me stories about how his dad would yell at him out of nowhere over his socks on the bathroom floor. Not that he really cared about Grey's socks. Grey understands though and tries to be compassionate. His parents have a lot on their shoulders. According to Grey, Robert never lets anything he is thinking show, until it all comes bubbling up at once over something stupid. And on top of being an unemotional father, he doesn't hug or kiss or say he loves anyone. So, Grey compensates.

"I hate you," I say. "Can you not be so annoyingly you all the time?"

Grey laughs. "You loved me once, and you told me every random thought that popped into your head."

"Stop it." I turn my head to look into the trees to my right. I don't want to be reminded about how *much* I loved him. "You're not my boyfriend anymore. That was a long time ago."

"Then tell me why you hate me now as my ex-girlfriend," he challenges me.

"I hate you because you made me love you," I blurt.

I didn't even mean for it to come out. It just did on its own. Is that why I hate him right now? I don't even know. I've never had to actually have a reason why I hate him until now.

Grey doesn't twitch and waits patiently for me to continue. I go with what I'm feeling, because why not?

"You knew I wanted to go to Hawaii for grad school. I told

you my goals and my plans. We planned together. You knew we'd be far, *far* away from each other. You knew that it would take a whole day just to fly to see me, and you tricked me into falling in love with you anyway." I shift uncomfortably in my tube. Maybe I should have gone to actual therapy. I feel like my chest has been suddenly relieved from the cinderblock that's been sitting on it for four years. "Well, it was hard for me too, but I wanted to try. I did try. And I would have continued trying forever. You just gave up. And then you had the balls to literally fall off the face of the planet. So yeah, I'm mad at you. I guess I didn't realize how fucking pissed off I've been at you for four years."

"Feel better?" Grey asks.

I take a deep breath. "Yeah."

"I'm sorry, Ryan," he says in a deep voice and looks away. His arms finally drop to the tube when he holds eye contact again steadily. "I'm sorry that I made you feel like that—unwanted. I wanted you more than anything, but I still think I did the right thing."

I scoff and laugh and try to keep my rib cage from crushing my heart.

"How badly did you want to go to Hawaii for coastal engineering?"

"Badly," I say, annoyed. "You know that."

"Yeah, I knew how much you wanted that. I knew how hard you worked to get accepted. And every single day for a month when we talked while you were there all I wanted to tell you was to come home."

"You just gave up, Grey."

"I didn't give up. It was harder than I thought, for sure. But I couldn't be that guy. Groveling to you every day about how I can't stand not being able to kiss you or touch you or fall asleep next to you. Ryan, you *know* how I am. I couldn't ask you to come back and be with me. You would have resented me. You would've hated me—which you do anyway, but that's beside the point. You worked *so* hard, and that was something you needed to do for yourself. I know how hard engineering is and you graduated with honors."

I can't look away. It's more than I ever remember getting, but I didn't float this far away from the group for him to drop some motherfucking common sense on my irrational ex-girlfriend brain. That's not *fair*. I clamp my mouth shut, trying to let him finish, trying to tell myself he doesn't get to talk his way out of this one. Sunshine and rainbows are not in our near future.

"So, I did fall off the face of the planet because I didn't trust myself not to text or call you because I was so close to begging you to come back so many times. I knew it would be a long two years. Too long. I deleted my social media because I hated seeing pictures of you snorkeling or shark diving or surfing and looking happy. I had to let you go. I couldn't ever forgive myself if I became the reason you gave all of that up. It turns out, life without social media was much healthier for me, so I never got back on it. You needed Hawaii for yourself. It was your dream degree from your dream school. I am sorry, but it was the right thing to do for you, and I hated myself for wanting to take it away from you."

Breathe, Ryan. Breathe.

The Colorado air burns my bronchioles.

"That was a lame attempt at not being so annoyingly annoying all the damn time," I manage to say.

"I think I'd rather you hate me than regret me."

His words punch me in the chest. "That's profound," I joke.

"Well, it's how I feel."

"Okay," I say, nudging his leg. "I'll go on hating you. A little less though."

Grey smiles. "I can live with that."

×××

GREY MANAGES TO catch us back up to the remaining twelve tubes, that I've counted multiple times already, by freestyling while I kick. I really am always doing math in my head. It's a curse.

He hooks us back to Sage, who actually does look asleep until she pops her head up and says, "Don't think about trying that again or I'll sink my nails into you." She holds up her American stiletto shaped nails.

"Girl trends are so crazy," Grey chuckles. "How do you type with those things?"

Sage lays her head back down and sighs. "Do I look like someone who types?"

"She's not lying," I say. "Coincidentally, she's also the worst texter, and she won't admit it, but you see that scratch on her cheek…"

Sage flips me off.

"Your nails do look great though," I laugh.

"I agree," Grey says and motions to Brett two tubes over. "Pass us two Trulys, will you?"

"Yeah." Brett holds his dark bangs back with one hand while he ice-fishes with the other. He comes up with two cans that he passes to Caleb, who passes them to Grey.

Grey looks at both and hands one back to Caleb. "Ryan doesn't like cherry. Grab a mango or a watermelon."

They repeat the process—while my nerve endings ignite through every pathway in my body because of the littlest gesture— until a Watermelon Breeze Truly, opened by Grey, is in my hand.

I should say thank you.

"Thank you."

"Don't mention it," Grey replies.

I should stop looking at his smile.

"Brett, how was the honeymoon?" I ask, tearing my eyes away from Grey's lips. "I've been dying to hear, but I didn't want to be that person that texts you while you're on your honeymoon."

They both look almost as tan as I did when I lived there. Caleb's already sporting a wedding ring tan line that's poking out from beneath his shifted gold band and his hair is even more golden from the sun.

"Oahu was everything you said and more." He takes Caleb's hand. "Seriously, I'm not sure any vacation can ever top that one."

"We wouldn't have had such an amazing time without your suggestions," Caleb says.

"Favorite memory?" I ask.

Caleb and Brett smile seductively at each other.

"Other than those," I add.

"Mine was the shark cage," Brett says back in reality.

I groan. "You didn't do the free dive?"

Caleb rolls his blue eyes. "He was too scared."

"Okay, fine. I get it. It took me like three cages until I mustered the confidence," I concede. "But you still should have listened to me. It's safe."

"Ha," Brett scoffs, "because sharks are so predictable. They would never bite someone's leg off."

"True," Caleb says. "I compromised with the cage."

"Who's the better surfer?" I tease.

Brett levies a serious courtroom look on me. "Who do you think?"

I consider it for a few seconds as I assess them. They both work out a lot, but Caleb is lankier. They are both athletic. Brett did play football, but Caleb used to skateboard.

"Caleb," I guess and hold up my hands when Brett frowns in offense. "Only because he knows how to skateboard."

"Brett's good too," Caleb laughs affectionately. "But we didn't see any sea turtles."

"Oh my god, Grey," I say, turning to him, "I surfed over a sea turtle once, me above water, it below, for forever"—the end of my sentence slows—"and it was amazing."

That tumbled out of my mouth way too naturally, and as soon as I looked at him, it registered that he has been intently listening to our conversation and smiling as he drinks.

He only knows one month out of my twenty-four months of stories, and he seems raptured.

"Have you kept up with surfing in San Diego?" he asks.

I smile at the genuine interest in his voice. I'll tell a little version of a white lie since I don't want to talk about any of my exes right now. "I have. Mostly by myself, but now maybe Brett and Caleb will come with me." I turn back to them with a sly, pleading look.

Brett shakes his head. "Caleb will," he offers before he remembers something. "Oh, and we went to that awesome restaurant you told us about, the one where she takes your menu."

Grooves form between Grey's eyebrows. "Why would she take your menu?"

"Because," I say, "the owner asks if you've ever been in, and if you say no, she takes your menus and asks if you're allergic to anything and how much spice you can take, and then she showers you with delicious food. Duh."

Grey laughs. "How many times did you get away with saying no before she recognized you?"

"Four. But then she loved me. Actually, I kind of miss her." I pause to take a long sip before I ask Brett, "Did you try poke and musubi?"

"Poke, yes." He makes a gross face. "Musubi, no."

"What's musubi?" Grey asks Brett.

Brett gags. "Spam."

"Hawaiians love Spam," Caleb laughs.

"It's good!" I insist. "It's grilled Spam on rice and wrapped in seaweed."

"I had no idea such a thing existed," Grey says.

"I didn't either until I moved there."

Grey tries the word on his tongue. "Mu—su—bi. I love that you know what that is and that you like it."

His eyes hold on mine. I hold them right back.

I've never felt such gratitude in a moment that is so insignificant but seems wildly and equally significant while talking about Spam.

I once loved Grey so much that I do think I would have moved back if he'd asked me to. If he would've given me an ultimatum.

I would have caved for him, given up my independence—my independence which I'd always thought he resented me for.

And where would I be? Instead, it would be me resenting him to his core? Hating him for sacrificing myself in the process? Nothing good ever comes from relationship ultimatums.

I'd have none of these memories. I'd have none of these amazing experiences. I wouldn't have met so many awesome people.

"I have so many stories," I tell him, "if you want to hear them some time."

"Yeah, I'd love that."

My life seems to have splintered in the last second from a realization that had never dawned on me before.

Maybe Grey has been right all along.

And I should actually appreciate him.

<u>5</u>

Monday Night

COLORADO JUNE NIGHTS are still pretty cold.

I'm bundled up in my oversized green Hawaii hoodie, but I still need to sit close to the fire to feel warm enough.

We've taken over the outdoor sofas and chairs around the largest rectangular stone fire pit the hotel has.

I'm in a best friend sandwich with Evie on my right and Sage on my left, nestled back against the white cushions.

I don't know that Grey is sitting across the flames. I haven't noticed him at all. And I definitely am not straining my ears to try to catch every word he's saying to Elliot and Alana.

I realize Sage is talking to me. "What?"

"Did the talk help?" she repeats softly. "I started to resist, but I ended up letting him. I figured it might be good to ease the tension."

Grey laughs and unravels a ball of yarn in my stomach. I keep my eyes on Sage.

"Yeah," I say. "I think so. I wouldn't say I feel closed though."

"And?" Evie asks. "I missed the whole thing!"

"Evie, this is your wedding week. You don't need to be consumed with my drama. This is the most ridiculous thing I could have dreamed of. Both of us are just tiptoeing around each other trying to get through the week."

"Please," Evie huffs. "That doesn't mean I don't care or don't want to hear about it. Actually, give me some drama. I mean, just look at Elliot."

We all watch Elliot smile into the fire as he roasts a marshmallow.

That was the same smile he gave me when I made them late for a movie when I was crying over a breakup and he told me he knew I needed Evie. That was the same smile he gave me when he hugged me and told me he was so happy Evie had me as a friend. He's like our collective honorary boyfriend that we all adore.

"Have you ever seen him frown?" Sage teases.

Evie giggles. "He cried at the end of *Marley & Me*."

"That's because he's related to Marley," I say.

We cackle like lunatics until we can't breathe.

Evie widens her eyes. "Do not tell him I told you that."

Sage and I zip our lips, but Elliot would probably just smile if we said anything.

"God, I love him though. Now back to you," Evie says. "What did Grey *say*?"

"It was surprisingly… nice?" I laugh. "When we broke up, I don't even remember what he said hardly. I wasn't listening. I was too busy sobbing and telling him to stop talking. Eventually, I just hung up on him."

"Reasonable," Sage says with a shrug.

"It was nice to hear it when I wasn't so emotional, and maybe I get it? Like where he was coming from."

"So mature," Evie quips. "So wise. So ol—"

"Don't you dare call me old." I narrow my eyes at her. "I can't even date Tube Inflater Ben."

Evie looks at me like I'm crazy. "That kid in the shop today? Ew. Why would you want to date him?"

"I don't!" I exclaim. "It's that I *can't*—based on the age rule— and he called me ma'am. The point is I looked like a *ma'am* to him."

Sage shudders. "Fuck, we're not old. I promise to slap sense into the first teenager who calls me ma'am. Also, don't say Tube Inflater Ben again. That sounds weirdly sexual."

I cover my face and laugh. "Jesus. Can someone get me a marshmallow to roast? I have arthritis in my back from sitting in a tube all day."

I use Evie's and Sage's thighs to push myself up in the hunt for s'mores ingredients.

Caleb and Brett have abandoned their roasting sticks in favor of canoodling on an oversized chair. They're technically still on their honeymoon since they spent less than a day in San Diego re- packing appropriate clothes before they came here. I snatch their sticks off the table without them noticing.

The marshmallows are in a bag at Alana's feet. She sways and giggles into Jourdan's shoulder as they whisper with their heads together. Day drinking on top of s'mores on top of night drinking probably hasn't done her any favors. I smile at her as I grab three from the torn hole in the plastic.

And of course, the chocolate is on Grey's lap.

"Can I borrow some chocolate?" I ask.

"How are you going to return it?"

I smirk. "That depen—"

"Don't," he cuts me off with a chuckle.

He knows me too well, and I know he'd gag just from me say- ing the words "throw" and "up."

Elliot surveys our moment. "How did you two meet?"

My eyes jump to Grey's.

The full memory comes and goes in a matter of milliseconds.

One Taco Tuesday six years ago, Grey and his fraternity brothers sat down in my section at Nacho Mama's Tacos, where I was a waitress.

By the way, I will never serve the general public again. People suck. I'd rather calculate the maximum total drag and the maximum total inertia force on the piles used for a pier any day.

Grey's friends were no exception.

They kept getting drunker off the two-for-one margaritas, but Grey only had one. He kept apologizing for them, flashing his smile, and calling me by my name that he read off my name tag.

I thought he was one of those guys that used his charm to get himself out of any situation.

You can't possibly get annoyed with us when my lips look like this, can you? his smile seemed to say. I'd ignore my stomach clenching every time he'd look up at me and the blue dot in his brown iris seemed to get brighter. This had to be their shtick—using him to win over doe-eyed waitresses.

After they'd left, I found a napkin under his plate that he'd written *Ryan, I'm sorry my friends are assholes - I promise I'm not* on. No name. I looked at his receipt, and he'd scratched his freaking name out.

I didn't work again until that Friday.

He came in after the lunch rush. I saw him first. He scanned the restaurant and found me standing behind the bar to the right of the entrance.

I looked at him like I had no idea who he was and I hadn't been wondering what his name was for three days before I went back to balancing my register.

When the hostess greeted him, she laughed. "Four days in a

row? Our tacos are not *that* good," she remarked as she handed him his takeout food and he paid.

Instead of leaving, he casually walked over to the bar and rested his forearm against it.

"Ryan, what's your middle name?"

Looking back, I wished I had said something more intriguing, sexier. Or maybe something more elusive because I didn't know his name. But I'd been so caught off guard by his question—like Grey has always had a tendency to do to me—that I picked my head up and said, "What?"

"I have to know." He smiled. "I can't not know. It's killing me."

Stomach clench.

"Walker," I told him. "I think my parents wished I was a boy."

Which isn't true but sounds like it could be. Walker is my mom's maiden name, and my dad thought Ryan sounded cool for a girl.

"What did your parents name you?" I asked. "Mary Elizabeth?"

"I'm glad you're not a boy," he said and walked out the door.

Yes, he scratched out his name on that receipt too.

I had to wait two Taco Tuesdays before he came back with his annoying-ass friends. He knew what he was doing, making me so curious I couldn't stand it, but I wasn't going to act like I was. I refused to ask him what his name was again, and that time he paid cash.

He isn't charming, I told myself. *He's playing games.*

But I'm curious by nature. I can't help it. I love games, riddles, and challenges, which is probably why I'm so good at math. I swear he'd already somehow figured me out, what made me tick.

As soon as they left, I looked under his plate.

His napkin said, *Ryan Walker, if you text me your last name, I'll tell you my full name,* along with his number and a little drawing of an iPhone that was *really* good.

I made him wait one day longer than he made me when I texted him, Ryan Walker Copeland.

Grey Thomas Beckett, he replied.

And the rest, as they say, is history.

I wonder how he met his recent ex-girlfriend.

"Oh, you know," I say to Elliot, "same old. I waited on him and his friends in college."

"Must have been memorable for you to win her over that way," Elliot laughs.

Grey tears his distant eyes off mine and shrugs.

I bend down in front of him to pick up the chocolate at the same time he reaches for it and my long hair brushes his hand.

Both of us freeze.

Like we're touching and we shouldn't be. Even though it's only my hair.

He winds a strand through his fingers effortlessly, lightly, like he's testing out if he likes the way it feels. My hair had been dirty blonde like Evie's when Grey and I dated. He's never seen me as a strawberry blonde. It's almost as if he didn't mean to, but he couldn't help himself because it was my fault for touching him with this brand-new hair. I grasp at the chocolate, missing it the first time, and pull back. Why does this nonsense almost feel erotic?

"I like the color of your hair," he says.

The softness in his voice spins my heart like a pinwheel.

"Thanks. It's new."

This is not new.

He is not new.

I have two years and one heartbreak out of him. I should not feel like this.

I'm already infected. I'm supposed to be immune.

×××

FOUR S'MORES AND two drinks later, it's almost midnight.

Brett and Caleb went up a while ago to continue their honeymoon. Elliot and Evie went up to celebrate their pre-honeymoon. Andrew and Sadie will definitely be hooking up by the end of the week, and Sage has made it her mission to try to make Mitchell laugh. I'm sitting across the fire listening to Alana and Jourdan flirt with Grey while I pretend to be interested in my phone.

Their conversation could also be construed as normal talking, but I'm biased.

In so many words, it's:

Jourdan: *I've never been to Austin. Tell me more.*

Grey: *It's a whole vibe. Eclectic and hip and vibrant. There's tie-dye everywhere, and you should see the cool bats.*

Alana (slurring): *Tell me what you do for fun.*

Grey: *I have Texas football season tickets, I play golf, I lift weights to make my torso look like it's carved from stone, and I dabble in making girls laugh on the side with my witty commentary and smoldering heterochromic eyes.*

Alana and Jourdan: *Giggle, giggle, giggle.*

Grey: *Tell me about you two.*

Jourdan: *We're from Denver. We went to high school with Evie. We both snowboard because we're way cooler than skiers. I'm a wedding photographer, but I can't do Evie's because I'm in the wedding, giggle, and Alana's a nurse. We're edgy in that way guys like. Which one of us do you choose?*

I took some liberties.

Alana throws her head back to laugh. When she comes back, she sways and puts her palm against her forehead. "I don't feel well."

Jourdan steadies her with an arm around her shoulders. "What's wrong?"

"Too much sun. And alcohol. I ate like six s'mores," she whimpers. "Why'd you let me eat six s'mores?"

All my real attention is on them now.

Grey says, "Do you need anyth—"

Alana retches and slaps her hand over her mouth.

Grey turns ghost white and looks away. I feel kind of bad now for almost making a throw up joke earlier.

"I think I just threw up in my mouth," Alana mumbles behind her hand.

Grey closes his eyes as his throat muscles quiver. His chest expands slowly and deliberately as he takes a huge breath through his nose.

Jourdan stands and helps her up. "Let's go back to the room for some water. It's late anyway. See you tomorrow, Grey."

He half attempts a wave without opening his eyes as they stumble away.

I rack my brain for anything to say to distract him. I know how hard he is working to not throw up. Inhaling through his nose, exhaling through his mouth, focusing on controlling his gag reflex and stomach. He will avoid it *at all costs.*

"We just finished this project at work," I hurry out when a feeble, weak noise comes up from his throat. "It was a reef restoration project. Some reefs along California's coast have been damaged due to pollution and sedimentation, so we brought in huge rocks and placed them on the ocean floor, like over fifty acres. It's going to create this rocky ecosystem that will restore the fish's habitat and help with the growth of algae."

Grey nods. I think it's helping, but maybe he's nodding off from boredom.

"We got the rocks from a quarry, and it was, like, fifty thousand tons."

"How far down?" he whispers.

"About twenty-three meters," I say.

"American, please."

"Twenty-five yards in the Imperial system."

He opens his eyes and finds mine immediately.

For a flashing moment, a memory surfaces and I wish there wasn't a fire in between us so I could reach out and touch his face.

"That's really cool," he says.

"Or boring," I joke, "depending on who you ask. You should've seen Sage's face when I told her *all* about it."

"No, it's cool. Do you get to scuba dive to it later and check it out?"

"I have never even wondered that," I laugh. "That would be even cooler, but I doubt it. I'm the lowly engineer. I'll have to settle for photos."

The color is starting to come back into his face.

"Do you love it?" he asks.

I smile. "I do."

The look of admiration Grey gives me settles low in my stomach.

"I get to problem solve every day," I continue. "My favorite is brainstorming ideas no one has thought of; figuring it out to see if it works. And then I get to use or drive by the things I design, and it makes me feel like I bettered something—left a crazy Ryan mark. It's fucking hard though."

Grey laughs. "You wouldn't like it if it was easy."

"I know," I sigh. "And I love San Diego—did you know I moved there? Of course, it has its cons like any city, but the pros outweigh them. What about you? How's work? Your graphic design business is going well? Do you still doodle on everything?" I take a deep breath. "That was a lot of questions."

They keep coming rapid fire in my brain. Four years is a long time to not know someone you used to know so deeply you could finish their sentences. I have a lot of questions.

"I did know," he says, seemingly unbothered. "About San Diego. Patrick told me."

Patrick, our friend from college, lives in Los Angeles. I guess that makes sense, but it's not like I'm still close with him anymore. He was Grey's friend more than mine.

"Actually, I've slowed down on graphic design. I did an intense coding course about two years ago, and I've been doing freelance UI/UX design work."

"English, please."

"User interface and user experience design. Like how apps work, how you would use them, and then I work with coders to build it all out."

"No shit," I say.

"Yes shit."

"That's way cooler than anything I do."

Grey shrugs. "Yeah, it's cool."

"Any apps I've used?"

He cocks his head to the side. "Do you use Fuse?"

I bark out a laugh. "You created that? That app is huge."

Grey nods slightly. "I didn't create it though. I designed it; how you use it, how it works, and how you as the user feel and what you experience when using the app. It was the first major project that I led. I'm actually pretty good at it." His eyes scan my face. "What?"

"Grey, there is something a little fucked up about me using a dating app created by my ex-boyfriend."

I'll be deleting it off my phone very shortly—after I inspect it closely from a new perspective—because Grey will not be indirectly setting me up on any more dates.

He chuckles. "I'm not pimping you out."

I am beaming. "But that is like *really* awesome."

"Honestly, I kind of feel like I've channeled my inner Ryan. It's like artistic problem solving.”

My heart lunges toward him. I wish I could hug him, because I'm so damn proud of him.

Grey never felt like college was for him. It was more of a necessity, an obligation. He had a full-fledged graphic design business by the time he was a sophomore. His clients included his fraternity, the school, his father's company, and twenty other businesses he'd juggle in between school. He is the most talented artist I know.

One of my favorite things was opening a textbook in class and finding some picture he'd drawn in the margin: me or a flower or some civil engineering marvel from the paragraph next to it.

“And yeah, I still doodle on everything,” he finishes.

My brain goes a little numb. The comfortableness between us suddenly thawing from the heat of the fire or from the heat swirling inside me.

I look around, realizing we're alone.

“That's nice,” I say. *That's nice?!*

Grey's smile flattens. “Super nice.”

“It's late.” I have no idea what time it is.

He looks at his watch. “Yeah.” He clearly doesn't think it's late. We're both night owls.

“Full schedule tomorrow though,” I say, standing up and trying to correct my lie.

Grey's head follows my face before he rises.

I hesitate. He wants to walk me back to my room. I know he does. He's too polite.

“What room are you in?” he asks as I walk around the fire.

“Sage and I got one of the houses.”

We take the path that winds to the right. Silently. Because I ruined it with my *That's nice.*

Eventually, some thought makes Grey spring his head up. He raises his eyebrows playfully. “It's nice not to be a poor college kid anymore. Remember when we packed into that one-bedroom beach condo in Galveston?"

Seven of us—four girls, three guys. The girls slept like sardines on the king bed. Grey and I snuck out to his car multiple times to have sex.

Why is that what I think of?

Maybe because I haven't quite found another *him* in that department either. He still shows up in my dreams, even sometimes when I've been dating someone. Maybe because he looks just as good now in his tan sweater that's hugging his broad shoulders, and his face looks better with a few years aged into it.

I hate men.

No, that's not true in the true sense of the word. How about… men are annoying—in that way that I'm always thinking: *not fair.*

"I remember," I say as I look up at him, wondering if he's thinking about the same thing.

I thought I might be over it after our talk, but this doesn't feel right anymore. Maybe closure for us looks like sleeping together one last time.

I should think about *anything* else right now.

"How long has it been?"

Grey gives me a bemused look.

"Since you *you know*," I clarify and use my hand to make a waving vomiting motion.

"Thanks for distracting me, by the way, and you're the one who's good at math. You tell me," he says.

My smug eyes drop to the ground in front of me at the confirmation I wanted to hear. I don't know why—I'm sure it's the unhinged ex-girlfriend side of me—but I wanted to know that I had a very weird piece of him that the other girl didn't; that he didn't stare his phobia in the face for her. I wonder if he never got the opportunity to.

It's halfway out of my mouth before I realize I probably shouldn't say it, but curiosity is a very strong emotion, and in my case, a very prominent trait. "Your ex never got sick or hungover?"

I blame my catty alter-ego.

This time Grey's eyes drop to watch the ground roll by as we walk, probably wondering how much I've been told. I think he might not answer me, but after a few seconds, he says matter-of-factly, "No, she did."

My catty alter-ego likes that answer even more.

"This is mine," I say, motioning to the front door of our little sloped house that must look like even more of a fairytale when it's snowing.

I decide not to turn around, not to make the end of the night a big affair. Just go inside with a simple *goodnight*. Easy.

"Goodn—"

Grey grabs my hand, spins me, and curves his other hand around the back of my neck before I can process the motion of events. I'm frozen, thinking he's going to kiss me, thinking he's going to push me against the door like he can't take not touching me any longer. I think I'm going to welcome it, because I can feel the heat unfurling between my legs.

But his hand keeps going around my shoulders, and instead, he pulls me into a hug.

I don't know how but my arms are around his waist. I like what I can feel beneath his thin sweater. We've always fit perfectly together, like the tab and the blank of two puzzle pieces. He nestles my head into his neck.

Like always, he whispers something unexpected into my hair, "I thought if I ever saw you again, it was going to go differently."

My body is still prickling from the simple act after he pulls away. My hair is standing on end everywhere he touched, trying to cling to him.

"Goodnight, Ryan," he says.

My neurons are zapping back and forth, misfiring from the shock.

"See you. Morning. In the morning. After I sleep," I ramble to his back as he walks away. "Goodnight."

Yep, I might have to get him out of my system one last time.

There might be no other way.

Two birds. One sex stone.

<u>6</u>

The Second Ex

A S SOON AS my co-worker tells me she's going to be out today because she caught the stomach bug from her three-year-old, I feel hot.

The rest of the day my stomach is twisted into a knot.

I try to brush it off. I convince myself that I just need to use the bathroom; that I ate something at lunch that didn't agree with me. I never sweat, but my dress keeps clinging to my armpits.

I'm not sick, I tell myself, because I very rarely come down with anything. In fact, it's been years, and I have quite a few perfect attendance awards.

I'd rather get the flu one hundred times than have the stomach bug. You never know how it's going to play out. Is it going to come up? Go down? Both? I don't want to be sitting on the toilet with a bucket in my lap. Next comes the chills, the fever, the fatigue. It's torture. Then goes away as quickly as it hits.

When I finally make it home after work, I know I'm going to throw up, and I won't be able to hold it down much longer.

Brendan is waiting for me at my apartment on my couch in his white button down and navy chinos, ready to go to his friend's birthday dinner.

We've been dating for a couple of months. I met him at the bar at the beach volleyball complex. He's a supportive boyfriend and comes out to cheer for me every week. I like his strong features mixed with his deep voice, and I'm lucky to have found someone so genuinely caring because he's always thinking about me in little ways.

"I can't," I manage to say. "I think I got the stomach bug from Sarah."

The look he gives me makes me instantly think of Grey—the same pained eyes and shallow gulp.

I try to shake it from my head. I hate when he pops into my brain like that—inserting himself inadvertently.

"Are you going to… you know?" Brendan asks me.

I nod and sit on my couch. He stands like he doesn't want to get too close.

I wave my hand toward my kitchen, feeling pale. "Can you get me some water?"

Brendan navigates around the room in a large ten-foot arc and pours me a glass of water from the fridge. He places it on the side table next to me and steps back.

"Look, I can't deal with all that. I'll *you know* if you *you know*." Brendan takes another step back. "I also can't get sick right now. I have that big meeting at work next week. And I want to go tonight. Not that I don't care. I do."

Maybe it's stronger the second time because I am already thinking about Grey, but my stomach rocks from an earthquake— separate from the rumbling happening from a virus—and I look away because I'm not looking at the person I wish Brendan was.

I know it's over. He can't redeem himself—even though there

are things I don't do for him, even though I'm not that mad. I understand. He just looks different. He doesn't like me *enough*, doesn't care *enough*, and I don't want to look at him anymore.

He tries to stay and talk from across the room after I break up with him in one hurried sentence, but the effort is useless.

Finally, I've just had enough.

"Okay, just go. Because I'm going to throw up," I say.

He gags and sprints out the door. I welcome the bathroom floor.

When I am finally able to keep a few sips of water down, I crawl into bed. The green send button waits for me like a comforting heated blanket—no, like a bucket for my word vomit. It's already therapeutic at this point.

Remember when my roommate caught the stomach bug from the little boy she babysat and then got me sick?

I called to tell you I couldn't make it to the football game with you, so you blew off your friends and came straight over.

You said you hadn't thrown up in over ten years, that you do everything within your power not to throw up because feeling nauseous is better than your stomach coming up through your esophagus.

I told you to stay away, but you insisted on taking care of me. You brought me Gatorade and crackers and held my hair back while I heaved into the toilet and you gagged. You were able to hold it in until I was finished, and after you threw up, you slept next to me and held me the entire night. Then you paid heavily for it less than forty-eight hours later and failed your test that week.

I remember.

Fuck you.

I cannot date a man who won't:

X order me girly and ridiculous sounding drinks

X hold my hair back and watch me throw up, even when he has a huge vomit phobia.

7

Too Early Tuesday Morning

OUR HERD IS standing outside the hotel, too tired to talk, waiting for Hunter and Hayden to pull the rental van around.

Yes, I did turn my phone on 'ring' last night and put it on my nightstand—fighting sleep and hoping that Grey might text me. I wasn't going to stare at it, but when I woke up, it was the first thing I looked at. I would have been happy with another simple 'goodnight,' but I know that is hoping for too much.

There's nothing that could be said that doesn't open up a huge can of parasitic, mutant worms.

Hey is a huge dare to flirt. Any simple, innocent word that is texted is like an invitation to take things further. I'm not good at this.

What does a cup of coffee say?

Because Grey is walking up with Elliot and Evie and laughing, with a coffee cup in his hand that looks suspiciously like it's for me.

He holds it out when he reaches me. "Flat white still?"

"Thanks," I say while I tell myself that I only feel warm because my hand is wrapped around a hot beverage. "Some things never change, and you even knew I didn't have any yet."

Grey smirks. "I know hotel coffee machines don't make flat whites."

I swear I'm not high maintenance, but it's painful to drink anything else. This one probably tastes more amazing than usual because it was in Grey's hand.

As we shuffle into the huge white van to go fishing, somehow, I get caught in the middle of Mitchell and Sage when we slide in, and we're forced to the back row.

Grey takes the seat in the first row with Elliot and Evie, and with the multiple conversations in between us, I can't eavesdrop.

I catch every fifth word when the van isn't rattling or there's a lull in everyone's laughing at the same time: *and...that's...believe...rocks...cold.* Riveting stuff.

My attempt at a nap is futile.

Hunter is driving and Hayden's riding shotgun. No, Hayden is driving, I think, and he's whipping around the mountain curves like a bat out of Austin's Congress Avenue bridge. Grey is lucky none of us get car sick.

I lift my head and look out the window until Mitchell decides he wants to converse.

"Ryan, I haven't gotten to talk to you much."

I smile at him. Sage presses her foot down on top of mine, silently challenging me to make him laugh. I'd settle for a polite chuckle.

"Being split thirteen ways hurts. Actually, fourteen because I talk to myself too."

He blinks.

I admit it was lame, but the socially acceptable thing to do is laugh anyway.

His entire look is one that if he committed a crime, he'd never be caught because he has no distinguishing features and the cop bulletin would read: white male, brown hair, serious, five-ten to six feet, clothed.

"I think I'm going to elope, you know?"

I don't know where *that* came from, but of course I don't stop myself from saying more ridiculous words because Mitchell continues to blink.

"Somewhere exotic. Low-key on a beach. Not all these people… you know?"

Sage holds back her laugh and looks out the window so she can't see my face.

Maybe I should try saying 'you know' a third time.

"What about your parents?" he asks.

Finally. But not exactly a topic I want to discuss.

"I mean, I love them, but I don't think it would bother any of us if they're not there. They would be welcome to though. I think I envision it as a handful of people."

"Are you one of a million children?"

"No," I laugh. "Only child."

Mitchell clicks his tongue like he doesn't understand.

I elaborate, "I've always been really independent. My parents never coddled me. I played by myself a lot. This is great, all this fun stuff and parties and outings. Evelyn is made for it, but I hate attention. I'd just prefer to do something away from everyone." I shrug. "I think it makes sense for me."

And really, my family does love each other in the way you're supposed to. I call my parents on their birthdays. My parents send me a card on mine. We get together for the obligatory holidays and go on family vacations. But it's just that—obligatory. I'm not quite sure any of us actually *like* it.

In fact, my mom visited me once in San Diego. It was shortly after I moved there and a few days after I'd broken up with Chase. I'd felt homesick and invited her on a whim because I didn't have the time off from work to go to Dallas.

We went out to dinner the last night of her three-day stay, and she tipped back one too many gin martinis. Which is a total of two.

With no alcohol, Kathleen Copeland is quiet and uptight. One drink makes her more fun, a little less rigid, but two makes her tiptoe along the edge of too honest.

It was after her first (where she'd been complimenting my apartment, my job, my new city, my friends and sympathizing with my breakup) and three sips into her second when she told me, "Ryan, I'm really proud of you."

"For what?"

She laid her hand flat on the table, not quite touching mine. "For going out and experiencing things. For following through on your dreams."

That tidbit of honesty hit me a little too hard, so of course, I joked, "Engineering is a boring dream," but as soon as my mom's eyes fell back on her drink, I changed my mind. "Why do you stay?"

My voice was only a scratchy notch above a whisper. When she didn't flinch, I thought she hadn't heard me. I could pretend I never said it, never pried into something that was too personal.

But after a stretching second, she drew her hand back and sighed. "It's not that simple, but sometimes there are more important things than happiness."

Anger prickled up my neck. I was not a reason to stay. I wanted loving parents who wanted to spend time together and enjoy life as a family. I wanted that for my children. Otherwise, what is the point?

Of course, I always tried to keep the peace.

"Sure, Mom," I said. "And why stay now?"

She couldn't pin it all on me. I'd been out of the house for years. She was still "young"—spending another year the way she lived seemed crazy to me, and she had a lot more life left to live.

But another three sips and she pulled out the full-on brutal honesty.

"It's not like I expect you to understand now," she said, unable to look me in the eye, "but maybe one day you will be forced to because he's not coming back."

I swallowed my stomach back down, hoping she didn't see it written all over my face. Yes, I'd hoped when I graduated that I would have heard from him. I'd spent hours wishing I would hear my phone ring and his name would be scrolling across the top of my screen. I once googled my own name to confirm that my new address popped up, so I'd sit on my couch thinking he might find me and knock on my door.

I gave up hope after three months, but Kathleen Copeland had me pegged wrong as her daughter. She might have stopped looking, but I wasn't about to.

I decided then that I would be dating until I found another Grey, until I found what I had with him, and if I never did, then so be it.

Life is too short to be unhappy.

Later that night as I was lying on my couch, I listened to her drunkenly snoring in my bed. I didn't have any resentment toward her or my dad. They did provide well for me, and I'm sure I had an easier life than a lot of people. I wouldn't be where I was without them, but I wondered why I had been homesick in the first place. No one at home was ever truly happy.

Mostly, I just felt sorry for them.

Mitchell shakes me out of my depressing daydream, and thankfully takes the focus off of me. "I'm an only child too, but my mom has been planning my wedding since I was a baby."

"Does your future wife get a say?" I tease him.

"My mom probably wishes I were a girl so she won't have to compete. She's…" Mitchell trails off, trying to choose his next word carefully. "Overbearing. Her way is the only way kind of thing."

Well, this is interesting. I'm almost banking I know what he's going to say when I ask, "What's your dad like?"

"Passive," he states without hesitation. "A man of few words."

Does no one else even try to break this vicious cycle? Do people not realize what we slowly become if we're not careful?

Am I the only one who notices and refuses? Please tell me I'm not the only one.

Actually… my eyes flicker to Grey smiling at something Evie said. He notices life's awful sense of humor and refuses to complete the circle.

"Are you in a relationship?" Mitchell asks.

My eyes can't pull away from Grey's face. "No."

Grey glances over his shoulder like he can feel me watching him. The blood in my cheekbones burns slightly less than between my legs. He smiles, like he knows exactly what I'm thinking.

Maybe he does.

You want to ravish each other tonight? I try to ask with my eyes. *You make me come. I make you come. Win-win.* I mentally dust off my hands. *Welp, that's that.*

But no, the lines of communication in our eyes are rusty. His confused lips curl up while his eyebrows flatten. *What are you thinking?* he's asking me amusingly.

Mitchell tries to talk over my thoughts. "Have you ever been fly fishing?"

I shake my head.

"I can help you, if you want."

"Uh huh," I mutter, half listening.

He's throwing out words like bobbin, imitative and impressionistic flies, stripping line, and clinch knot.

I'm thinking about stripping off each article of Grey's clothing and the tight knot forming below my belly button.

This isn't something I'm accustomed to. I have never slept with an ex in my life, but break-up sex is fairly common, I think. Ours is just four years late.

The sooner I can make this happen, the better. I need Grey out of my bloodstream. My veins are sticky and hot, and I can almost feel the sludge trying to pump through the constricted space.

I have to pop this bubble between us, but this is brand-new territory for me. I don't exactly know how to navigate us to 'Want to hook up one last time?'

I smile back at Grey and turn my phone over in my lap to text him. I push down the sting that I am the first one to text, and it almost feels surreal that I am now about to text him for real. His phone is going to vibrate in his pocket with my name across it for the first time in four years.

We're the only two people in the world who aren't going to turn out like our parents. How does it feel?

I look up to see him pick his hips up off the seat and, I suspect, pull his phone from his pocket.

He types until my phone buzzes in my hand.

Feels fucking fantastic… although my dad does like to fish. Alone.

Good thing you're not alone, I say.

I can only see the back of his head now.

Are you going to fish with me? comes after a few seconds.

I consider my reply, wondering how much he wants me to fish with him or if he's just trying to be nice.

I've never fly fished in my life. I'll probably suck at it. I was thinking about lying out on a rock instead.

I can dangle bait at least.

I'll teach you, he says. I promise I'm more fun than Mitchell, and I made

Elliot rent a pair of teeny tiny waders.

I'm not the only one trying to eavesdrop, and maybe I'm not the only one who is irrationally jealous.

Just for me? You shouldn't have, I joke.

Of course, for you. Never for anyone else.

Ajoskycgsbwisym, my brain thinks in a sludge of letters.

He's supposed to be working himself out of my system, not burrowing further into it.

One and done is the way.

I'm not sure I can put together a coherent or socially appropriate text after that.

So, I don't reply.

× × ×

MITCHELL CAN'T BLAME me for semi-ditching him. I wasn't in the right state of mind when I muttered in agreement at him.

And I'm not in my right state of mind now either as Grey holds up my XXS waders with a giant smile.

I gravitate toward him, not of my own accord.

They match the pair he's wearing exactly. Light gray with a dark gray pocket on the chest and a red zipper across the top. There's a buckle on the front of each strap.

He has on a thin light blue hoodie underneath his waders, and his sleeves are pushed up to his elbows.

Such. Nice. Forearms.

"I just have a bikini on under here," I say, running my hand down my sundress. "I wasn't planning on getting in the water. It's freezing."

Grey rolls his eyes. "I bought you clothes."

Why am I surprised by anything he does anymore?

He hands me the waders and crouches down at my feet to rummage through his bag.

A seafoam green hoodie appears in front of my face followed by leggings, socks, and a sleek spandex shirt.

"You bought me all of this? How'd you know I wasn't going to take Mitchell up on his offer?" I mutter, awkwardly holding the ball of clothes.

Grey smirks up at me from his knees while he zips his bag closed. Jesus, nothing he does doesn't remind me of some time we've had sexual relations.

"That guy never laughs."

"True," I say.

I swivel my head one hundred and eighty degrees. I don't know where to change. We're in a gravel parking lot off the highway. There's no bathroom or shelter or coverage besides trees and bushes lining the outer edge.

Grey stands and waves his hand to the space between our white van and a silver SUV. "Go back there, and I'll stand in front of you."

I walk as far back as I can until I hit the bushes. Grey turns his back to me and takes up the entire space between the two cars. He puts a hat on while I slip off my dress. I stuff it into my tote bag and pull out underwear and a sports bra.

"Working on any new cool apps?" I ask to fill the silence.

I put my underwear on over my swimsuit before I do girl magic and slip my swimsuit bottom off.

"Maybe," he says. "Patrick has been raising capital for an idea he's been working on. We'll see how it goes. Right now, I've just been doing freelance UX/UI on top of graphic design."

Same magic goes for the top. "What's the idea?"

"It's an app where you order and pay your bar tab all from your phone."

"That's awesome. I love things that make us less and less likely to interact face to face and more and more lazy. How long does it take to raise money?" I lean against the van to put the tight black leggings on.

"Whatever I can do to contribute to society and have your face even more glued to your phone," Grey jokes. "And probably six to nine months, if I had to guess."

"I also love how remote jobs are fairly common now. I have a few co-workers who work on the east coast."

"Yeah," Grey says absently. "Clothed?"

I tug the shirt over my head. "Clothed."

He turns around and patiently waits for me to put on my waders while he folds my tote bag into the smallest square he can and stuffs it inside his backpack.

The shoes are ridiculously clunky, but everything fits. "How do I look?"

Grey cascades his eyes down my body as he stands. "Like the cutest fisherman I've ever seen."

I scrunch my nose. I don't want to be *cute*, but arguably, I see the inappropriate thoughts in his eyes.

"Just cute?"

Grey laughs and brushes me off. "Stop trying to read my thoughts. You don't know me anymore."

"Hmph," I say, ignoring his playful mimicking tone and squeezing past him. I know what I saw.

He doesn't move as I slide beside him. He just stands there smirking as a wall of muscle and warm skin and masculinity that I try to pretend isn't guiding my body in like a lighthouse.

"Can you walk in those things?" he asks to my back.

I clomp through the gravel like a Clydesdale. "Doing just fine."

He sidles up next to me, picking up what I suppose is two fly fishing rods in cases (though it looks like someone had a sense of humor and designed it to look like a penis and balls), before we take the path into the woods.

I just make out Sage's and Mitchell's bodies as they round a curve twenty yards in front of us and disappear.

"How long is this walk?" I question him. I glance behind me where Andrew and Sadie are bringing up the rear. They're so far away, like they don't want to be seen with their embarrassing "parents."

"I think about fifteen minutes per the guide," he says. He opens his mouth again but knows from my face not to push the shoe issue.

We walk in silence for what seems like fifteen minutes but is actually less than a minute.

Fifteen minutes is a long freaking time to walk in silence with your ex-boyfriend who you last saw when he screamed he loved you, turning multiple heads, after you walked through TSA… after having sex in the back seat of a car in an airport parking lot.

I can already tell I'm going to be terrible at initiating closure sex.

"How's Lily?" I ask.

Grey picks his head up and smiles brightly. "She's great."

My heart melts like a scented wax bar in a warmer. This Grey is one of my favorites, when he shows you in his face how much he loves someone and something.

"She still asks about you," he says.

I hold back the unexpected tingle of tears. "I miss her too."

"She just turned twenty-three, and she's been taking classes through a program at UT."

"Really?" I gush. "That's awesome. What kind of courses?"

"All sorts of stuff. Science, humanities, music, cooking. Her favorite was one on the solar system."

I pout. "I didn't rub my math off on her?"

"She doesn't like art either," Grey laughs. "No matter how hard I tried, she's definitely a science girl. And they also learn professional and social skills that focus on career development. She's met so many other people with disabilities and has new friends. She even has a job now."

My eyes light up. "Doing what?"

"You remember that coffee shop near my parents' house? She greets people and offers samples, cleans the tables. She loves it."

"I'm so happy for her," I say.

"Yeah," Grey says, "she's thriving. I don't feel like this many opportunities existed for Lily even five years ago." He pauses like he's not finished, but it takes a few more steps for him to speak again. "She wants to move out."

"Wow, Grey. That's amazing for her. How do your parents feel?"

He runs a hand through his hair. "Nervous. Anxious. Not ready. But also supportive. Lily has a lot of friends who live in supported living facilities. We'll see how it goes. There are a lot of steps in the process."

"Like what?" I ask.

"It takes a long time for it all to line up. Like funding, agencies, and finding the right fit and staff. Then the waitlists are long, but Lily is excited."

I resist the temptation to bite my nails and ask, "How do you feel about it?"

From the look of relief mixed with misery he gives me, I don't think anyone has asked him this question yet.

"Lily is excited," he repeats too happily.

"You said that already," I press.

Grey chews on his bottom lip, so I lure him with silence until one long breath comes out with, "Conflicted." And then he can't hold it in any longer. "I want to be excited. I don't want to feel like her third parent. I'm supposed to be her big brother. And then I feel guilty for even thinking that because I love her so much. She deserves it. I wish I could say that I was only happy for her that she has the opportunity, and I am happy, but I'm also terrified." Our fingers brush past each other, and for a fleeting moment they find one another again. I wish I could grab his hand, hold it in mine, squeeze him to give him any reassurance that I could. Then we swing arms again, because it's awkward walking with them stick-straight, and he smiles. "Mostly, though, I'm really proud of her."

It hurts that I didn't know all of this. I don't know why. He's not mine anymore. I'm not privy to anything that goes on in his life. I shouldn't care so much, but having someone who was so intricately tied into your life ripped from you as suddenly as Grey was hurts. Things in our relationship weren't bad. They were strong; stronger than I knew was possible. There was no gradual everyone-saw-this-coming demise.

And I guess it hurts for a long time.

"I'm really proud of her too," I say.

He pulls his phone out of his pocket and grins into the screen. "Here she is with the solar system model she built. She said I was being annoying and wouldn't let me help."

He hands me his phone, and it takes everything in me not to spill tears all over it. I beam at it instead. Lily and Grey smiling into the camera that Grey must be holding out, and she's holding up the model. She looks just like him but with long hair and soft features. The same brown eyes without the blue spot. The same brown hair.

"She doesn't look like a teenager anymore," I say.

"Yeah," Grey laughs. "I'm going to have to worry about her boyfriends next."

"Maybe you'll be less stressed if she does long distance," I tease.

Grey stops short, but he can't hide his smile.

"Too soon?" I joke. "Come on. Four years is not too soon."

"You are not funny."

"I think your lips beg to differ."

He scoops me up and throws me over his shoulder.

"Grey!"

"We'll get there in half the time without you stomping along like the world's slowest elephant."

"Are you calling me fat?"

He lifts me up by my hips high above his head to make a point. "Those shoes are fat though."

"Fine," I huff, but I can't keep the laugh out of my voice. "You better teach me to be the best fly fisherman and make sure I catch the biggest… what are we fishing for?"

"Trout," he tuts.

"Trout," I repeat.

I dangle from his shoulder and watch his muscular ass tense under his waders with each step.

My face is too close to it, but I have nowhere else to look, so I prop my chin up on my elbows and let myself enjoy the view. I don't know what it is about his tight ass that makes me want to sink my fingertips into his butt cheek and then find out (like, I didn't know before) that I can't make it budge any deeper than the layers of his skin.

By the time I realize I'm extremely turned on, my body has let off so much steam inside my waders, even though it's a cool seventy-one degrees out, I've increased the humidity between us to one hundred percent.

Grey's hand is so large it almost completely covers the back of my thigh, and it's hard for him to ignore the sticky, muggy feeling between us.

His hand shifts upward, inward.

Closer.

My mind shifts downward, laser focused on the feeling that his fingers digging into me is eliciting between my legs.

I can only think of that primal, sweaty sex that's almost always spontaneous. The kind where you peel each other's clothes off like you're wearing latex. The energy surrounding you is animalistic, greedy. The bedroom feels like a steam room and a drop of sweat rolls down your skin. A drop of his sweat falls and mixes with yours. You'd think it was disgusting if it wasn't so damn good. It's hard. It's fast. And you're glistening in the dark, slipping and sliding against each other. Every self-conscious thought has been released, and all there's left to do is get completely and deliriously lost in—

My body thunks. Grey drops me to my feet on the ground like I burned him.

Or maybe he put me down gently (I'm not entirely sure) because we had emerged into a clearing, and I hadn't noticed, in the middle of the most gorgeous landscape—a rocky river with greenish blue water rushing over and around them, full lush trees lining the mountains looming over us, snow caps covering the highest mountains in the distance, and a gorgeous bright blue sky that makes me feel nothing but happy endorphins.

There's even a huge white-tailed deer across the river that everyone is enamored with.

I smell clouds and wet rocks. I feel the sunshine and wind whispering against my skin. I can taste the mountain air.

No wonder everyone standing around is silent. This is an assault on all five senses.

My senses are already going haywire, weakened from the previous attack.

And to top it off, Grey is looking at me like we got our wires crossed.

I guess my ass was too close to his face too.

✕✕✕

NO SURPRISE HERE, but I'm terrible at fly fishing.

The words Grey tries to teach me don't make sense. The rod isn't a normal fishing rod. I keep getting my line stuck in the branches overhanging the opposite bank of the river.

I don't like being bad at things, and I'm frustrated as hell but in that way you brush off everything with a sense of humor and give up.

"This sucks," I sigh as my fly line gets stuck for the seventh time.

Grey laughs and follows the thin white line thirty feet across to untangle it before he scolds me. "Quit tugging on it."

I still my antsy self. "What's the point of this? The fish just swim right by the little thingy, even when I get it in the water every fourth try."

He holds up the tiny wispy brown fly that he claims he made. "This little thingy is called an Elk Hair Caddis."

"That looks like something I pulled out of Sage's hairbrush."

Grey drops his jaw and feigns offense as he reels himself back into me, grabbing a foot of line with each step.

I can feel his movements in my hand that I'm gripping the rod with, and that vibration is knocking through me like I'm a tuning fork.

When he reaches me, he steps in front and angles his head down close to my ear to chuckle, "Maybe the trout would like a fly made from your hairbrush better."

"Creep," I tease.

My stomach clenches anyway, and I make the mistake of looking up into his smirking eyes.

"Let me help you…?" he asks with a slight question mark on the end.

I nod, and before I can remember how to exhale, he circles around to stand behind me.

Grey wraps an enormous hand over the back of mine. Warmth cascades up my arm.

"Hold it here," he says, repositioning the cork on my fingers instead of my palm. He jiggles our hands. "Light."

"Light," I repeat breathily.

"Thumb here." Grey slides his thumb down mine, nudging the pad of it into position at the top end of the handle. My body is so hot it's going to boil everyone alive who's standing in the river. He mimics casting with my new grip controlled by him.

"I'm a pro already." I roll my eyes, ignoring every inch of my burning skin. "Should I have stuck with Mitchell?"

He hitches one eyebrow and smiles. "You know, fly fishing is all about physics."

"Hmm, talk dirty to me," I joke. "I'm listening."

"Newton's laws of… moving?" he replies.

"Motion," I say. "Newton's three laws of motion. But continue. I'm still hot and bothered."

Literally.

"What's the first one?" Grey asks.

His face is so close to mine, it takes me a second to recall it. "If a body is at rest or in motion at a constant speed in a straight line, it stays like that unless acted upon by an outside force."

"Yeah," he laughs. "That one. So, your *Sage* Hair fly is still at the end of the line." He points to it sitting on top of the water. "Think of it like you're sending momentum from your arm through the rod to the line as you cast to send the fly forward."

"Potential energy," I smile. "Momentum. Okay, got it."

I test out flicking my wrist once. I don't get stuck in the trees at least.

"Better," Grey says nicely. "And the second law?"

"Force equals mass times acceleration."

"The fly is absorbing water as it lands."

"Its mass is increasing, and I need to change the rate of acceleration?" I ask but I already know the answer.

Grey lets his hand drop to my hip. "Go on," he urges me as he traces his thumb over the top curve of my ass.

Nothing is going to get done if he keeps this up. My brain can't focus on both the momentum of fishing and the momentum of our newfound I-don't-how-to-label-it relationship at the same time.

I shift my hip into him as he draws me closer with his fingers. My butt rubs against his crotch and there's a swish between the fabric of our waders.

I try my learned technique, landing my fly just above a fish chilling in the water teasing me. He doesn't react.

I groan. "Newton's third law is when two objects interact, they apply equal and opposite forces on each other. How does that apply?"

Grey laughs, and I feel it down my spine. "How the hell should I know? Catch that fish."

I pull my arm back again and cast. Once, twice. I let it float above the fish again. Grey reaches out and lets out some of my line from the reel, and suddenly, my fly disappears under the water.

I gasp. "Did I get it?"

Grey pats me on the side of my butt and grins. "Pull him in."

I blink up into his face. He isn't looking at me, but I can't move. I'm stuck in place, the track of my brain skipping. Grey. Teaching me to fish. Using physics he doesn't understand.

He cradles his arms around me when I continue acting like a statue, hooks his finger around the line to hold it, and pulls the fish into us.

When he lifts it out of the water, he whistles softly in my ear. "Beautiful. He's huge."

It is—a speckled brownish green slimy-looking fish, shining in the sun, with a red line down the middle.

I finally smile when Grey unhooks it and places it in my hands. It's slippery and wriggles as I hold it up and beam appreciatively at him.

He holds his eye contact, pride pulling on the corners of his lips. "See, I still know you."

His soft words whoosh through me.

"You got lucky," I smile.

"I know," he says, eyes scanning my face slowly.

"You guys are cute."

Grey and I both whip our heads to the side, where Jourdan is taking a picture of us in our moment.

She shrugs with her face in her phone. "Elliot said you two weren't a thing anymore."

"We're not," Grey and I both breathe out hastily at the same time and create distance between us.

Our eyes connect, now five feet apart. Ouch. Even though I said the exact same thing he said, the words still nip at my heart.

Jourdan lifts her head and looks straight at Grey. "Oh." She smiles bigger. "My mistake."

Goddammit. I don't need any sex competition. This whole thing is awkward enough without it, but I'm grateful for the snap back to reality.

Grey and I are definitely not still together—no matter how well he thinks he still knows me.

<u>8</u>

Tuesday Afternoon

ELLIOT SCOFFS IN the face of rest and relaxation.

After fly fishing and a late lunch, we pile back into the van to go straight to the high ropes course.

I think Grey and I both make a subconscious effort to stand as close to each other as we possibly can this time so no one will step in between us.

It's those subtle things your brain and body do without question—like submitting to the forces of gravity. Neither one of us will acknowledge it openly, but I can feel it happening, and I'm choosing to ignore it, because I just plain want to.

When we settle together in the back row, we flip through all of the pictures we took of one of us holding up a huge brown or rainbow trout before I slowly let my head down on Grey's shoulder.

He's my personal pillow—not the one you get when you go on vacation and curse yourself for leaving yours at home because the one you have to sleep on for a week is too flat or too fluffy or too firm. Nothing compares to the one left on your bed, and whether I like it or not, I'm already too comfortable.

I don't even overanalyze the fact that Grey shifts to let me nuzzle further into his neck. The soap on his skin smells better than the ridiculous three-hundred-dollar reed diffusers that Evie sells in her boutique.

I don't think anything of it when his arm wraps around my shoulders and warms me with friction from my wrist to my elbow. His body warmth feels better than a weighted, heated blanket.

I'm blissfully out of my mind and finally able to nap after he whispers into my hair, "Get some sleep before Elliot comes up with a car game."

When we make it there after what feels like two seconds, Sage wakes me up with a violent push, and we all tumble out to stretch our legs.

High above our heads are endless contraptions. They disappear into the canopy as each platform around a giant tree goes further up and down the slope of the mountain in a large maze.

"We're actually doing this?" I ask, looking up into the treetops.

Elliot shoots me an exasperated look, while still smiling, of course. "Yes! Have you done a high ropes course before? This one has a great zipline at the end."

"It's just a giant puzzle, right?" I scan the ropes and wooden platforms, trying to calculate the distances between some of the planks. "I don't seem tall enough to do some of those things though. That low ropes course over there looks great."

Much more suitable for short people, it has a spider web similar to what I've seen on school playgrounds.

"You'll figure it out," Elliot teases. "You always do."

I roll my eyes at everyone else's eyes five to twelve inches above mine. They've been blessed with height their entire life, and I often find myself wondering what the world looks like from up there. They can actually see what's on top of the fridge or use the top shelf in their closet.

The ropes course instructor calls the guys over to harness up, so I saunter over to Sage and Evie.

I give Sage a knowing smirk and joke, "Does Mitchell laugh when he comes?"

Her eyes widen in wonder like she hasn't thought of that. "I'll have to try that tonight."

"What did you try?" I ask.

"Your sex stone joke totally fell flat. He blinked at me. Just so you know."

"You'll never be as funny as me," I tut.

"Where are we on the plan?" Sage asks, ignoring me.

"What plan?" Evie huffs. "Why am I not involved in the plan?"

I wave a hand at her face. "Because you're getting married this weekend."

"We're orchestrating closure," Sage tells her before she raises her eyebrows toward me. "You two were in your own world last night and this morning. *And* on the drive over here. Any progress?"

"Last night was comfortable until it wasn't," I say. "Today is comfortable until it isn't. We just fall back into our known rhythm. I don't know what I need." I squeeze my eyes shut and lower my voice. "There was a moment last night where I thought he was going to kiss me. I'm cringing right now thinking about it. I was thinking maybe we need to, like, hook up one more time… or something. I'm trying to be casual, break the awkward ice."

"Break-up sex!" Sage hisses. "You never got it."

"Can closure be dynamic?" I ask.

"Is everything in your life dynamic?" Sage teases. "Yeah, we're changing the action. Screw talking. Just screw."

"I can't just flirt with him."

"What have you been doing all day?" Sage questions me.

I shrug. I'm not sure what we were doing—trying to be nice, not make things awkward, be friends again?

Evie gawks with a wide-open smile. "Why not? Look at *that*."

I follow Evie's eyeline to where I see Grey in a harness, and the harness tight around his groin.

My eyes bulge—not nearly as big as *that*.

"Jesus," I groan. I already know what's there, and my leggings suddenly feel constricting. I wonder how often he's pictured me naked the last couple of days. "Seriously, what if he doesn't flirt back?"

Sage shrugs. "I'm not sure how you define what you've been doing, but you won't know if he will until you try."

"The alternative is being humiliated when he shoots me down."

"So?" Sage waves me off. "You won't see him again for another four years after this. No big deal if he does."

"Besides, you're, like, the perfect rebound," Evie adds. "Casual, live across the country, you already know each other, and you're hot. There's no way he will turn you down. Make him think with his dick."

No less than five memories flood my brain: a trampoline in his parents' backyard, on the hood of his car in a field on a road trip, in the walk-in freezer at Nacho Mama's Tacos, his car after a football game, in a dressing room at the mall.

Grey used to think with his dick a lot, but we were young, dumb college kids. He couldn't keep his hands off me. Now, we're twenty-six-year-old professionals who have real jobs and actual things to lose if we go to jail for indecent exposure. I think making him so horny he can't help himself will be a little harder—pun intended—to accomplish now.

The thoughts alone are turning me on like a gas stove though.

I can almost hear the clicking of the ignitor before the flame catches. If Grey was any closer, I'd combust. *I* certainly haven't changed that much when it comes to him.

"Okay, maybe I can do that," I say. "Not on a ropes course though."

"Lay down the groundwork. Low-key flirt," Sage suggests.

I'm wincing just thinking about it. "Yeah," I say as the instructor calls us over to strap up.

After he's done showing us how to tighten it and comes around to make sure it's snug enough, I stand there awkwardly. It's too tight and gripping me in all the wrong places, so now I have to worry about having a camel toe. I can't feel sexy enough to flirt when I'm worried about having a camel toe.

Life is cruel.

✕ ✕ ✕

I'M NOT AFRAID of heights, but I am having trouble finding my balance on this tiny rickety platform.

And there's seven more after this first one.

This is the last obstacle before the zipline at the end. All of the others were relatively easy: a spider web, unstable bridge, inclined log, line bridge.

Every time I try to reach my leg across the gap that is twice my height (literally, I swear) to the next one, the whole thing rattles from the two ropes it's dangling from.

If I fall, I'll be stranded, hanging from my harness and further toeing my camel. Was there no better way to design these black straps other than squeezing my groin?

I glance behind me, where Grey is waiting patiently from the platform built around the tall tree trunk.

"Quit looking at my junk," he says, leaning against the bark and crossing his arms over his chest.

I double take, lingering on it for another second, before I pull my eyes up to meet his. "I can't help it. It's just… there."

He makes no movement to try to shield it. "There's no mystery there for you, Ryan."

Like that matters now. It's not about the mystery with him. I know what I get from Grey until suddenly, I don't. I think he will always surprise me, no matter what. He throws a curveball into the equation every single time.

He scopes out my predicament, smirking, as I internally laugh at the puns popping into my brain.

This is the way my neuro pathways work:

I like a little zero mystery.

It's still so hard to look away.

Shove your junk wherever you want.

"How are you going to get across?" he asks.

Across your crotch? Easy. My thighs will be your harness.

"I'm thinking about swinging this thing, but I'm probably going to fall. I don't see any other way though."

"Let's see it."

I grab onto both ropes and push my legs to create momentum. After a few swings I'm close enough to reach a foot out.

I test it, putting the ball of my right foot out, but the second wooden plank tips from the weight of my leg. I change my mind and swing back.

"I just need to grow a few inches really quick," I say.

"Jump off," he laughs.

I turn fully around and narrow my eyes at him. "You could walk across this normally."

He sticks his long leg out and pushes the edge of the wood piece I'm standing on hard. When I swing back to him, Grey grabs the ropes right above my hands and smiles. His fists slide down to rest against mine.

All I can think about as he pulls me into him inch by inch is what it would be like to kiss him again. The taste, the urgency, the feeling. He's one of those kissers that makes it sensual every damn time because his lips move with the perfect pressure. It's not too firm and not too soft. He used to make my legs liquefy, and then he'd have to hold me up by the small of my back so I didn't puddle to the floor.

"Hey," he says softly when our bodies are separated by a space you could only slip a piece of paper through.

My breath hitches. The ends of Grey's shaggy bangs almost graze my forehead as he looks down at me. A playful spark singes the edge of his smile.

Then he pushes me.

An aggravated exhale escapes my lips that I hope he didn't hear.

When I pivot back, he gives me another push by my hips and says, "Turn around and jump."

Right. I forgot what I was doing.

I'm loopy as I slowly turn, trying to balance, trying to focus on the next platform. My foot makes it, my hand does not.

"Shit," I hiss as I slip and fall.

The anticipation of what I know is coming is probably worse than the actual act, but I'm still surprised by it. My heart leaps into my throat and pulses as the line I'm attached to catches me three feet later. The force and suddenness jostle me violently. My harness gives me a deep front and back wedgie, and I've definitely bruised my pubic bone. It aches between my legs from the straps digging into me. Finally, I settle, and the line spins me slowly, suspended in mid-air, to face Grey.

I blame him because my mind is still gloop. He was flirting. With me.

"Ouch. Are you all right?" He buries his smile in a look of fake concern.

"I'm fine," I laugh. "My vag on the other hand…"

Grey chuckles and steps out onto the first wooden platform. He crouches slightly and extends his hand out to me.

Our bodies will be touching if he picks me up. There's no way they won't be. He's too large and the rectangular piece of wood is too small.

"Come on," he says, hoisting me up.

All in one swift motion, like I'm a girly, pink, three-pound dumbbell, my feet are laced with his and the front of our bodies are pressed together.

I try to hold my shoulders back as much as I can and avoid looking him directly in the eye.

"How do you want to do this?" he asks.

I definitely have a sex swing joke swirling in my head right now.

I need a clear mind if I'm going to get through this. His proximity is so overwhelming that everything will become a sexual innuendo, and I am not going to flirt with sexual innuendos.

Grey senses my hesitation. "Ropes courses are about teamwork, aren't they?"

I nod. I mean, they are.

"Okay," he says into my ear as I turn around, "let's be a team."

Before I can respond, he bends his knees, pokes his butt out, and heaves us forward. Two swings later, and all I have to do is take half a step.

I spin to face him after I've successfully stabled myself on the second piece of wood. "That was almost too easy," I joke.

His eyes light up. "Let's play a game."

The words are spoken. I can't not play. It's how I'm wired, which Grey already knows.

"What're the rules?" I ask.

"Simple. Each rung we have to get across differently."

"Seven more scenarios seem like a lot. Can there be that many ways to cross a ten-foot gap?"

"Put that mind to work, Ryan." He steps onto my platform easily. "And it is not ten feet across."

"Semantics." I raise my eyes to the line above our heads and test if the carabiner slides easily. "You think we can glide across?"

"I'm an excellent pusher," Grey says.

"I'm an excellent puller," I reply.

I grab the rope above my head that is attached to the harness and hoist myself up into a ball. Grey stands there smiling distractedly, but I don't have time for that.

"Push me before my upper body strength wears out. I have only milliseconds left."

Grey uses one hand on my hip and gives me a small push for momentum before he shoves me across. The top carabiner does glide but catches slightly just before I reach the next platform. I lower myself down and reach out a long leg. I'm able to pull the rope of it with my foot so I can grab it and stand.

I grin at Grey when I turn around. "Halfway there."

When he pulls up his body into a ball with one arm, I'm not focused on his outstretched arm. Instead, I'm watching his bicep strain against the hem of his shirt and wishing I could curve my fingers around it.

He waves his free hand in my face after a second. "I don't want to just hang here all day."

I certainly wouldn't mind.

I tip my body and lean out with my free hand while clinging to one of the ropes. Palm to palm with him and leveraging my legs against my tiny swing, I jerk his weight forward.

He doesn't slide as easy—I guess because he's heavier—so I

have to pull him a second time.

"Two down," Grey says, lowering himself into the tiny space next to me. "How do you want to do this one?"

"Your turn to choose."

He reaches an arm high above him and grabs the top line. "Think you can sort of monkey bar across it?"

My lips pull down skeptically. "Are you going to keep overestimating the strength of my arms?"

"Five-year-olds can swing on monkey bars," he challenges me.

"And if I fall?"

"Climb back up your rope attached to your harness."

"This isn't an '80s P.E. class."

Grey scans my arms. "Doesn't look like you've stopped working out in the last four years." His eyes rise to the sky like he didn't mean to say that out loud. "Can I lift you up?"

I have to admit I'm proud of myself with that tiny bit of female smugness. He notices me just as much as I notice him.

"Sure," I say, trying to sound seductive and womanly and god knows what else—anything but clever. He wraps an arm around my upper thighs and raises me until I can grab it.

"I'll go first so I can lower you down," he tells me. "Keep your momentum up."

"Thank you," I huff as he grabs on and shakes the rope I'm desperately clinging to. I can't help but watch his butt as I start to traverse behind him. "I've played on a playground before."

Grey stops abruptly and turns to smirk at me.

"I can't keep up momentum when you stop." I kick him in the side, trying to use the violence to gain it again. "Go."

Three more arm grabs and he's there. Three of his arm grabs equal five of mine. The rope fibers are prickly and uncomfortable in the palm of my hand, but I don't fall.

When I reach him, I slide down the front of Grey's body slowly. He has his arm wrapped around me loosely enough to allow me to descend, but his fingers are lingering everywhere he touches. The tips dig into me at my thigh, my hip, and lastly my rib cage, like he's drawing me closer. His eyes are locked to mine, and he has to be able to feel my heart in double time, banging against his chest.

We're almost face to face, and he's looking at me like he has a thousand times—like I'm his girlfriend and he's about to kiss me.

Neither of us move. Neither of us are breathing. His pupils are ink black, focused so intensely on mine, and the one dot of blue in his iris is highly contrasted. Peripheral vision has become obsolete.

I slide down a fraction of an inch more, but our helmets clank together, and the sound seems to startle him into this reality, the one where I am not his girlfriend anymore and he can't go around putting his lips on me like he used to. He releases me to fall a few inches to my feet while I cling to his neck.

"Sorry," he whispers.

I don't think he has anything to be sorry for. The speed of my pulse tells me I want him to kiss me. The knock below my belly button tells me I've missed that intense look of hunger that I've only ever gotten from him.

Maybe this won't be as hard as I thought, and I'm supposed to be flirting anyway.

I run my nails lightly down his arm. "Carry me across the next one."

Well, I wish I could suck those awkward words and the tone of my voice right back into my mouth, but Grey doesn't laugh.

Instead, his eyes follow the path of my fingers, and we both watch as goosebumps appear across his skin.

He lets out a strained breath and regains his composure quickly. "Climb on."

So, I do. My arms go over his shoulders. My legs go around his waist. I smile at him before I place my cheek to his so he can see what he's doing.

His chuckle tickles my ear, but he doesn't say anything.

"I almost made a sex swing joke earlier too," I confess.

He laughs harder, and the weirdness between us seems to melt away. The old and new versions of us fusing together.

"I've missed you and your mind," he says, stepping across the gap like it's the easiest thing in the world.

"I've missed you and your ability to take a ten-foot step," I say as he puts me down.

And a lot of other things, I can't help but think.

"A handy skill I can use once a decade."

The last few are harder to figure out. We go backward on the next, then we sit and only use our legs, where I almost topple over but Grey catches my arm. For the final swing, Grey has the wild idea to use them as trapezes, and I'm surprised we actually accomplish it. Lastly, we simply jump to the next tree trunk platform since it's not a ten-foot-wide space.

"Want to zipline together?" Grey asks me as we circle around to the other side.

The tree canopy opens up to a gorgeous landscape. The leaves slope downward for what seems like miles and rustle in the breeze.

Grey and I exchange looks like we're the only two on this platform, but we're not. We're just in our own little world.

I smile genuinely. "Yeah, I do."

The instructor, who has been patiently waiting for us to snap out of it, hooks our carabiners to the zipline and shows us how to sit in the air. Grey cradles me between his legs before we launch ourselves off.

The wind rushes around us as we fly through the sky. I stretch my arms out wide and lean back into him.

I'm that kind of happy where I wouldn't choose to be anywhere else at any point in time except here. It surprises me, but I think I know why.

"I miss playing games with you," I say.

I'm not sure if he heard me. My eardrums are vibrating from the wind whipping against them.

But I know he did when he slides his hands down my arms, places his palms against the back of my hands, and laces his fingers through mine.

9

The Third Ex

IT'S FRIDAY NIGHT, but I'm exhausted.

This past week has been draining. I stayed late at work every day trying to finish a project for a deadline.

I don't want to go out to dinner anymore, so when Ian texts me, I tell him to come over to my place instead.

Ian is the third guy I've dated in San Diego. He's got a mousy brown buzz cut that I love to rub my palm over. He's a little stuffy and works in IT, but he's really sweet and he likes to problem solve as much as I do. Everything he says about networks and VPNs tends to go over my head, but I try hard to soak in what I can about computers when he talks because I care about him and he doesn't go cross-eyed when I talk about work like Sage. We met on a dating app. It's not my favorite way to meet people, but we ended up having some mutual friends through my job. Things have been good over the last four months.

I spend two hours preparing. I stop by the grocery store on the way home. I steal some dice from a game in my closet. I draw and

94

color little pictures of different candies and sweets on cards and make a whole unique game board complete with little figures of me and Ian as game pieces.

I'm not an artist at all, but I think it's endearing in a terrible way.

When I open the door for him, I'm beaming with pride. He kisses me and makes a beeline for my remote, not catching my excitement, before I can even get my words out.

He picks it up to turn on the TV.

"Want to play a game?" I ask him playfully.

Ian glances at me and punches in the numbers of the channel he wants. "The MLB playoffs are on." He falls back on my couch, puts his feet up on my wooden coffee table, and pats the seat next to him. "I'm glad you wanted to stay home. I kind of didn't want to go out either."

"I have a better idea than that though," I say, lowering my voice seductively. "Like your favorite board game when you were a kid."

His eyebrows pinch, not picking up on my tone. He cocks his head toward me but can't tear his eyes off the television. "Why would I want to play that? I'm not a kid anymore."

His tone isn't mean—I'd peg it more as indifference.

"I had this idea…" I trail off.

His eyes are trained in front of him, the light from the screen illuminating his brown eyes blue. He curses at the umpire.

Finally, Ian notices I'm still standing here rooted in my spot next to the table. He smiles sweetly. "I don't want to play a game. I want you to come cuddle with me on the couch."

I know he doesn't know what I have in mind. He might be more open to the idea if I tell him it is actually a sex board game. Candy and chocolate and popsicles and peppermints. Nipples and earlobes and lips and necks.

I shouldn't blame him.

No—I actually blame myself. And Grey.

Anger hits me square in the throat. What was I thinking? Why would I try to take something Grey did for me and introduce it into this relationship? It was never really my idea. That memory is mine and Grey's. Not Ian's. I shouldn't cheapen it.

I look back at the game I set up on my kitchen table and feel dumb. I don't want to push it anymore. I don't know why I wanted to play it in the first place. Was I testing Ian? That wasn't what I had set out to do.

But even if I wasn't, he doesn't pass the test I've inadvertently administered.

"It was going to be much more fun than this," I say, sitting.

Cuddling seems ridiculous now. If he doesn't like games, I don't like him. If he's not going to challenge me and push me, then I'm bored. I think I've been bored for months.

I break up with him after the baseball game is over.

As soon as my head hits the pillow, I can't go to sleep until I've texted Grey. It doesn't matter how long of a week I had or how tired I am. I will not be able to turn off my brain until I get it out. Hopefully, it's out forever and never comes back. My therapy is cheap.

Remember when I texted you and asked if we could stay in instead of going to the basketball game because I was exhausted from studying all week for my mid-term?

You told me of course, that you had something you've been dying to play on our next game night anyway because you'd finally finished it and your roommates were conveniently out of town.

Little did I know, it had taken you weeks to create a sex version of my favorite board game. The board looked like a bird's eye view of your house. You made a card for each room, a card for each sex toy, and a card for each piece of lingerie you bought me in a different color.

And we had to play to find out how the night was going to end.

We did it in the laundry room with the blindfold and me in the scarlet red lace teddy.

I remember.

Fuck you.

I cannot date a man who won't:

X order me girly and ridiculous sounding drinks

X hold my hair back and watch me throw up, even when he has a huge vomit phobia

X get excited about game night and play silly and sexy board games with me, even when there is a game on TV.

10

Tuesday Night

BACK AT THE hotel, we all squeeze around their outdoor pool bar.

Everything is cast in a blue hue, and the lights ripple as the water reflects across the bar and the bottles of liquor lined against the wall. The bar is heated from the electric lamps hanging under the pergola, and the pool is heated from the looks of the steam swirling off the surface into the cold air.

I am perusing their cocktail menu when Grey appears over my shoulder.

"Pomegranate martini?" he asks.

I place the menu flat on the bar. "I've changed *some*, okay?"

"Really?" Grey sits beside me and swivels his chair to face me. "What's different?"

The bartender smiles at Grey. "What can I get for you?"

Sage pokes her head out on the opposite end of the bar and gives me yet another thumbs up.

I scrunch my nose at her, telling her to stop posing like a lame dad, until Grey blocks her from my view unintentionally.

After he orders for us, I say the first thing that pops into my head. "I like pickles on my pulled pork sandwiches now."

He gasps.

"I know," I say, "but they have to be those really good, like made in-house, crunchy ones."

"All pickles are good," Grey says. "No bad pickle exists."

"While I admire your effort to attempt it, you haven't tried every pickle in the world," I joke.

"I'll accomplish it one day." Grey's thigh presses against mine as I turn to pick up my martini off the bar. He does the same, picking up his glass, and our thighs get intertwined together, one of mine between his. "What else?" he asks, facing me.

"I'm one thousand times funnier."

He purses his godforsaken lips and shakes his head. "Is that what you tell yourself?"

"How am I different to you?" I ask, pinching his arm.

His chuckle turns into a laugh. One hand rests his glass on the bar, the other squirms out from my pincers. He barrel rolls his arm around mine to grab my hand and rests them together on my knee.

And then he just leaves them there. Together.

I hold my breath and don't move a muscle. Other than my thumb that links with his. Other than my insides melting from the internal blaze.

"You seem more confident," he says, squeezing my hand gently. "Like you know what you want."

I shrug. "Maybe."

Is that what my list is? My dynamic list of things I once had, still want, and won't compromise on?

He's talking about sex though. I think my eyes may be desperately screaming, *You! No one else is you!* so I close them for half a second. "What else?"

Grey takes two full seconds to sip his bourbon, buying time. "Mostly you're the same."

"How so?" I press.

His index finger traces the ledge of his lowball glass. His eyes follow the path. "You're still passionate and courageous. Smart. Logical but imaginative at the same time."

The bottom of my heart drops open like a trap door and blood is flooding my stomach. I cannot let myself get sucked into Grey. I can't let him trick me again.

I need to focus on what I'm trying to accomplish: R.A.C.E. Not swoon over the reasons he used to love me.

I tip my head back to gulp down the rest of my drink and motion for another one. I need it to feel loose. "Are you any different?"

His eyes lift to mine, piercing me with his pinprick pupils. "Maybe in one way. But no, not really."

"Not really?" I repeat.

"I thought I had changed, but I haven't." The edge of Grey's lip lifts in a smirk. "It's hard to change, isn't it?"

"I think it depends on what you're trying to change about yourself."

"How so?" he parrots me.

"Some people's personalities are fixed. They can be a result of genetics or their childhood or experiences. I think some of those things would be extremely hard to change, but a bad habit like biting your nails or being late for work might be easier to correct."

Is not being able to do long distance a bad habit? He's practically telling me that he hasn't changed one bit. He's the same Grey, his hands always on me somewhere with the look of *I have to have you right this second* in his eye. Doesn't work fifteen hundred miles apart.

His fingers wiggle themselves in between mine without looking down. Grey drags his thumb heavily up the side of my hand, and my entire body feels pulled in two different directions—the sting from the fact that he does just want to have sex with me, and the warmth from the fact that I still want to follow through with it.

Neither of us is paying attention to the bartender, but two more drinks appear in front of us.

"True," he says, "but I think it's more about how much a person wants to change."

"Deep," I joke. "I was having an internal crisis over how the pickles felt about not being liked."

"Salty," Grey quips.

I can't help but laugh. And tip back more of my martini to muddle his goddamn charm.

He continues. "If you don't want to really stop biting your nails, it won't happen. Maybe temporarily, but most people will fall back into old routines. I think if someone desperately wanted to change something about their personality, they could."

I play the "How so?" game.

"Being self-aware mostly. Then being intentional about enacting the change, behaving differently."

"Self-awareness," I snort. "I'm not sure humans are that self-aware. I'm not sure I even truly know what that means. It's just one of those buzzwords that sounds good."

"Exactly." Grey tips his drink toward me in agreement. "How do you change then? You don't really want to deep down, you don't know how to be self-aware in the first place, you fall back into your same routine."

Am I any different? It doesn't seem like four years has changed anything. We're the same two people, doing the same thing, acting the same way.

"Did you get a psychology degree in the last four years? *That* would certainly be one difference."

A smile leaps onto his face. He untangles his hand from mine and slowly reaches up toward my face to sweep the hair that fell in front of my eye back.

"You have strawberry blonde hair now." His tone is deep and just above a whisper.

Our eyes are frozen together. I see it just beneath the surface, his longing.

I can do this.

"Do you want to go back to your room?" Internally, I cringe. That was painfully unsmooth and one of the cheesiest things I could have gone with, but my words are out in the world now.

I catch the beginning of his smile faltering before someone's shriek startles me so badly, I almost fall off my stool.

It's a rush of bodies, and I can't find Grey's face anymore, but I can hear him laughing.

I don't know who gets thrown in first, but before I know it, all fourteen of us are in the pool. I don't know who I pushed. I don't know who pushed me. It's just squeals and laughs and splashing and warmth.

I feel hands on my body, but Grey isn't near me. I know it instinctually. I spin to see Mitchell wiping water out of his eyes.

He takes his hand back. "Can you stand?"

"No," I splutter, "but I can swim."

I dip my head under water and open my eyes. I find Grey's blurry legs immediately. He's slowly wandering toward the shallow end on the opposite side that everyone else is swimming toward. His calves are flexing, his Achilles tendons are making me feel weird inside like they always used to. Am I the only woman who strangely thinks they're one of the sexiest male body parts? All taut and strained when a guy takes a step. They're panty-dropping hot and sexy as hell. Side note: Grey's are perfection.

The two pomegranate martinis I had have led me down a daydream about mankles and given me a lot of liquid courage. I can make him think with his dick, and the pool is the perfect place to do it.

He's the one who flirted first. He's the one who grabbed my hands on the zipline. He's the one holding my hand and tucking my hair behind my ear. He's the one who flirted last.

He doesn't get to go around looking disappointed in me. We're in this together—him just as much as me.

I kick toward him as I watch him walk on the balls of his feet up the sloped gunite bottom of the pool. He turns when he's chest deep and must see my body swimming underneath the water because his legs stop mid-backward-step.

I pop my head up in front of him and grin. "Why are you over here?" My feet float through the water. The side of both my calves brush against his shirt and down to his hips. His fingers reach out and trace lightly down my shins before I let my legs drop.

"You can't stand here," he says hoarsely, backing up, thinking I'll follow.

The art of the chase. I swish my arms and legs back and forth in the water. I'm going to make him show me how badly he wants me. This way, I won't be rejected if he's not thinking what I'm thinking.

I stare at him.

He takes a step into me. His arm slices through the water and finds my waist. He curls the tips of his fingers into my side. My hand curves around his forearm and slides up to the crease of his inner elbow.

I take a breath and disappear under water before I swim around his body. He turns to follow my direction, then appears underwater.

I smile playfully, letting little bubbles escape my mouth, but he doesn't react. His face isn't so much serious as it is intense. Intensely inquisitive. I can see the lust that I've seen thousands of times easily in the golden brown of his irises, but he's trying to figure me out and read the thoughts I'm drawing like a blueprint.

We both surface at the same time. I back up until my spine hits the side of the pool. Grey takes two large steps, closing in on me.

The internal dilemma is written all over his face. Take what he wants or not?

"Want to have a handstand contest?" I ask slyly before I push myself off the wall and try to swim past him. I let my fingers trace his abs. I let my legs and feet tickle his thigh. It's enough to rouse him, allow him to do whatever he wants. Just as I think he's going to let me go, his large hand wraps around my ankle and pulls me back into him.

He turns and holds me tight. His hands slowly grab my leg, one handful at a time, until he reaches my upper thigh and rests his back against the side of the pool. He manipulates my body against him, nestled against his chest. I'm happy I chose to change into my sundress after the ropes course.

Grey could never keep his hands from roaming. Constantly. And I welcomed it. Now, he has easy access.

His hands grip my inner thighs as he brings my ass against him. He's so hard I can practically use his dick as a chair.

"Ryan," he rasps against my ear, "what are you doing?"

Even as he says it, one hand comes up under my flowing dress and fans across my stomach to press me against him firmly.

My heart is knocking around inside my rib cage like he slingshot it.

I clamp my inner thighs around him, and impossibly, he gets even harder. "You mean what are *we* doing?"

He drops his face into my neck and groans as his hands cradle my hip bones. I couldn't squirm out from his iron grip if I tried.

Grey creates friction. "Fuck. You know I will be inside you after another thirty seconds, and I won't give a fuck that there are a dozen other people across this pool."

My mistake. His sex drive has absolutely not changed in the slightest.

He nibbles at the sensitive skin below my ear. I suck in a breath as the scrape of his teeth light a match like I'm his striking surface.

"What are we doing?" he tries again. He's breathing heavily, swaying me back and forth slightly in the water from the force of his chest.

I lace my fingers through his and drag our hands up between my legs. "That's obvious."

His fingers don't match his hesitant voice. They're pressing against me in slow strokes like he is savoring me in the most unhesitant way ever.

His mind lapses for a second. I can tell from the new growl in his voice, demanding and steady, that he's thinking with his dick. "No one else fucks you like I do, do they?"

I lie back against his shoulder and shake my head. Now we're getting somewhere.

He gives me a satisfied hum and bites my earlobe. "Tell me that no other guy makes you feel like this."

"Grey," I whisper into the steam rising from the surface of the pool, "it's only you."

His lips rest against the cartilage of my ear, and his rational thought overpowers. "Tell me what's going on inside your brain."

"I don't know right now," I whisper, arching into him. "Can't think straight."

His other hand roams across my breasts, grabbing handfuls, before he dips below my bra and pinches my nipple, rolling it between his finger and thumb. I let out a soft moan as the long-lost fire comes raging back.

"Fuck, Ryan. I've missed the way you sound. I want this so fucking badly, but you have to tell m…"

We grind into one another, and Grey loses the ability to speak. If it defies physics to have sex with clothes on, Grey would still somehow accomplish it. We're both lost in it momentarily. Both a simple push of two articles of clothing to the side away from sex.

"I'm going to do something we'll regret," he says gruffly, suddenly flipping me around. He pulls my thighs around his waist. I think he's trying to not slip his fingers inside me, but I'm not entirely sure why he thinks it would be better to face each other. It's a whole lot easier to slip something else inside.

His face turns dark. "We've been drinking."

"I'm not drunk. I know what I want."

"Talk to me about what you want then."

"I won't regret it," I say.

Grey lets out a frustrated breath. "This is about sex?" His eyebrows furrow deeply, but his hands settle on my butt cheeks. He's working his fingers into me, cupping it like he's been starved of a good ass for years. His eyes trace my lips.

I lick them, daring him to taste me, because I think he'll taste better than he did four years ago. I'm only now realizing how much I've been starved for years. No one else makes me feel this *good*.

I nod. "Let's just have fun this week. I want you to fuck me, Grey. I get closure. You get your rebound."

"Shit," he breathes out, pressing his hips into mine.

"See?" I agree back with my hips. "Perfect arrangement."

His eyes search my face. He's an infuriating mix of hesitancy and lust.

Fine. I can be bold.

No wonder people have break-up sex. The beginning of a sexual relationship is so awkward; trying to figure out what the other person likes, trying to feel okay enough to use your voice, hoping they know what they're doing, hoping they're receptive and listen, praying they'll be able to make you come.

This is obviously different. We've been through it all. We've learned each other intimately. Nothing's left up to chance, only familiarity. The comfortableness is almost too easy.

I wrap my hands around his neck and whisper, "I still have dreams about you."

Grey swallows hard. The muscles in his neck cord, making his Adam's apple bob.

I cover his hands with mine and lead them down and back up my thighs. "The way you take me wherever and however you want. How hard you make me come." He closes his eyes, so I run my tongue over his earlobe as I twist my fingers into his hair. "I want your face between my legs."

The muscle in his jaw leaps. "God, I'd do anything to see those eyes roll back in your head again, feel your fingernails claw into my skin." The tips of his fingers are digging into me, restraining himself, at the crease where my upper thighs meet my hips.

I go ten percent.

"Ryan," he says almost inaudibly. I stop moving. It sounds like a warning. He licks his lips as he stares at mine. "I can't taste you again without losing all control." He loses approximately half control for a second as he rakes me across his erection. "God, *fuck*," he mutters under his breath meant for the porn star side of me—we all have one, and Grey knows I used to like to embrace mine. "I want to watch you ride my cock while you moan like a good fucking girl about how much you've missed it."

My breath catches in my throat from the spurt of electricity that runs through my body. I feel like an excited teenager first discovering how to make myself feel good, how much my mind and body respond to dirty words, because I guess I forgot. Grey sure didn't.

"You're going to make me come just from this."

"No one else makes me this fucking hard." His tone is like a pleasing groan. Grey bites my neck as we dry hump (wet hump?) like we've figured out we're too cool for the skating rink and graduated to our first girl-boy party.

He pulls back. I wait for him to kiss me, but he doesn't move. Obviously, he wants me, but I know from the look in his eyes that he's not going to budge.

"Don't you want this?"

The outer edges of his irises burn bright. "I want to fuck you until you can't add one plus one." Then they quickly fade. He finds my hand under the water and kisses the bottom of my palm. "But you could never be a rebound for me."

I lightly graze my fingernails across his arm, trying to ignore the fizz of my heart. I remind myself he didn't mean it like that, and I don't want him to mean it like that. "Okay, so you need closure like I do. We never got it. Now we have this opportunity to help each other put our relationship behind us. One in four ex-couples do it. I googled it." I arch against him, trying to prove my point. A moan escapes my lips, and I actually might come from this alone. I place my cheek on his. "Take me back to your room. I want you inside me now."

"God," he hisses. His voice sounds pained, a total contrast to what his body is doing in pleasure against me. "You have no idea how badly I want that, but you have to stop. You don't understand." Grey pulls himself off the wall and smushes my back against it, pinning me under his weight. "*This* isn't what I want, Ryan. I can't put you behind me. Ever."

I blink. "What?"

"I meant it when I said I didn't think I could ever stop loving you."

I trip over my words. "When did you ever—what?—when did

you say that? When you first told me you loved me? Everyone says that the first time."

I quickly remember that is not entirely true, but I'm not about to bring up one of my exes at a time like this.

Grey closes his eyes and takes a deep breath.

He also told me that when he broke up with me, apparently, while I was wailing into the phone. He just doesn't want to say it out loud.

"I tried to not love you," he whispers. "I just can't. I'm sorry."

"But you've had another girlfriend for years."

"I know."

"But you live in Austin," I stammer.

He sighs. "I know."

"But you can't do long distance."

"I know."

He releases the pressure he's using to pin me against the wall, slips out of the pool by pushing himself up with his arms, and walks off into the dark—awkwardly, I might add, and adjusting his shorts every six steps because he has a raging hard-on.

It doesn't matter how badly he wants me or even how much he loves me. I still get rejected by Grey Beckett up, down, and sideways.

$$\underline{11}$$

Technically Wednesday Morning

I HEAR THE door to our house open.

The living room is only lit by the moonlight coming in through the two windows on the far back wall. The sad fire I'd started in the fireplace has died down to just crackling embers, but the room is still warm.

Someone flips on the light.

I squeeze my eyes closed and groan. "Please explain to me how I can make a guy's penis so hard I could snap it in half, but I'm still lying face down *alone* on this gross leather couch."

Maybe there's a math equation that can answer it. Like hardness divided by force: 8==/==D.

Jesus. I'm like a tween boy spelling out 5318008 upside down on a calculator.

Someone reel me in.

"I told you she wasn't having sex in the pool," Evie's voice insists.

"It certainly *looked* like she was," Sage's voice chortles.

Leave it to your best friends to put you in your place. I can't even imagine what Grey and I looked like in the pool.

Two pairs of footsteps approach me.

My best guess is Sage sits under my feet and Evie sits under my head. And my best friends are the best. Sage massages my feet, Evie rubs my scalp.

"Just talk when you're ready," Evie says.

I wonder how long I could get away with getting this massage before they catch on. I start counting.

The balls of my feet unwind their tension. The veins in my head slow their throbbing against my skull.

Numbers and my best friends.

Both constants in my life. One plus one always equals two, and Sage and Evie will always be there for me. Never changing. True to who they are.

Just like everyone, including Grey. He's not special, and he's not going to change for me.

Case in point: Sage mutters, "Don't milk it," when I reach fifty-three, and Evie laughs and switches to petting my hair before she says, "My fingers were getting tired, but *I* wasn't going to say anything."

Three more seconds and, "Okay, I'm ready." I sit up, curl my knees up into my chest, and pull my oversized black T-shirt over them. "That was humiliating. I'm going to be thinking about how massively embarrassing that was for a really, *really* long time."

Exactly how you think about something from middle school when you're in your freaking twenties and *still* flush. I'll be forty and my cheeks will turn red when this moment randomly pops into my head.

"So happy to have provided the group gossip for the week," I add. "I'm going to run into the woods and live off the grid now."

"I mean," Sage says, "Grey was all over you. We're not considering that some type of win?"

"Is it considered a win in the PR world when you get seventy-five percent of the way there before it all crumbles around you?" I ask her sarcastically. "That's lawsuits in the engineering world. I put myself out there—vulnerably and awkwardly—and he walked away."

"How did you plan for it to go?" Evie asks.

"Sex," I state, mimicking it with my fingers. "P in V."

"Not what I meant," she laughs. "The whole thing. The whole week. We've got four more days until the wedding."

I was so focused on accomplishing my task of one and done, I hadn't thought that far ahead—very unlike me.

But I know immediately that I actually thought that we'd just have fun for the next few days; slipping in and out of each other's rooms, sneaking off to have sex wherever like we used to, definitely not involving our emotions, and flying home on Sunday, never to communicate again. That it was the magic cure-all.

I guess that was way too optimistic.

"I thought it was going to go how break-up sex is supposed to go. Not messy."

"Not messy?" Sage questions me.

"Filthy, tangled, sticky shambles," I say. "It's a long list of synonyms, but I don't think there is one that can capture just how messy that was."

Sage gasps under her breath. "Wait, he still has feelings for you?"

"I think that's what he was saying, but *he* broke up with me. He's the one who hasn't talked to me in four years and completely cut me out of his life. For fuck's sake, he's had a long-term girl-friend for years. I feel like a bitch. He was flirting with me, and I thought we were thinking the same thing, on the same page. He kept saying people don't change, and I even took it slowly and let him initiate. How was I supposed to anticipate that he was going to say he can't stop loving me? So, he can't have casual sex with me because he cares too much? He even admits he shouldn't love me. God, what am I supposed to do with that?" Evie's and Sage's eyes go wide as I look between them. "Don't look at me like that. I'm not a bitch. Right? I just wanted this behind me."

"You're not a bitch." Sage gives me an intent look. "But is that what you actually want?"

My throat stings. "Yes."

Sage and Evie study me skeptically, but I mean it.

Grey and I live over a thousand miles away from each other. He doesn't want to move. I have built a life for myself in San Diego. I have a good job and great friends. I'm supposed to give that up for him now? Maybe two years ago if he had told me he missed me, I would have considered it. When I'd actually wanted him to reenter my life. I could have moved to Austin instead, but the last time I checked, there are no coasts for coastal engineers in Austin either.

"Our lives don't fit together anymore," I say. "Maybe they never did, and we were too young and in love to realize it." Evie looks like she's staring straight through me, so I bury my face in my knees because I don't like it. "Let's not talk about this anymore. It's your week, and we should be talking about that. About how great today was."

"Ryan," she says. "Stop."

I look up at her sheepishly because I know she's not going to let it go.

"Do either of you know anything about each other's lives over the last four years?" Evie asks.

I shake my head. "I didn't want to go there."

I don't want to go there at all. That seems like a good way to let him back in, to pick at the scab around my heart that never truly healed, and then I'm left bleeding out because there's no happy ending for us.

"Maybe you should," Evie suggests.

"Such a serial monogamist answer," I joke. "Sage?"

"Ryan, you've been keeping a list of reasons other men aren't him," she laughs. "Which you never told us about, and I'm a little offended. My answer is to never get yourself in a situation where you have a reason to keep a list in the first place. You aren't the loner. You don't want to be the loner. But I also don't think you want to be the serial dater either. I say talk to him. Four years is a long time. You both might see things differently now, and if you don't, you may find the closure you're looking for."

"Did I say you were both smart before?" I tease. "Dumb. Dumb friends. You're going to let him eat me alive."

Grey won't even mean to. It's his nature; raging like a tornado and pulling in everything around him.

They both wrap their arms around me tight—Sage at Evie's urging.

"We love you," Sage says, squeezing me tighter.

"We want to see you happy," Evie says, smiling against my hair. "And if Grey still loves you, I know that's all he wants for you too."

"I'm scared," I whisper.

"Of what?" Evie asks.

"Of… everything."

Scared Grey will let me go and not let me go at the same time. I'm not sure I will be able to let go of him myself, and there's endless possibilities and opportunities where I know Grey will surprise me.

Because his track record is to hook me, then love me, then completely fucking wreck me—and he does it all better than anyone else.

If he catches me off guard, there is nothing I will be able to do about it, except spiral into the depths of *him*.

No one else is Grey, and I'm mostly scared he will prove to me that no one else will ever be able to come close.

Where does that leave me then?

I guess it leaves me in my own personal serial dating hell— where the Xs never stop.

× × ×

JUST AS I'M about to drift off, my phone buzzes.

It's not a text. It's probably an app notification. Reddit always buzzes to show me contagious laughter or perfectly timed screams. I'm not going to look. I'm not going to doom scroll. I try to ignore it. If I look at the bright screen, I'll be wide awake. It's *not* a text.

Two minutes later (yes, I counted one hundred and twenty sheep to make sure), my phone reminds me that someone did indeed text me.

Don't look, I tell myself again. *Don't slip*.

Of course, that's too hard, and I never listen to my own brain. My arm's already going for my phone before I finish the first word.

Grey's name sits right there at the bottom of my screen, and I have to know what it says.

I hate me too.

I'm annoyed that all his text does is shove in my face how much I don't hate him at all, not even a tiny freaking bit. He doesn't get to be the Heath Ledger in my story just like that.

My list of reasons is way longer than ten things, I reply.

He infuriatingly responds with, 1. I don't wear combat boots.

I add, 2. The fact that you watched chick flicks with me and remember that.

Even though this is not on my list, I know that it easily could be. I'm *self-aware* enough to realize I'd break up with a guy if he told me he wouldn't watch one with me—because Grey did it all the time. I'm that far gone and delusional.

My phone buzzes in my hand. I hate me for everything. For being in a relationship for the last four years. For feeling like I will never move. For being so physical I can't stand long distance. I'm sorry I misread the situation. Do you hate me enough to ignore me the rest of the trip?

No. I try to leave it at that, but I don't. I slip further and text him again before he responds. I hate how much I like seeing your name on my phone screen again.

The gray bubbles flicker for a while. I hold my breath. He either can't decide how to respond or he's writing a wall of text.

His big gray box appears on the screen, and it's "gray" in more ways than one.

I thought if I ever saw you again you were going to be indifferent toward me. Then on Sunday, I got what I've wished for every damn day for four years—you weren't here with some other guy, and you were mad. And anger isn't apathy. Fuck, that made me so happy. I'm happy because you feel something, anything, toward me. Indifference would have meant you didn't care about me, about us, about our relationship anymore. It would have meant that you were over it. Apathy would have crushed me and has always been my biggest fear. So, I was happy that you hated me. Because for me, you hating me is better than you feeling nothing. I'm sorry I walked away tonight, but I wasn't thinking about having casual sex with you. You will never be casual to me. And I'm even more sorry, but I don't want you to be. I have a hard time keeping my brain level around you, and I shouldn't have flirted with you or led you on in any way. I can't change into someone who doesn't love you, because I can't make myself want to. I still can't push you to the back of my mind. At this point, I don't know if I ever can.

The emotions in my stomach pop like the dice inside the dome in a game of Trouble. There's mostly guilt and regret for what I said and did—and a million other emotions trying to win out. I know I'm already in deep, deep trouble, but at this point, I don't know if I care. We're halfway through this week, and I have to finish it.

I'm on an uncontrollable slip 'n slide covered in liquid soap, and I won't be able to get up until I reach the end.

No, I'm sorry. Of course, I care, Grey. You are not casual to me either. I don't know what I was thinking. I feel like a bitch. I wish we could erase that from everyone's memory, including ours.

Ha, he replies, no thanks. I don't want that.

Glad your ego is intact, because I am completely mortified, I retort.

Ryan, it's me.

He's right. Honestly, when I see him tomorrow, I know it's going to be like it never happened. We're two people who don't ever have to get embarrassed in front of each other. We've seen it all. We're open books. We reached a point in our past relationship that I have never reached with anyone else, and I wish it didn't feel like we picked up right where we left off. It shouldn't.

Can we talk tomorrow? Like normal? Four years is a long time.

Talking is good, he replies.

It's just talking. Innocent.

Nothing else.

I will not spiral just from a conversation. A conversation has to happen.

Otherwise, I'm going to go back home, and I'm going to have an infinite list that I can never move past.

A list that I want to move past and don't want to move past at the same time. I can already feel that in my heart, and I know it's the truth—no matter how much I hate that fact.

Is it even possible to accomplish both?

I wish I could embrace our past relationship, respect that we loved each other deeply, and not be so affected by his presence.

That's what closure is supposed to be.

But at the same time, I wish it could be different.

<u>12</u>

The Fourth Ex

I STILL GET butterflies five months into my relationship with Preston. This is the one that's going to stick. We're going to make it past that hump I can't seem to clear.

Joke's on Sage for making fun of me for being a perpetual dater.

It's ironic I think he's the one who's going to cure me. He's been right in front of my face the entire time I've lived in San Diego. I've crossed paths with him so many times in my apartment complex where we both live—in the elevator, at the pool, in front of the mailboxes—and he never smiled, never muttered a hello.

He's hot—he's got that dark hair, dark complexion, bright blue eyes thing that girls love—but I thought he was an asshole. Turns out, he is just extremely shy.

Something feels different about tonight.

Maybe because it's Christmas. Maybe because something always feels so different during the holidays. But maybe I just feel like I could really fall for him.

"Don't be nervous," Preston says as we step up on the front porch. "My parents are going to love you."

I'm not so sure about that. Their house is luxuriously modern and enormous. Hard right angles, all glass and stone with one of those cool frosted glass garage doors, and palm trees everywhere. Their Christmas lights are immaculate and were definitely hung by a professional. It's a block off the beach and must be worth millions.

I didn't realize he came from wealth, but now I'm imagining his parents as people who certainly won't like me.

I smile up at him and his soft blue eyes with fake assurance and kiss his lips. "I'm not nervous."

Preston rings the doorbell and the twelve-foot door swings open noiselessly.

His parents are nothing like I'd pictured.

His mother, Kris, is wearing a huge smile and flowing linen pants with dried paint smeared all over them. She pulls me into a giant hug, rocking me back and forth, and tells me how sorry she is for getting so carried away in her art studio that she didn't have time to change and how excited she is to finally meet me.

His father, Julian, is booming loud, but in a good way. He claps Preston on the back and practically picks me up off my feet when he hugs me.

They're so down to earth. I didn't realize parents could be like this.

I learn that Kris is an artist. She spends her days painting the ocean and selling her artwork on Etsy.

I learn that when Preston said he works with his father as an architect, that he meant his father owns the company and is rather well-known.

They are warm and welcoming, nothing like my parents, and the entire night goes by as quickly as a breeze through their palm trees in their backyard, where we've sat the entire night eating dinner on their heated porch.

This is it, I think over and over on the drive home.

I wasn't headed for doom. I see the light at the end of the tunnel. It's close, and I feel happy, content with where I am right now.

Until we're walking up to my door and Preston spins me around by the hand.

He cradles my chin and kisses me hesitantly. "I think maybe I might love you, Ryan."

I feel like he's reached into my throat and pulled out my vocal cords. This is all wrong, and I have no words to express it. My brain's losing computing power, drained from the energy he just sucked from the hallway.

Finally, I whisper, "You think. Maybe. You might. Love me?"

His smile inches slowly downward as he nods.

"Have you been in love before?" I ask.

Who cares anymore if I screw this up by not giving a canned response back? Not me.

I know I don't love him yet, because I have been in love, and I know what it feels like.

Before Grey, I would have said I loved him back. I'm sure of it. But now I know, that's not how I want someone to tell me they love me.

He's confused but answers, "Yes."

"Did you tell her the same way?"

Preston's eyes widen as it clicks where I'm going in my mind. "No," he says sheepishly.

"I don't think you love me then," I choke out. "I'm sorry."

And I am.

Of all my San Diego boyfriends, this one hurts the most. Maybe he didn't mean it. Maybe he was nervous and got tongue-tied. But the moment for me is tainted. I want someone who confidently says he loves me and has zero doubt.

I try to let him down easy, but he's still standing on my "An Awesome Engineer Lives Here" welcome mat (courtesy of Sage), mouth wide open in surprise, when I shut the door.

I crumple to the floor and sob so loudly Preston can probably hear me. I'm not shedding any tears for him though. It's the hole in my heart that no one else can fill.

I cry alone in my bed until no more tears come, and all I have left is the words I need to get out.

Remember when you kissed every inch of my skin to wake me up before six a.m. that one Saturday morning and said you wouldn't apologize because you hadn't been able to sleep at all?

You laid your head on my chest. You brushed your fingers over my stomach, across my arms, down my legs. I ran my fingers through your hair and gave you goosebumps across the back of your neck. We just lay there as the sun rose through my bedroom window. I have your words memorized.

Ryan, I am in love with you every second of every day. I can't sleep because I don't want to not think that thought long enough to drift off. My mind has this hold on you, no matter what, like I can't let you go to the back of my brain for even one second because it's not worth it. You are always with me, even when you're not. And I won't ever stop. I will love you forever because no one else is you.

I remember.

Fuck you.

I cannot date a man who won't:

X order me girly and ridiculous sounding drinks

X hold my hair back and watch me throw up, even when he has a huge vomit phobia

X get excited about game night and play silly and sexy board games with me, even when there is a game on TV

X say he loves me outright because 'think,' 'maybe,' and 'might' aren't good enough anymore.

13

Wednesday After Sleeping

THERE HAS BEEN no time to talk.

Well, there has but not alone.

It's been only surface-level stuff because we are both on mountain bikes for most of the morning and I have to focus on not falling flat on my face.

Grey tries to help as best as he can. He stays close at all times, checking for me out the corner of his eye. He waits for me when I start to struggle, and as I start to lag, he joins me in the way, way back.

My helmet slips down in front of my eyes. He stops pedaling and leans over his handlebars.

"Tighten it so you can see, Ry."

I stop because I can't breathe as well in this ridiculous altitude. He slows to a halt and digs in his backpack for me.

"Do you need help? Let me get you some water so you can rest."

He holds back a leaf-covered tree branch so I can pass. I smile at him as I wheel underneath it.

"Don't smack your face with this branch."

He smiles when I look back at him before panicking. His face scrunches up from the anticipation of what I don't see.

"Watch the rock!"

After a sudden thrashing, I'm crumpled in a ball, whining in pain. He's cradling me, checking all of my body parts for injuries.

"Shit. Are you okay? You scared me."

So, even if my limbs are jelloid, I'm happy I am now trading my mountain bike for my good old trusty legs and feet. I've got a nice bruised and scraped knee, but Elliot bandaged me up with his first aid kit (saving me from being cradled in Grey's arms and looking up at him like he's my knight in shining helmet) and gave me some Advil, so I'm all good to hike.

And we're going to be doing a lot of hiking.

Elliot's idea of a bachelor party is to include the bachelorettes on a three-day hike.

I blame the fact that he and Evie are so in love for why they think this is a good idea.

Us girls went to Cancun a few months ago—planned to perfection by me and Sage. No hiking involved. It was all beach days and catamarans and snorkeling and alcohol.

Elliot should have gone to Vegas—or even the local strip club—so I'm not stuck sleeping on the hard dirt in a sleeping bag. But dammit, I love him almost as much as Evelyn does.

He's packed every girl's small backpack and made every man carry the heavy loads including the tents, the stoves, the food, and the alcohol. I have a tiny black backpack with my sweatshirt in it that weighs as much as, well, a sweatshirt because Grey even took my water bottle for me.

So, this isn't going to be so bad.

And it's beautiful.

Never mind Grey's calves, which are equally as gorgeous. Don't get me started on his Achilles tendons again—they are my Achilles heel—so I should be staring at the scenery instead.

The trail is dry and rocky and zig-zags back and forth as we go up the mountain. There are so many fallen trees, I have to constantly straddle my legs over them to get across. Occasionally, we will pass patches of last-to-melt snow, a creek that delights us with the sound of running water, or open spaces where I can see the vast mountainscape.

I turn back to Elliot behind me. "What's this hike called again?"

"Lakes of the Clouds," he says. "We're going to camp near one of the lakes. It's incredible. I haven't done it since I was a teenager though."

"Ohh, Teenage Elliot and Teenage Beck," I say. "Spill the tea."

In front of me, Grey laughs. "You know all of mine already."

He has a point.

I'll spare him any real embarrassment, but my favorite is when Grey decided to sign up at my gym in college so we could work out together, first he fist bumped the guy behind the desk who just wanted to take back the pen he was using to sign his name and then Grey proceeded to say, "You too," after he told us to enjoy our work out. Every time we saw him afterward, Grey would die a little more inside and beg me to switch gyms.

"There is no tea," Elliot jokes. "I am a man without a past. I wasn't living until I met Evelyn."

"I should buy you one of those giant bumper stickers that says, 'I eat ass,'" I tease.

"Ryan!" Evie exclaims. The tips of her ears turn pink, unrelated to the exertion of energy.

"Evelyn!" I exclaim right back.

Elliot and Grey appreciate my sense of humor.

Grey turns and walks backward for a few steps. "She kisses her grandmother with that mouth."

Grey's pulling out inside jokes. My father's mother, Lucille, is one of my favorite people in the entire world, and Grey knows she probably eats ass herself and would tell me all about it.

The sexual tension in her senior assisted living facility cannot be unfelt. They are like teenagers, playing dominoes, dancing in wheelchairs, and fucking every free moment they can find.

And she thinks Grey is quite the looker.

"She's dead," I deadpan.

His face falls with lightning speed, and he stops so short, I almost run into him. Dammit, I can't keep the smirk off my face long enough, so I scrunch my nose at him.

"Fuck," he laughs. "You suck."

I shrug nonchalantly.

"Did you have a high school girlfriend?" I ask Elliot.

"Eighth grade through senior year," he says.

"Five years? Evie isn't even your longest relationship, and you're getting married this weekend," I say.

Elliot makes love eyes at Evie. "I love her a hell of a lot more though."

"Did you break up because you were going to different schools?" I ask.

"No," he replies and laughs. "Actually, she went to UCLA the year after I started USC. We just always knew that we had an expiration date. It was high school."

"Lots of people marry their high school sweetheart," Evie points out.

"There's a lot more to life after eighteen." Elliot shrugs. "We hadn't lived yet. We both knew it and agreed."

Grey glances back. That blue spot seems to scream at me, begging me to not be mad at him anymore—or I just see what I want to see because I'm tired of being mad.

Maybe Grey felt like he had more life to live after twenty-two. He was not a one-girlfriend-throughout-high-school kind of guy though. I'd been his first long-term girlfriend—but I'm certainly not his only anymore. Maybe he thought he needed to make sure there wasn't something better out there for him.

"Elliot, did Grey actually get dumped during junior prom?" I ask, staring at the back of Grey's head as old conversations flood back.

Elliot chuckles. "I forgot about that. Why was that girl crying in the bathroom again?"

"Nina. I went to get us drinks," Grey replies, "and only came back with mine because she slipped my mind. In my defense, I was shooting the shit with Coach Carl and totally forgot. That was just the last straw though. She said I did stuff like that constantly, but I dunno. I don't remember."

He gives me an are-you-satisfied smile over his shoulder.

I never truly believed deep down in my heart that his stories like this were one hundred percent factual.

He told me about the girl he forgot to buy a homecoming corsage for during his senior year of high school. He told me about the girl who broke up with him because he chose his frat brothers and a football game over meeting her parents. He told me about the girl he ghosted right before he met me because he didn't like her laugh.

I'd tease him and ask why he told me he wasn't an asshole on his napkin if he'd always been such an asshole. But he'd tell me that he just knew from the beginning that I was different; that as soon as he saw me, something changed, and he felt like he'd come alive.

I couldn't make sense of it, so I always took them with a grain of salt. Those stories were opposite of the Grey I knew, the Grey that was my boyfriend.

My Grey stops at the creek we have to cross and extends his hand out to me. My Grey gets his feet wet (so I don't have to) and lets me hold onto him as I walk across the tree trunk bridge. My Grey asks me if I'm thirsty and want to sit after I jump down. He hands me my water bottle, and of course, he takes it back when I'm finished because he doesn't want me to carry an extra pound.

Elliot ruffles my hair and calls over his shoulder as he walks past us. "Don't sit for too long or you won't make it to the lakes before dark."

Both Grey and I smile at each other. We don't make any attempt to move or get up from the log we're sitting on.

Let them go ahead, his smile says. *We can talk.*

I've missed talking to you, mine stupidly says back.

He finally stands and holds his hand out. "Don't worry. I picked you up a headlamp. I know you're going to wander off when the sun goes down anyway."

My Grey seems to include me in every thought he thinks.

I wonder if he included her in every thought he's had over the last few years.

The thought can't help but be thought.

I feel like I'm competing with a mirage. I don't know her name. I don't know what she looks like. I've never pictured Grey with anyone else. It was always just me and him in my head. It's still always me and him in my head. Even when he'd tell me about the stories from his past—I knew he'd never truly loved anyone before, and I never considered the possibility that we would break up.

When I moved to Hawaii, I thought he'd come visit over the holidays. I thought we'd suck it up for two years. I didn't care how hard it was going to be because Grey would be waiting for me at the end. I'd graduate and move back to Austin. I envisioned working in consulting, commuting to Houston or Corpus Christi.

Maybe that was a pipe dream and I never realized, but I thought it could have worked—or maybe we were always doomed to fail because we were the right people at the wrong time.

What happens if I can't ever find another right person? Because all it's been for two years is wrong person, right time. I told myself I'd never give up, but will I eventually?

I stumble like I kicked myself in the stomach.

Fuck.

I settle.

And if I settle, I turn into my mother.

× × ×

I STUFF THAT thought deep down into the depths of my mind as we walk and walk some more.

Birds chirp. Water trickles. Leaves swish.

It makes the silence more silent between me and Grey. Just because you miss something, doesn't mean it's easy when you get it back. We finally have a moment alone. The world is only the two of us.

And I don't know what to say.

It's a little harrowing when you realize the universe is going to win. This whole time I thought I had the upper hand—I wasn't settling. I was dating and breaking up and dating and breaking up; suffering through it because that's what I had to do to find someone better. But none of them will ever be the one for me. I already had my one. Those ones don't come around often—we're lucky when we find *one*. The universe doesn't give that freely.

And I already felt myself struggling against the quicksand, letting the world swallow me, letting myself succumb to the fight. That's why I wanted to pause, take a step back, work on myself. Marriage isn't everything. I was putting too much pressure on myself to find the right person who had to compete with a non-existent Grey.

"Were you happy in Hawaii?" Grey asks out of nowhere. "At least, after a while?"

I smile. "*After a while*, I was."

He seems grateful for my answer and slows to walk beside me.

"Thank you," I say.

Four years is a long time to come to terms with how grateful I am for what Grey gave me. I wouldn't be the same person without it.

"For what?"

"I didn't realize it for four years, so in a really weird way, thank you for breaking up with me. I understand where you were coming from now. I think if I had known you were miserable, I would have been miserable. I'm not sure I would have lasted two years out there. I would have come home if you'd asked."

Home echoes in my head. I'm surprised how easy that came out and how right it feels saying it. But it's not Austin that feels like home, and now I'm regretting the words that came out of my mouth.

"Yeah." Grey shrugs. "You wanted an adventure. I couldn't give you that back then. I don't necessarily feel good about it though."

"But you did give it to me," I insist. "I've been to all eight of the largest Hawaiian Islands. I hiked Diamond Head almost every weekend. I visited Pearl Harbor. I've eaten the juiciest pineapple in the world from a roadside stand."

He laughs. "How'd you get on those two islands you're not al-lowed on?"

"Legally, I swear," I say. "I saved up for the helicopter tour to Niihau, and I volunteered to plant 'Aki'aki grass on Kahoolawe, the uninhabited island."

"What's 'Aki'aki grass?" Grey asks, careful to pronounce it like I did.

"It helps protect the sand dunes against erosion because it's drought and salt tolerant." I nudge into his side. "Grey, did you read about Hawaii?"

"Of course, I did," he says. "For hours. I looked at every Google image I could find. I even took online tours of your campus and Honolulu. I wanted to be able to picture you there, walking to class, driving down the street. I hated not being able to see you there in your element. When you'd tell me something, I realized how much I hated not being able to form it in my mind. So, I googled everything you told me about in that first month." He pauses. "And I drew you doing it."

I study my feet and try to let go of the anvil hanging from my heart. I wish with every part of me that I could see those pictures.

"Like what?" I ask.

"You sitting in a classroom. You in front of your apartment building. You on the Dole Plantation pineapple tour. You and that beached seal."

"Do you still have them?"

Grey flattens his eyebrows and sighs out a, "Yes."

If only I could have shown him Hawaii in person instead. He could have drawn it all from memory instead of piecing his imagination together with Google images.

But I'll settle for anything I can think of to tell him at the moment.

"There's this Banyan tree that's been in a ton of movies. *Pirates of the Caribbean, The Hunger Games, Jumanji.* It's enormous. I got to see that. And I learned how to scuba dive. I saw whales and stingrays and sea turtles. I swam and explored waterfalls, ate so much Polynesian food I thought I'd pass out, went to luaus. I made lifelong friends. And I loved every minute of my engineering classes."

"What are your friends like?"

"Hanna was my roommate for both years. She's from Florida and moved back after we graduated. She was one of the few girls in my program with me. And Caroline was my other roommate. She moved in the next year. She was a senior art major and kind of like you, spent more time painting every sunset than going to class. She still lives in Honolulu, painting and working as a dive instructor. All three of us still talk a lot and have our own group text. But you know how it goes when you live on opposite sides of the country. We try, we make an effort, but life still gets in the way. We've grown apart some, but phone calls and group texts… make it a little better."

I can't pick my head up to look at Grey. That was the last thing that should have come out of my mouth, but it's the truth. Growing up, living in different cities, marriages, kids—that gets in the way sometimes with long-term friendships.

You wish it could be different, but not actually seeing someone has an effect whether you want it to or not.

Out of the corner of my eye, I see him look off to the side, away from me.

"Have you been back?" he asks.

"No," I sigh. "I'm trying to plan a trip for next year. I haven't had the vacation time, and now all these weddings."

"It really is sort of a once in a lifetime trip I guess for most people." Grey laughs. "Yours lasted two years. I hope I can go one day."

"I hope you can too," I say. "So… yes, thank you."

Grey wraps his arm around my neck, pulls me into him, and chuckles into my hair. "You're welcome."

I slip my arm underneath his backpack in the space against his lower back. We take a few slow, awkward steps before both of us come to a stop.

His hand cradles the entire left side of my face. "Can I take a little credit for you having awesome friends and a cool job in San Diego? Anything to not make me feel like such an asshole."

I nod as he runs a thumb over my cheekbone. "You're not an asshole. You're a very annoying non-asshole actually."

Grey's scoff gets stuck in his throat. He can't land his eyes anywhere, bouncing around to every one of my facial features like he's just as scared as me about what will happen when we finally actually *look* at each other. "I'm sorry I didn't love you enough. That I love you too much. I don't even know sometimes."

I breathe in and lay my chin on his chest. "Grey, we loved each other more than we thought we were capable of. I know that."

Finally, he catches my eyes.

"I don't hate you anymore," I whisper.

Grey holds me tighter.

I'm questioning now if I ever truly did.

<u>14</u>

Wednesday Evening

I GASP WHEN we emerge from the path into a wide-open lake.

The mountains that surround it give off the effect that we're standing in a crater filled with water.

Maybe we are. I have no clue.

The trail turns to grass in front of our feet. Patches of trees over hilly ground dot the edge of the lake, and patches of ice unfold up the mountainside.

And the water is so… green.

"Why is it so green?" I whisper.

Grey is just as stunned as I am. "Do I look like I know the answer to that question?"

We take a few moments to absorb our surroundings.

The rest of the group is on the other side of the lake, maybe a football field up on a rolling hill, setting up tents.

"Let's take a picture!" I exclaim, grabbing Grey's forearm. I release it like he tased me. "I mean—sorry—will you take a picture of me?"

"Yeah, of course."

I hand Grey my phone before I gallop down the hill to the edge of the lake. It's even more emerald up close.

I turn around and smile wide for the camera, although I'll look like an ant in the picture because I'm so far away from Grey.

I'm out of breath by the time I trudge back up the incline. "Jesus. I thought I was in shape. I could never live here."

The corners of Grey's lips do a weird up then down motion, like he's unsure of his feelings. "Are you thinking about moving?"

"No," I say. "I was just spewing thoughts. I'm happy in San Diego. I love my job. My friends are my family. Sunshine year round. It's great."

"And expensive," Grey says. "The cost of living is crazy."

"Do you scope out Realtor.com?"

"Favorite pastime." He shrugs. "I googled the pros and cons of living in California. Do you have an earthquake survival kit?"

I look at him like he's crazy. "Of course, I do. In a plastic bin in my closet."

"Water?"

"Three days' worth."

"Non-perishable food?"

"And a can opener."

"Battery powered or hand crank radio?"

"We've already established I have less than ideal upper body strength."

"Whistle?"

"Check. And a solar cell phone charger. I'm nothing if not prepared. Chase even helped me bolt all my furniture to the wall so I won't get squished."

"Chase?" Grey asks.

Dammit. *He wasn't you. I promise,* I immediately think like I have to defend myself. But I don't. I don't have to feel guilty for trying to move one.

"One of my exes," I mumble.

Grey leans closer to me as I speak, trying to catch the words tumbling out of my mouth.

"Oh," he says under his breath when he comprehends them. "Chase."

He hasn't backed up. He hasn't pulled away.

That little wedge of blue in his right iris flares brightly. *You're mine,* I swear it growls.

I'm afraid the heat that loops behind my belly button tells me that he's right, that I'll always be. The reality of my situation is that maybe I can't imagine not being his.

"Why are you googling the pros and cons of living in California?" I accuse him.

Grey smiles softly. His lips don't part until he barely breathes out between them, "Because I never stop thinking about you."

Everything inside me twists like a paperclip. Grey is a magnet. My chin tips up toward his smile involuntarily.

"You promised you wouldn't," I whisper.

I get it now. Everything we do blurs the lines. Past and present run together. Like neither one of us has ever let the tether go.

We've been walking through life connected to each other, giving the other person all the slack they need, so much that we couldn't even feel it. But it was there the whole time, tied around our waists.

It's taut now. Pulling us together.

I'm not sure I have enough energy to stop the world's two slowest freight trains that end with our lips crashing together.

My hands land on his chest. His face dips down. He's licking his lips as he stares at mine.

"Hey, you two!" Elliot screams from across the lake.

I jump. Grey's hand, which is millimeters from my face, drops.

The *you two* echoes off the curves of the crater, but Grey's whisper of a, "Sorry," echoes off of my eardrums louder and drowns out Elliot's, "It's getting dark!"

It is dark. Not that I noticed before.

Grey's eyes go out and glance over my shoulder to where the group is. "Let's set up our tent. I mean—sorry—our separate tents." He smiles apologetically, like he's been caught doing something he shouldn't. "Bad habit."

The almost kiss or using the word our?

Either way. Bad, *bad* habit.

I need a squirt bottle like I'm a dog in training.

I mentally blast myself in the face. *No jumping! Do not climb him like a tree. He is not yours. He can't be. We cannot kiss. And we both know it.*

It stings that he knows it too though.

× × ×

I'VE CALCULATED THAT the distance between my and Grey's tents is approximately twenty feet.

We've all set them up in a haphazard circle with a fire pit in the middle. Evie and Elliot's tent lies between mine, that I'm sharing with Sage, and Grey's, that he's sharing with no one.

It just kind of happens that we're all sitting in front of our respective tents around the fire pit after dinner and drinks when Hunter—no, Hayden—pulls a box of charades cards out of his backpack.

Elliot excitedly assigns teams. He shouldn't have put Grey with me and Sage for the sole reason that we will kick everyone's ass.

"I don't lose," Sage tells Grey when he sits beside her on the tree stump.

"Funny," Grey quips. "I only win."

Sage gives him a satisfied shit-eating grin. "Good. And we have the advantage." She traces a triangle in the air. "Ménage à trois."

Grey chuckles and bumps his fist against my outstretched one before he realizes he just walked straight into that.

He pushes my fist. "Get that shit out of here," he laughs. "That fist bump still haunts me, and I need to focus."

He's just as competitive as me and Sage. And we do have an advantage. Grey and I used to play charades a lot, and when we played it, we played it with the inside knowledge of our relationship.

"Cards have either a book, movie, or TV show on it. You choose which one you want to act out," Elliot announces.

Hunter picks a card first and smiles at his teammates, Hayden and Alana, as Elliot flips the hourglass.

Hunter holds out his hands like an open book.

"Book!" Alana exclaims.

Hunter nods and pretends to lick his hand.

"Mouse!" Hayden screams. "*Of Mice and Men!*"

Hunter shakes his head and puts his hand out flat closer to the ground like he's measuring something, then repeats licking his hand.

I think he means it's for kids, but I'm not about to help them. He looks more like a cat to me. Oh, I know.

"A cat?" Alana asks.

Hunter beams and nods enthusiastically.

"*Cat's Cradle?*" Hayden asks, confused.

Vonnegut? I'm actually impressed Hayden knows that book.

Hunter pretends to put on a hat.

"*The Cat in the Hat!*" Alana screams.

"Oooh, just made it," Elliot laughs, studying the timer. He marks a point on his piece of paper. "Grey, your turn."

Grey slides a card off the stack in Elliot's palm and smirks.

He looks right at me and holds up a one with his finger.

"First word!" Sage yells intensely as Grey kisses the air. She doesn't take a breath, so I don't have time to tell her he didn't mean that was the first word. "*Never Been Kissed! The Kissing Booth! The Last Kiss! French Kiss!*"

"Sage," I laugh, trying to cut her off, "those aren't even ones with kiss as the first word." I focus back on Grey. "*Breaking Bad.*"

"Yes!" Grey makes an I-told-you-so face at Sage as he sits. "Don't question me, Sage."

"*Breaking Bad?*" Sage questions both of us anyway. "What the hell was that?"

Evie is studying me through the fire.

I shrug. "Inside joke?" That's not necessarily true, but I have no idea what else to call it. "Inside memory?"

Memories we shouldn't be revisiting—but now I am while Grey and I smile at each other. It's blurry. Swirls of something inside my abdomen are looping in tight circles.

I'm not just revisiting it, I'm reliving it.

Breaking Bad *playing on TV. Under a Sherpa blanket. Grey's arm around my shoulder. Pressure of his forearm tight across my collarbones. My back nestled against his chest on a couch. We're the only two not really paying attention in a living room filled with my friends and their significant others.*

Grey's fingers playing with mine. My other set of fingers tracing the top of his thigh.

When I look up at him and smile, he pulls the blanket over our heads.

"Hey," he whispers.

I instantly know. I lick my lips and hold my eyes on his, committing to it. That little piece of blue is mine. I hope our children have it.

"Hey," I whisper back as permission.

His other hand traces my jawline lightly. "I love that smile you give only to me."

Before I can give it to him again, his lips press against mine. Everything is soft. The way he moves like he's restraining himself. His tongue slick against my bottom lip. His palm resting against my neck. His thumb on my pulse.

Inside, I'm nothing close to soft. It's violent.

I'm seeing a montage of explosives behind my eyelids. My heart can't keep up. Something inside my stomach has ruptured.

He makes a short deep rumble in the back of his throat that turns me on so much I could set the blanket on fire. Our tongues taste each other. But it's not enough. Then again, we're in a room full of people.

He breaks away.

"I couldn't go another second without kissing you," he says in my ear, barely above a whisper. "But now I know, I'm always going to feel like that."

Memory Lane is a horrific thing to travel down.

Well, not so much horrific as it is dangerous.

I missed Caleb and Brett's turn completely, and I haven't been paying attention to what Jourdan was miming until now. Based on the responses she's getting it must have been a dog.

"Time's up," Elliot says.

"Ugh," Jourdan whines. "*Secretariat.*"

"That was not a horse," Mitchell insists.

Evie takes her turn. She mimes a book and points between her and Elliot before mimicking walking down the aisle.

Elliot excitedly screams out, "*The Seven Husbands of Evelyn Hugo!*" when he figures it out.

I'm proud he knows that book. Sage, Evie, and I read it in our book club a few months ago, so maybe he actually picked it up and read it. He would.

"One husband for this Evelyn though," he teases as she sits in his lap.

"Bullshit. There's no way that was actually on the card," Sage grumbles into my ear. "And I'm supposed to not call them out just because it's their wedding week?"

I shrug. "Let them have it."

Then I smile as they do their usual lovey-dovey shit. No one wants to interrupt them rubbing their noses together and whispering about this weekend.

Except Sage. "All right, Ryan's next."

I'm actually nervous as I take the top card from the pile. I think I could take a memory from anything this card says and turn it into a charade.

I steal a look at Grey, and another memory lights my brain like a plasma globe.

Grey holds me in a tight hug across the console of his car. Nerves are shot. Anxiety imploding in my chest.

"I want to meet them, Ryan."

"I'm scared you won't love me anymore."

A laugh reverberates against my scalp. A kiss that's perfect. He somehow pulls me across his lap effortlessly.

"Do you think that's possible?" he asks seriously.

Tears well, and I nod.

"It's not," he assures me. "Unconditional means unconditional."

Tears fall, and I decide to argue, "You can't define a word using the same word."

"I just did." Grey raises his thumbs to wipe them away off of my cheeks, then his hands settle underneath the hem of my dress across my thighs. "I know you are not your mom. I know you are not going to turn into your mom. I want to meet the people who raised you. Besides, you still love me after meeting my family," he says.

I wipe my cheeks with the palms of my hands, trying to make myself stop crying.

"Relax, Ryan." His tone has turned playful, deepened. He swipes his thumb over my underwear, which makes me release a frustrated and content sigh. The pleased hum he gives me makes me bite my lip. "We're going to go eat dinner with your parents, and I'm going to charm their heads off the entire night. And the whole time it will be our little secret that we're both really

thinking about how wet I made you in the car earlier."

He applies pressure against me in circles. Increases the friction. My underwear is moved to the side, and he slips his middle finger inside.

"Turn your brain off. Don't think about anything else but this." The end of his finger circles my G-spot. "How it's going to be my cock inside you when we get home." I claw into his shoulders and moan in appreciation. "That's it." He pulls me in by the back of my neck to talk against my lips. "I love you. Forever. Nothing and no one will ever change my mind." He's hit that perfect spot, perfect rhythm, using his thumb in perfect unison. I'm bucking my hips. I'm so wet that it's all over my inner thighs and I'm going to have to go to the bathroom to clean up before I sit down, but I don't give a shit. It turns me on even more. "Fuck." His other hand slides around my throat, and he gently applies just enough pressure to make me lose my rational mind. "Come for me, Ryan."

His grip is tight, holding me right where he wants me. When I start to shake, he plays his little game where he counts how long he can drag out my orgasm. I can see in his eyes his brain doing the math, and it only makes the electricity run deeper, longer, more intense, because I play the game with him every time I notice and try to beat our high score. It only happens when he's pleasing me this way. Otherwise, he's too distracted.

After we're done, he pulls his finger out and sucks it into his mouth. "Never mind, I'm going to be thinking all night about how much I wish I could go down on you under the table."

While we eat and Grey charms my parents' heads into a guillotine, he lets his fingers linger on my wet underwear under the table no less than twenty times.

I don't think a thought about my mom fussing at my dad for not putting his napkin on his lap. I don't think a thought when my dad tells my mom to quit nagging him like a child. I just don't think about my parents' awful marriage.

I think about dessert.

Because Grey is equal parts sweet and spicy and refined and filthy.

I shock myself back to reality. My underwear is damp. I peel my eyes off Grey's inquisitive ones, which are wondering what I'm thinking about, and look at Sage intently.

I make the book symbol. I point to me and her and Evie.

"Book! Friends! Best friends!"

I pretend to put on pants.

"Pants!"

I motion to her to keep going.

"Jeans?"

I nod. *Keep going.*

I pretend like I'm an airplane.

"Plane?" She taps her foot, looking confused, until she shouts, "*The Sisterhood of the Traveling Pants!*"

When I sit, Grey smirks. "What the hell are traveling pants? I've never heard of that in my life. What was the other one?"

I don't look him in the eye, but I suppress my smile into his shoulder. "*Meet the Parents.*"

Strangely, Grey laughs.

But that's what we need, I guess. Humor to get through this week. Laughter fixes everything, especially the laughs that come from Grey's throat.

Nothing else needs to be said.

15

The Fifth Ex

MY LEGS ARE splayed across Austin's (yes, I see the irony that I used to call this city home, that this is where Grey lives) lap when his phone rings. He pauses his video game to answer, so I continue reading my book.

I had to go through so many painful conversations before I matched with Austin on the new Fuse app. Every single person is on it, so I might as well be, and it is a breath of fresh air for a dating app. But I think he was worth it.

He has dimples and warm brown eyes, and he makes me laugh. Bonus that he's actually sweet. He'll randomly leave me notes or, even better, a cupcake. Without warning, he'll show up at my office to take me to lunch.

When he puts his phone on speaker to keep playing NBA Live on his PlayStation, I sit there thinking his entire exchange is a joke.

"Sweetie," a woman's kind voice coos, "are you coming to help today? It's already one."

"Oh, I forgot," Austin says absentmindedly. "I don't really

want to."

The woman sighs. "You promised."

"Dad can help," he insists.

"He cannot lift all of that furniture with his back, and he already has bad knees. You're supposed to do it with Jack."

Austin is momentarily distracted by his game. "I'm sure Jack has friends."

"I'm sure Maddie would like to see you too," she says sternly, motherly. "We'd all like to see you."

Never mind. This isn't a joke.

"I'm super busy," he lies. "I'll see her later. Tell her I said hi. Love you."

Austin doesn't even bother to hang up on the call. He's too super busy trying to dunk the ball. I can hear his silent mother on the other end of the line hesitate before the call disconnects with a beep.

"Today was the day you were supposed to help your sister move into her new apartment?" I ask.

He shrugs. "I guess."

"I can go with you if you want," I offer.

I've been wanting to meet his parents and his sister, get a feel for his family dynamic.

Austin scoffs. "Maddie has her boyfriend. He can get some of his frat brothers to help. I don't really want to."

"You said the other day your sister told you she misses you."

Another shrug, but no response.

I sigh, and Austin double takes.

"What? I don't want to."

"I don't know," I start. I feel like if I press it, I'll be starting our first fight. I'm not sure I'm ready for that. "I wish I had a sibling."

He laughs. "You hardly talk to your parents."

No fighting, I tell myself. *Not yet.*

I ignore the low blow. "Yeah, and I love them, but I wish we talked more. I wish I had a family like yours. Someone who cares enough to move furniture for me. It's more special than you realize. That's all."

Then it hits me. He isn't Grey. Not even close.

Austin could never be my family. It wasn't even me who made him forget about his plans.

And just like that, we do get into our first fight, which is also our last, because I don't care anymore. I know he won't come close to being someone I want to make my own family with. I will not constantly bicker and nag him to do things he doesn't want to do. I'm not setting myself up for that.

I will not be my mother. I will not live in a marriage like hers.

I have to keep reminding myself. It seems like I forget for a minute. I have to let him go when I know that dragging this out is the furthest thing from what I want.

When my tears dry up after hours of crying, my phone comforts me.

Remember the first time your alarm went off when we were hanging out? I asked you what it was for, and you said it was so you wouldn't forget that you were going to dinner with your little sister.

You said you needed a reminder when you're with me because I distract you so much that you didn't want to forget.

For the first time, you invited me along so I could finally meet Lily and your parents. I was already so in love with you, I didn't think it could be possible to fall even more in love.

Of course, you proved me wrong.

I'd never seen someone so loving and patient, and I'd never seen you so proud.

And it hurt so much in a good way. That kind of hurt that made me cry a myriad of emotions I couldn't explain.

You asked me what was wrong, but I didn't know. All I knew was that I wanted a family like yours, a bond like yours, and I wished in some weird, messed up way that I could be in your family (while legally having sexual relations without it being gross).

But you said I already was. That we were our own two-person family. That one day it would be official.

I remember.

Fuck you.

I cannot date a man who won't:

X order me girly and ridiculous sounding drinks

X hold my hair back and watch me throw up, even when he has a huge vomit phobia

X get excited about game night and play silly and sexy board games with me, even when there is a game on TV

X say he loves me outright because 'think,' 'maybe,' and 'might' aren't good enough anymore

X set an alarm to hang out with his sister because he loves both of us so much he needs it.

<u>16</u>

Still Wednesday

U SE PROTECTION," SAGE mutters.

I stop unzipping the tent and glance back at her burrowed in her sleeping bag. She's perfected the art of looking like she's asleep.

"I'm still on birth control, and I'm not going to have sex with him," I grumble. "Besides, I'm not even going to see him. I'm going to the lake."

"Yeah, okay," she says skeptically.

I ignore that and slip my new headlamp around my head as I step out into the dark, cold air.

But maybe if I stomp right by Grey's tent, he'll instinctively know they're my footsteps and follow me.

I do before I wind downhill between the trees toward the lake. My headlamp is extra bright, lighting the path in front of my feet with a huge circular halo of white light so I don't trip.

It's not that I want to have sex with him anymore. Well, I mean I also don't *not* want to have sex with him either, but I really want the connection back. I want to spend quality time with him. I want to hear his voice and see him smile at me and feel his body close to mine.

It's hump day (the non-sexual one) and I've made it halfway through. Only halfway more to go. I feel like I can do this. I just haven't figured out yet if my week is half full or half empty, but having Grey back for a slice of finite time is suddenly exhilarating.

Which is why my heart blooms when I see him sitting on the shoreline, lying on his back with his arms behind his head like he already knew I'd show up here.

He didn't need my footsteps. He's always one step ahead.

Grey squeezes his eyes shut when I loom over him. "I'm glad I got you the ultra-high lumen one."

"Impressive vocabulary," I say, sitting beside him and switching my light off.

"It's no jetty or Loranger measurement."

I laugh. "*Lagrangian* measurement."

"Right. That."

A breeze blows through my hair and the entire forest creaks and groans. I can feel it move across the lake.

"Are there bears out here?" I whisper.

"They're not going to bother you."

That's highly suspect. "Are you going to let me run first while you die?"

"Obviously," he says.

The water is still so unexplainably green, but it's reflecting the moon and stars across its shimmering surface and creating a silver light across the shoreline. I bend my knees and pull my sweatshirt over them, pretending to be enamored with the night sky.

The only thing I'm actually enamored with is the rise and fall of Grey's chest as he breathes silently. In person. Physically next to me. Seemingly impossible a few days ago.

"Is this okay?" I ask out of nowhere.

I don't know how to process the fact that Grey still has feelings for me. I don't know how to act. Clearly. Hot and cold is the only thing that makes sense. I can't do anything right.

"I'm not going to freak out, if that's what you mean."

I stifle my laugh and narrow my eyes at him. "Grey," I breathe out.

He grins at me, letting his hand fall on my back. His warm palm presses lightly into my spine as his fingers play with the ends of my hair. I stay curled up in my ball and let myself enjoy it.

"It's okay, Ryan," he chuckles. "I can handle it."

Obviously, he's more emotionally intelligent than I am.

"I never thought I'd see you again," I say.

"I always wished I would."

I look back at him and furrow my eyebrows. "You did?"

"When things could be different," he adds. "Once about a year ago, when I was visiting Patrick in L.A. I drove halfway to San Diego before I turned around."

I widen my eyes. "You *did?*"

"I did," Grey says amusingly.

A year ago. When he was with her. I should probably be less happy about that than I am. Is this another part of the secret club we're all in—secretly wishing he still thinks about us sometimes? Don't say it out loud though. Rules.

"What's her name?"

He stares at me, wondering if he shouldn't tell me, but he does anyway. "Kennedy."

Damn. I like that name. I wonder if she looks like me. Let's call it morbid curiosity, but I also probably wouldn't ask if we hadn't been drinking all night. Yeah, right.

"Can I see a picture?"

"Ryan," he laughs, "she doesn't look like you."

I roll my eyes at him. "That wasn't what I was thinking."

"Yes, it was." Grey's hand wanders down my back before he digs in his pocket and produces his phone. "But you wouldn't be you if you weren't so curious."

I can't help but smirk. "I want to be able to picture her when I think about you for the last four years."

He hands it to me without unlocking it, but a generic faded blue lock screen stares back at me, so I type in his code before it even registers what I'm doing.

For a split second, I panic that he's changed it—but no, it's still his birth month, 08, and mine, 03. His apps blare bright in the dark exactly in the order they've always been in. It's the little things that remind you that people are who they are deep down. Change is scary, and people never welcome it eagerly—right down to the way their iPhone looks.

Grey sits up behind me and hovers over my shoulder. His body is almost curved around mine. I feel his arm settle against my back as he props his weight up. With his other hand, he touches his photo app and scrolls once before he sees a picture of her.

It fills the screen, and I have no idea which emotion I am feeling. It almost feels surreal because she's simply not me.

I'm a lunatic.

A lunatic that can't deny how gorgeous she is.

Her dark brown hair is long and straight, and I'm not sure if her teeth are really that white or if it's an optical illusion against her flawless tan skin. Thankfully, she's not in a bikini so I don't have to go down the very dark road of comparison. It's just her on a couch with a guy I don't recognize, smiling wide.

"She's beautiful," I say, turning my head up into Grey's face.

His eyes don't stray from mine. We're inches from each other, desperately trying to pull thoughts from the other's eyes.

"Yeah," he whispers eventually.

And I'm desperately hoping he really means me—in my sexy headlamp and wild, breeze-knotted hair.

Grey drops his chin to my shoulder when I lock his phone. "What else do you want to know?"

"How y'all met."

"Through Michael at work."

I think I've met him once, maybe twice, with Grey at a bar. Personable, center of attention kind of guy who is a decent graphic designer that Grey employs.

Grey lies back, and my body suddenly feels cold without his arc of warmth.

"He was sick of me being depressed and brought her to a happy hour after work, trying to set us up. He thought he was doing me a favor. It was only a few months after you'd moved—just way too soon. I ended up leaving after one drink. Then maybe eight months later, she came to Mike's birthday dinner, and it went from there."

Okay, not really four years. One blind date, a long hiatus, and three years.

My throat shrinks when I realize she made it longer than me.

It's not like I expected Grey to sit around and mourn our relationship. I sure didn't after a few months—mainly because I knew it wasn't healthy—but I also couldn't bring myself to be with anyone anymore when I figured out that I would never love them as much as Grey.

He anticipates my next question. "We broke up a little over a month ago."

"I'm sorry," I say. Seems like the right thing to say, although I don't really *feel* sorry. He'd be here with her—Kennedy—if they hadn't, and that would have been a bigger clusterfuck. Or he wouldn't be here at all. That thought burns through the pathways of my brain as I comprehend my emotions. I think I'd take him here in any circumstance over nothing, other girlfriend included.

"I was," he says. "But not that much anymore. Well, I take that back. I am sorry, but for a different reason now."

I lie back next to him. "Why's that?"

"Kennedy was right." Grey sighs. "Your name was… a point of contention in our relationship."

That isn't necessarily funny, but I fold my lips into my smile to keep it off my face. Not a single one of my ex-boyfriends has ever heard me say a thing about Grey.

"She knew I'd thought it was too soon initially to date, but I didn't realize how insecure she was about it until our first fight. I don't remember what we were fighting about until all of a sudden we're fighting about you. She thought we never broke up for a true reason, that it wasn't necessarily because I knew you weren't for me, that I was holding on to you. I tried to let you go. I lied to my-self, convinced myself I'd changed. It would work for a while, until it didn't. She didn't know I thought about you constantly."

"Grey, we fought too. We weren't the perfect couple." I sound like I'm defending myself against the woman I can picture but don't understand.

"Every time she and I fought, I knew I'd rather be fighting with you. But I was an asshole, no surprise, denying it left and right, thinking if I just had more time…" He shakes his head. "I realized on my drive from Los Angeles to San Diego, I wasn't looking for closure like I'd told myself. If I was honest, I was hop-ing that you still loved me. But then it had been three years. I didn't know if you had a boyfriend. I didn't know anything about your life except that you lived in San Diego and worked as a coastal engi-neer. I couldn't bear the thought that I'd show up and you'd tell me thanks, but no thanks."

My heart forgets how to work. I don't know what I would have told him if he'd shown up out of the blue, no matter how badly I wanted him, three years later. The time I'd spent wishing for it was long over by then.

But when I'm honest with myself, nothing has changed. We still live in different states, and he's already shown me that he can't do long distance. I'm not naive enough to think it turns out differently a next time.

Grey sighs. "I turned around. I shouldn't have stayed with her. But I did, because I knew I had to accept my fate. Then last month, out of nowhere, she broke up with me because she said she wasn't sure if I'd ever get over you, that she couldn't keep competing against you. She felt it, she said, in everything I did that she wasn't who I thought about. And when I saw you, I knew she was right. I never wanted to change. Not really. I would never have loved her as much as I love you." His humorless laugh is low and makes my body tingle. He talks about her in the past and me in the present. "I should have stayed single. I was such a jackass."

"Maybe you just needed more time. Or maybe a different person," I say.

He looks toward the sky. His lips form a thin, hardened line before he looks back at me, resigned. "No one else is you, Ryan."

My heart jump starts back, racing against my sternum. The warning signal in my brain is wailing and spinning a bright red light. I can't let the lack of oxygen affect my rational thought.

Nothing has changed, I think again, but the thought burns. *Why can't it change?*

"I'm sorry," I breathe out.

I know as soon as it's left my lips that it's the wrong thing to say. What am I even sorry for? That he went through that. That he still loves me. That I tried to have a one-night stand with him. That we can't be together. Or am I sorry for myself? That I empathize with him. That I know what that feels like. That I can't have him. What the fuck is wrong with me?

But Grey chuckles.

"Me too." He studies me cautiously, and I expect him to ask me about my love life for the past four years. I *know* he's thinking about it, wondering about the men in my life. I can see it in the wrinkles around his frown, in the shadows under his eyes. But instead, he asks, "How are your parents?"

Since it's the last thing I expect him to say, it only makes sense that I burst into tears.

He stares at me in shock as I try to wave him off and recover. I take a deep breath and laugh through my tears. Super attractively, I'm sure.

"Ryan," he whispers, pulling me down against his chest. My knees fall against his stomach, and he slips a hand into the crease between my calf and thigh. "Did something happen with your mom and dad?"

I shift into him, satisfying my craving, and let the scent of his sandalwood soap calm me in the way Grey has only ever been able to do.

"No," I sniffle against his shirt. "It's the universe. The cosmos is messing with me. Like a big 'fuck you' slapping me in the face because I thought I could actually defeat it."

"What?" Grey asks, bemused. "No one's sitting up there slapping anyone. We slap each other enough." He isn't going to let it go. "What happened with your mom and dad?"

One deep breath in is all it takes for it to all come out in a big rush. "Nothing. They're the same as always. No, they're worse. I wish something would happen. They fight over the smallest, stupidest things. They are aggravated with each other all the time. It used to be quiet in their house. Now, it's different. They aren't happy, but they won't *do* anything about it. I went on a vacation with them last year, and I swore I wouldn't ever again. Nothing about it was fun. I was stressed the whole time, stuck between them and their fucking fights about which table to sit at when we went out to eat or which way to take back to save fifteen seconds. Like who the hell cares? They only care about being right. I went home for Easter, and they ruined the day because they got into a fight about the dog. And I'm going to be my mother, Grey. I'm going to turn into her, unhappy with my marriage, unhappy with my life. I'm going to nag and be bitter. I'm going to sacrifice myself, because I'm going to settle."

"You are not going to turn into her," he says against my forehead. "And none of that is going to happen because you're stronger than her."

"I'm not so sure anymore," I argue. "I don't think I can be that strong forever."

"Ryan." He says my name as a command.

I tilt my head to look at him, but I shouldn't have.

We're both sucked into the black hole instantly. My tears stop mid-stream. His heart pounds underneath my arm laying across his chest.

His hand sweeps up my thigh and over my waist before it reaches my face. The pad of his thumb runs across my eyelashes to dry them.

My face follows his hand, not wanting him to pull away. Everywhere I want him closer. Every inch I want to connect to him, stick to him. I wish it would be so painful to peel ourselves off of each other that we just never do.

His thumb traces the bridge of my nose, then drops to my lips. I part them a millimeter in an attempt to breathe him in.

Grey smiles softly. I smile softly back.

We're going to allow ourselves just this little bit of the other. Let ourselves get lost in this moment.

"I wish I could have the chance back to never let you turn into her." His eyes lift from my lips and settle their gaze on mine. "I miss you so much."

I open my mouth to say that I miss him just as much, but he covers it lightly with his fingers. His eyes feel heavy, studying me so he can draw me from memory.

Grey brushes the hair on my temple back behind my ear, and I swear I can feel his touch in the strands of my hair. Everything I've missed about it, the intensity behind it, like he can't stand to not have his hand on me somewhere all the time. I feel like his power source again.

But for the past four years, the electricity has been cut off—until Grey suddenly switches my breaker.

His hand travels down the side of my body until it reaches my hip. All four of his fingers dig into me while his thumb circles against the skin just under my shirt, heavy then light.

I take a deep breath and let my hand wander beneath his. All the lines I knew were there, are. But there are new ones too. My fingers press into his dense torso, rise to his collarbones, and pop out of the neck of his shirt. I cup my palm around his neck, which makes his muscles tense when he sucks in a sharp breath.

His jaw hardens as he readjusts me, bringing my leg tighter around his waist, before he takes my hand in his and presses his lips into the bottom of my palm. He could brand me with his lips from the heat. "I love you so much."

I'm not going to say anything. This moment isn't about what happened or what's going to happen. It's just us, now.

I let myself trace his facial features. The stubble across his cheek is faint and lightly prickles my fingers. His lips. His nose. He closes his eyes when I sweep across his eyelashes.

His hand is back on me, fanning out across my thigh. He doesn't open his eyes, but he rests his forehead against mine.

"God, Ryan. I always will."

A corkscrew drives through my belly button. My heart burns

like a volcano erupting onto a frozen lake below.

"Grey," I whisper. Everything inside me wants him to kiss me for real.

No one else is you, my heart screams. I want to say I love him, but I can't. I'm not supposed to anymore.

His eyes flutter open, and his pupils dilate in time with his chest as he takes a deep breath. A look of sadness crosses his face.

One of his fingers curves below my chin and tips it up toward him. But I don't know if this is okay. Am I allowed to kiss him? We can't be friends with benefits. He said so himself, and I really am not a bitch.

"I don't think this is okay," I stumble out. "We're not on the same page, and I don't know what I can give. It's not fair to you."

"Ryan, it's okay," he answers. "Just be with me right now."

A branch snaps. We both freeze. The black hole spits us out, back into the real world.

Footsteps echo somewhere up the hill. I swear if it's a bear, I'll kill Grey myself. And then there's a giggle carried on the breeze.

Grey rolls out from underneath me as Andrew and Sadie emerge from the trees.

They stop in their tracks when they spot us, laugh awkwardly, and apologize, before they disappear to go hook up elsewhere.

We both stare at each other, the bubble that once surrounded us popped.

The now we'd found ourselves in is in the past, but there's no point in getting upset. It's better that we didn't kiss. We were way past dangerous territory.

"I knew those two were going to happen from a mile away," I joke.

"Oh, to be young again," Grey mutters into his hands as he rubs them over his face, "and naive enough to think your life will work out no matter what. One thing I definitely know now is there is no fucking cosmos that rights everything, that brings soulmates together at the end because it's meant to be. Nothing is meant to be. Who came up with that? 'If it's meant to be' is bullshit. We have to make the choice. We have to be the ones who will it into existence." He forces a morbid sounding laugh and sits up. His shaggy hair falls over his forehead as he shakes his head. "I'm sorry."

"For what?" I breathe out. There's way too many *I'm sorrys* going on between us.

"For that. I don't know what the fuck is wrong with me. I literally told you no a few days ago, and now I'm spouting about 'now' and how it's magically okay, but it's not. And for what I did years ago. For how I am. Because I couldn't be strong enough. And I just dropped you. Really, I'm sorry for so much. It's a long fucking list." He pauses to look out over the lake. "Being your friend is enough. It has to be."

Grey stands abruptly and pulls me up. His arms squeeze me flush against his body, familiar and warm.

"Friends," he says again.

"Friends," I repeat, stupefied.

Friends?! I cannot be friends with Grey Thomas Beckett.

We stand in this embrace with my hands wrapped tightly around his lower back (mainly because I can't move, but it's not like I want to), until he decides to relax his grip around me. When I look up at him, his palms glide around my cheeks, and he plants a slow kiss against my forehead.

"If I could go back, I would make a lot of different decisions." Grey smiles. But it's far away, like he's in his mind, traveling. "Starting with breaking up with you."

I'm the water. He's the drain.

Fuck spiraling.

I'm in a violent vortex.

<u>17</u>

I Can't Believe It's Already Thursday

I CAN'T BELIEVE this is my life right now.

My brain won't shut off. I have to rest one side at a time, never fully reaching a deep sleep.

I'm fully awake as soon as the sunlight hits our tent with zero hope of drifting back off.

Sage is actually asleep for once, so I slip noiselessly out of the tent and into the bright golden sun rays breaking through the trees.

Grey couldn't sleep either. He's sitting on a stump, talking quietly with Elliot and Evie, as Elliot cooks breakfast.

As soon as my motion catches Grey's eye, his smile reaches his eyes. I don't like it—it's a *friend* smile.

All three of them greet me lightly, careful not to wake anyone.

I sit next to the stump to join in on their conversation. "Good morning."

Surreality continues.

Our friendship continues.

Grey swivels and cocoons me in between his legs. I don't miss a beat when I lean into him, and his hand skates up my arm and settles on my shoulder. One thumb zig-zags into my hair and glides back and forth across the nape of my neck.

"Morning," he whispers into the top of my head before raising his voice slightly. "Elliot was telling me how he met Evie when he walked into her store with his mom."

"My favorite story," I say. "Mostly because he takes his mother shopping. But did he tell you that he goes to market with Evelyn and picks out all of the male clothes for her little man corner, *and* the candles because his nose has impeccable taste in scents?"

"No," Grey laughs, looking up at Elliot.

Elliot flips a pancake and smiles bashfully. "It's true. And the Thymes Frasier Fir candle will change your life during the holidays."

"Noted. I'll order one this Christmas," Grey jokes. "Evie, how'd you, Ryan, and Sage meet?"

As he says my name, his four fingers play with my clavicle under my shirt like he's strumming it.

Evie is trying to keep her eyes on our faces. "You haven't told him?"

You're supposed to be talking to him, she accuses me through telepathy. *What have you been talking about?*

I've been preoccupied, I beam back at her through my eyes. *Spiraling and trying to keep my head above water.*

"Sage and I knew each other from college," she says as she tries to go for bubbly and ignore the position Grey and I are in. "We both played volleyball. I was at San Diego State and she went to Berkeley, so we knew of each other, played against each other. When we both saw each other at Guava's four years ago, we formed a team with Amy—you'll meet her this weekend—and this other girl who eventually moved. That's where our short little Ryan comes in."

"I am not short," I retort.

"It's relative," Evie sings.

"Guava's is beach volleyball?" Grey asks.

Evie nods. "Ryan joined as our defensive player and wrapped our team into a nice bow. Look, she's even wearing our championship T-shirt from spring league."

Grey and I both look down at my royal blue long sleeve shirt with their logo on my chest and Spring Champs down my right sleeve.

"I've never seen you play volleyball," Grey says, pressing his chin into my hair.

"I'm not that g—"

"She's good," Evie interrupts me. "And fast. You should see her diving and rolling all over the sand. She really wants another T-shirt this summer."

I shrug. "Well, yeah. They're mint green this time."

"Summer league starts next week. I'll be on my honeymoon for the first game." She pouts before perking up. "Do you ever come to San Diego?"

Noooo.

Evie chews on her lip and shoots me an apologetic whoops look. If she'd tone down the room mother in her, she wouldn't be putting me in these awkward positions.

Grey shakes his head. "Just L.A. for work sometimes."

"That's only like two hours away," Elliot chimes in excitedly. "You should drive down next time. Evie can show you the boutique, you can come watch them play."

Fuuuckkk noooo.

"Maybe I can do that," he replies. "I should be in L.A. in a couple months."

"You can stay with us," Elliot says. "That's all right, right, babe?"

"Of course," Evie says, smiling, but her eyes flicker down to mine, trying to gauge my reaction.

Which is a fucked up form of hope.

I don't know what I'm hopeful for though.

I never thought about what comes after this trip or the fact that Elliot and Grey are friends.

I can't wish to see Grey a few times a year when once every couple of months isn't good enough for him. I will never get over him.

That form of hope gets stuffed deep down into my toes.

Hopefully, these two just fizzle out again.

"How did y'all reconnect?" I ask.

"I was in Austin a few weeks ago to help my mom with some of the final rehearsal dinner decisions," Elliot says. "I went out with another high school friend for someone's birthday dinner, and Beck was there."

"Elliot evidently never bothered to give me his number when he got a new one," Grey says.

"And *you* aren't on any social media." Elliot laughs. "It's both our faults, but you'll have my number from now on."

"Were you close in high school?" Evie asks.

"Yeah," Grey says. "We played the same position on our football team, so we hung out a lot."

"We definitely didn't talk as much as we should have in college," Elliot adds, "so we kind of grew apart, but now..." He grins. "I'm glad you came this week."

Goddamn Elliot and his heart-melting smile. I switch to looking at Grey's lips beautifully turned up in sincerity.

They could both charm someone to their death.

Now that I think about it, they shouldn't be allowed to be friends. It should be illegal for two men with such magnetic faces to walk around on this planet and talk to women because they have the upper hand. Always.

And then you put both of them together with their panty-dropping smiles, bouncing their personalities off of each other—God help us.

Grey gently squeezes my shoulders. "Me too."

I can do this.

If Grey wants to be friends, then I can be friends.

I can be the best damn friend to ever grace the face of Earth.

Elliot passes around the blueberry pancakes, which he's cut into little squares, lathered in syrup, and sprinkled with powdered sugar.

I hold my paper plate in my lap and stuff them into my mouth with my plastic fork.

"So good," I tell Elliot and smile psychotically.

This is what eating your feelings looks like. I'm barely bothering to chew, and my cheeks are puffed like I'm playing a game of Chubby Bunny.

I can hardly breathe.

But I will not be mad.

This is what I wanted.

✕ ✕ ✕

WHEN WE'RE PISSED off and lying through our teeth, do our laughs only sound different to ourselves?

Like that philosophical tree falls in the forest question—my laugh sounds like a tinny, high-pitched, ridiculous trill coming off my tongue. I can't stop, but I'm hoping no one else hears it.

Jourdan and Alana are scheming about something until they pull their heads apart and Alana announces giddily, "Last one in the lake… has to do something!" while Jourdan strips.

Oh, you guys, my laugh lies as everyone sprints down the mountain.

We're so silly, it squeals as I peel off my shirt and leave it behind me.

It's fun acting like teenagers, it cries when Grey kicks off his shorts.

When we reach the edge of the bright green water, I stop short while everyone else tumbles in, laughing and screaming at the biting cold temperature.

It looks freaking frigid.

Grey isn't watching me. He's joking around with Jourdan and Brett and splashing Alana.

Is this what it feels like being his friend? I'm standing here in my bra and underwear and he's not even interested. I won't be the center of his world anymore?

Trust me, I couldn't stop staring at him in his tight black boxer briefs and noticing the slope of his lower back and the groove of his spine.

Grey has been back in my life for five whole days and it's like he never left.

I want to be selfish, have him all to myself. He isn't anyone else's and I don't want to share.

But I have to, right? I can't have what I want. I'm not a selfish bitch no matter how hard my alter ego tries to win out. I can't have it all.

Closure is one step forward, two steps back.

"Get in!" Sage screams.

I muster every bit of courage I have, tear my eyes off Grey, and dart into the shallow water. "Holy shit!" I'm knee deep and it's like ice. Well, not ice because it's liquid, but just as cold. Is that scientifically possible? "No, no, no, no."

I turn to make a run for it back to the shore, but Evie calls in reinforcements. "Elliot, grab her!"

Elliot scoops me up by the waist before I'm able to make it

back to semi-warm land and cradles me in his arms like a baby.

"I'm breaking up with you," I declare.

"You'll love me anyway," Elliot teases, lifting me high above his head and tossing me through the air like I'm a paper airplane.

Story of my life is all I can think as the anticipation builds. I feel as if I can measure every inch that I fly, waiting, dreading.

Then suddenly I crash into the green lake so quickly that I was teleported. It sucks the oxygen out of my lungs, stinging me like a thousand bees, but it kind of hurts in a good way.

I try to sink and keep my body below the surface for as long as I can. People shell out hundreds of dollars for cryotherapy, and I'm torturing myself for free. I try to stretch out the seconds as my lungs scream for air.

Frantic hands find me submerged and yank me by an arm and a leg back up to the surface.

"Elliot," I whine, rubbing water from my face.

"Jesus, Ryan. I thought you were dying."

I am. On the inside.

"Nope." My entire body is one big goosebump. "But now I might because it's even colder out of the water."

Elliot wraps his arms around me, trying to warm me. "I know. Time for a fire."

Once everyone has made it back up the camp site, Elliot puts all the boys to work.

He and Caleb start working on the fire while Andrew and Mitchell have to go find kindling. Brett heats up some water on the stove for hot chocolate and Grey passes around blankets.

"Here you go," he says, handing me a plaid one and continuing around the circle.

Here I go—wrapping it around myself and scooting closer to the tiny flames that are finally starting to crackle.

Brett follows behind Grey with the warm drinks.

"I kind of want to go jump back into the lake," I joke to Mitchell, trying to distract myself from Grey who sits down three seats away next to Jourdan. "It felt good."

Mitchell, on my left, stays quiet long enough for Brett, who sits down on my right, to interject. "I think I speak for everyone when I say that it is so crazy that he is here at this wedding."

I laugh my weird laugh. "Have y'all been talking about us all week?"

"Of course." He shrugs. "What did you expect? He was a new toy that everyone wanted to play with and all of a sudden, you're not sharing."

"By all means," I comment snidely, motioning toward Grey.

"I'm a married man," Brett jokes, "and Jourdan beat me to it anyway."

"Joke's on her. He doesn't do long distance."

Brett raises his eyebrows. "What does he do?"

"Annoys the shit out of you mostly."

He laughs. "I think it's cool you've been so cool about it. Four years is a long time though, I guess. Easy to get over it and move on."

Hahaha, my laugh trills. *I'm super cool.*

"Grey!" Brett calls to him. "When are you coming to San Diego? We all need a new friend. Everyone's sick of everyone else, and Ryan annoys the shit out of me."

He pinches my thigh because he thinks he's hilarious. I smack him in the arm because he's not.

Grey flicks his eyes to mine and laughs. "I'll try the next time I'm in Los Angeles. I already promised Elliot." He looks around at all of us with his rich smile. "So, tell me the story of the friend group."

From across the fire, Sage joins in. "Evelyn is the glue."

"I take pride in it," Evie says. "It's hard work being the social butterfly."

"Nell paved the way first," I add, "and perfected the art of social interaction."

Sage looks up to the sky. "Thank you, Nell."

"She's not dead," Elliot laughs. "Anyway, Brett was my first friend in college. He was more fun when he wasn't a lawyer."

Caleb runs his hand through Brett's perfectly coiffed hair from back to front. "When his hair gets messed up though, you know he's going to let loose."

"How did you two meet?" Grey asks.

"Happy hour," Brett replies. "We'd both had long days. We bonded. His children are… children and my clients act like children."

Grey nods. "What kind of lawyer are you?"

"Divorce attorney."

"Wow," Grey says amusingly. "That's depressing."

"Or educational," Brett laughs and looks around at everyone around the fire with purpose. "It's the little things. Everyone remember that."

Evelyn and Elliot smile at each other. "We won't," she says, sickeningly in love.

"For instance, I'll divorce Caleb when he stops getting my oil changed when I'm too busy and stressed to recognize that I'm two thousand miles over."

"And you always have to buy my favorite cereal, even though you hate it," Caleb replies before he kisses Brett and whispers something in his ear. Everyone is getting too smushy for my liking.

"What about you and Alana?" Grey asks, turning to Jourdan and thankfully taking the focus off of the couples.

"We've only been snowboarding with everyone a few times," Jourdan pouts. "But we make it out to San Diego every so often. Maybe we can coordinate a visit together."

I roll my eyes internally. Even better. I'll be subjected to Grey and two much cooler than me girls flirting with him every time he visits.

"And Mitchell," I interrupt too haughtily, breaking their eye contact. I non-laugh. "He works with Elliot."

"Yeah?" Grey says. "What do you do?"

"I'm a financial analyst," he replies. "Lots of spreadsheets and data. Pretty boring."

"No," Grey insists. "That sounds awesome. The best decisions are based on data."

Leave it to Grey to make Mitchell come alive (for a split second). "I know!"

"Is everyone warm and ready to pack up?" Elliot asks, looking at his watch.

Slowly, we all rise to pack up.

Grey crosses in front of me. "You got your tent?"

"I got it," I say noncommittally.

He raises his hand in front of my face.

I'm shocked into silence. This motherfucker is motherfucking high-fiving me? Is this my life now?

Grey has never high-fived me in my life.

It takes everything in me to place my palm against his before I jerk it back and my laugh is one I don't even recognize, a sound I have never heard.

I turn quickly on my heels and float back to my tent to take it apart. I'm out of my body, hovering above myself and not aware of a single thing I'm doing, as I undo the poles and sit down.

"What's wrong?" Sage says, pulling me back into reality and picking up one side of the tent.

I ignore her and stuff a piece of it into the tiny nylon bag.

"Why do they make these fucking bags so tiny?" I seethe. "Like the machines that make every damn product puts these things in perfectly folded inside these narrow, tiny-ass bags, but once they come out, it's not going back in. Why can't they make the fucking bags bigger?"

"Whew," Sage whistles, letting the end of our tent drop to the ground—or I inadvertently ripped it from her hands.

She looks over my shoulder to where I assume Grey is helping Elliot pack up for our next leg of the hike.

I can feel her and Grey have a moment with their eyes, like the connection is bearing down on me.

"What's wrong?" she asks again. "Your laugh is fake and now you're seething."

"Nothing," I lie.

She scoffs. "I can tell when you're fake laughing. You're not fooling me."

"Nothing *should* be wrong," I correct myself angrily. "I shouldn't be mad. So, I'm trying not to be mad."

"I think you're way past that," Sage jokes.

I roll my eyes and get as much of the tent as I can into the two inch by two inch wide bag.

Seriously, who the fuck designs these things? All four corners are still spilling out, but there's no more room for them to go. I'm milliseconds away from tearing this thing to shreds.

I drop my arms and sigh. "I can't be friends with him, Sage."

Her forehead forms multiple creases before she laughs breathlessly. "That man does not want to be your friend."

"He almost kisses me," I say, "and then he tells me being friends with me is enough."

"You almost kissed him?"

"Yes, I think. Twice! Keep up," I insist. "But we didn't."

"Why didn't you tell me? We're supposed to be R.A.C.E.ing. We can't figure it out if we don't do the evaluating."

"Because nothing is working. He told me he wants to be

friends with me."

"Again, Grey is not interested in being friends with you."

"He's trying to be," I retort. "And he's going to come to San Diego and visit Elliot in a few months. Stay with him. I'm going to be subjected to him again and again."

"And that's a bad thing?"

"I can't get over him when he cuts off all contact for four years," I hiss. "How the hell am I supposed to get over him when I have to continually see him?"

"Does he know how you feel?" Sage asks.

"What? No."

She raises her eyebrows. "Don't you think he should?"

"He hasn't asked."

"Tell him you can't be friends with him. That he can come to San Diego and be friends with Elliot but that you'd rather not be around when he does."

My brain fogs. I squeeze my eyes shut.

I couldn't imagine Grey being in the same city and not seeing him. I'd know it through Elliot and Evie. I'd know he was there, only miles away. I wouldn't be able to take it.

Sage tuts. "That isn't what you want either. You know R.A.C.E.—as in the acronym for Ryan accomplishes closure effortlessly—only works when you actually *want* what you're trying to accomplish."

"None of my options are good," I say.

"Or you could tell him you still love him," Sage says matter-of-factly.

I recoil.

"Now you're not fooling anyone," she adds. "Except maybe Grey because he's probably too scared of the possibility that you tell him you don't anymore."

Anger pricks through me like reverse acupuncture. "Did you

ever think *I'm* scared?"

Sage doesn't skip a beat. She puts her hands on her hips and smirks. "Of course, you're scared. I get it. It's scary that the person you love lives across the country and swears off long distance."

"And what if he tells me no again? This is the life I'm meant to live? Pining for something I can't have from all of my goddamn endless boyfriends." I pause. "It's a shitty way to live, by the way."

"And what if he tells you yes?"

"Who moves? Who gives up something? Who resents who?" I look away. "It's always the wrong time for us."

Sage shakes her head. "If he's the right person, there is no wrong time, Ryan."

I feel like she's speared me with the tent poles she's folding together. "Don't mock me."

"I'm not," she says, registering my anger that's welling for her now. "I wouldn't do that. I'm serious."

"What are you saying? He's the wrong person?"

"No! Neither one of you have been able to move past it after four years." Sage laughs quietly. "For fuck's sake, Elliot tried to set you up with a man no one knew you were still in love with but is perfect for you. I don't even think you wanted to admit it to yourself. You love each other—still. I'm saying time hasn't kept you from anything." She senses she should probably leave me alone so she hands me the poles. "Just make Elliot deal with the tent."

I sit cross-legged in the dirt and stab the poles into the bag futilely as Sage backs away.

After a few minutes, I hear his footsteps approach behind me.

"Ryan?"

I stab harder.

"Is everything al—"

"No, I'm mad at you," I state.

Grey steps around me. "Can we talk about it?"

I raise my head to look him hard in the eye. "No. I need space. And I mean it. You can't help me sort out my emotions. We're not together anymore, and there's no air conditioning out here for you to turn down. So, give me space."

His smile is soft, and the blue spot in his eye glints back at me. "I'll figure out something else then."

Yeah, you do that.

The fact that I know he will makes me madder.

The hatred I have for him right now is the kind of hate that's only reserved for a person you love.

<u>18</u>

The Sixth Ex

I HATE FIGHTING.

I know it's necessary. Healthy, even.

And always inevitable, of course, since it's a byproduct of caring.

I care about Joey.

He's got shaggy blonde hair and loves to surf. He's in sales, and he does well, thanks to his ability to make someone laugh. We met on the beach through some mutual friends, and he's pretty laid back. I like him because he relaxes me, makes me see the simpler side of things. He doesn't know it but he helps me unwind my mathematical brain sometimes, because all of that stuff goes over his head in a way I enjoy.

Just like Grey—and Joey's the first boyfriend I've had that I've appreciated a similarity between the two. Progress.

But I really, *really* do hate fighting.

I want it to be over almost as soon as it starts, but that doesn't mean I don't retreat. Sometimes, I need a minute—to simmer, collect my thoughts, sort out my feelings about why I'm mad. I internalize it and try to solve it like a math equation.

Algebra. X means Y. Y doesn't mean Z.

Words aren't my specialty. They never have been. I want us both to apologize and move past it, but I just always need a little help to get to that point, because my instinct is to shut down. I don't know how to express what I'm feeling.

I need Joey to pull me out of my self-destruction, not detonate me.

We've been sitting on my couch in silence for forever because I'm trying to organize my brain.

He won't talk. I do something very unlike me and reach my hand out to touch his arm.

He pulls back angrily.

"I'm trying," I say. "I need help. Can we laugh or cuddle or something?"

"No," Joey says.

"Last time you walked out," I say, "and I forgave you."

I'm proud of myself and equally horrified for this. I didn't end it like I wanted to. Grey would never walk out on me in a middle of a fight. But I gave Joey another chance when he apologized. That's growth or it's settling somehow. I haven't figured out which yet.

"I need help sorting through my emotions. I have to make them equations in my brain. Line them up. Work it out in steps. Like anxiety plus this action times this attitude pissed me off or made me sad or whatever."

He stares blankly at me. "What?"

"Like root causes and parts of the whole, et cetera. Like math."

"I have no idea what you mean. Emotions aren't math equations."

"Everything can be a math equation. It's not that crazy."

This isn't crazy at all to me. This is how my brain works, and it makes all the sense in the world to me.

So, the look he gives me makes me snap—his eyes look so *judgy*—and I lose it.

Probably because I was already pissed off in the first place because he forgot about Caleb and Brett's wedding and made plans to surf with his friends. But it's more than that.

He doesn't *get* me.

And the only person who does lives thirteen hundred miles away and no longer thinks twice about me.

More tears. More fighting.

He doesn't understand anything I'm saying. I feel dumb, and I can't put my words together correctly to get out any point I'm trying to make when I'm not sobbing.

I break up with him.

Then he slams the door behind him.

My unread texts burn bright green, and I immerse myself into my phone. It's the only reliable thing in my life. The only thing I have to cling to. The only thing I have left of the man who left me behind to move on while I simply can't.

Remember that fight, the one where I realized you just got me?

Normally when we fought, you'd just wait me out, eventually get me under a blanket with you, then make me explain what I was thinking. My words always came out with plus and add and times and equals, and you said I got mad like I was solving an equation.

I'd never been told that before.

I think it was maybe the half-dozenth fight we'd had when I noticed the pattern: fight, retreat, freezing, blanket, cuddle, resolve. The same six steps every time. I'm good at recognizing patterns. As soon as you held the blanket up for me to slip inside next to you, I felt like my mind would clear.

When I jokingly asked you how you always got me out of my mind and under a blanket with you, you smirked and, after some prodding, admitted that you always turned the A/C down and waited for me to get cold so I'd come find you for warmth.

I remember.

Fuck you.

I cannot date a man who won't:

X order me girly and ridiculous sounding drinks

X hold my hair back and watch me throw up, even when he has a huge vomit phobia

X get excited about game night and play silly and sexy board games with me, even when there is a game on TV

X say he loves me outright because 'think,' 'maybe,' and 'might' aren't good enough anymore

X set an alarm to hang out with his sister because he loves both of us so much he needs it

X lower the air conditioner and pull me out of my own mind because he doesn't understand how it works.

<u>19</u>

Still Thursday

GREY DOES GIVE me space.

Enough space for me to walk and talk with every single person I've spoken less than one hundred words to this entire trip.

I work out lots of emotions—except the ones I have about Grey—as I hike and learn more about anyone else who is not a six-three male with just the right amount of thick brown hair and a blue eye-streak that physically weakens me.

I gain satisfaction because I figure out a trick to tell Hunter and Hayden apart. Hunter has attached earlobes so I'll be creepily checking out their ears for the rest of my life.

Then I ignore Sage's cutting glances.

I am impressed with Alana because she started school this year to be a nurse practitioner on top of her job as a NICU nurse. I could never do school and a full-time job at the same time.

Then I ignore Sage's footsteps too close behind me.

I'm in awe of Jourdan because she gave up a steady job in internal audit years ago to pursue her dream as a photographer. I wish I had the balls to do something like that.

Then I ignore Sage's pointed sighs.

And I'm totally envious of Sadie and her backpacking trip through Europe this summer. Full-time working adults deserve a summer break every so often too—like a summer sabbatical. It shouldn't just be teachers. Where do I sign the petition?

After hiking miles to our new campsite, I can't avoid Sage any longer as she hovers over me, silently judging me while I attempt to set up our tent by myself.

I think I should move into product design. I'd have a one-non-outdoorsy-woman, one-handed tent able to pop out and set itself up in under a minute—that came with an enormous bag. Instead, I'm on my knees underneath the tent, fooling with these poles and struggling to figure out which holes they go into because nothing is intuitive about it.

"If you'd let me help, we'd be done by now," Sage says when she's had enough of me.

I scoff at her through the mesh window that's tangled around my head and neck. "I'm trying to strangle myself."

"Maybe you should try setting it up from the outside."

"Genius," I mutter. It is taking me longer than it should for me to get the tent off my head before I give up. "I thought I could simultaneously reach all four sides from the center."

She raises her eyebrows. "He's inside that mathematical brain of yours."

"That's nothing new."

I resist looking at Grey through the mesh squashed against my eyes. Sage's serious face, trying its best to keep the corners of her lips from tilting upwards, suddenly stirs humor inside of my chest that forces itself out of my throat as a harsh laugh.

"Fuck, Sage. Something is wrong with me."

"That's an understatement." She giggles behind her hand.

"You look like a mermaid stuck in a net."

I beam—but I'm sure my smile looks more like a fish mouth pressed against glass. "I do kind of have red hair now."

Sage drops to her knees and starts searching for the edge of the tent.

"I don't even have to buy you dinner first?" I joke.

She laughs and disappears under the fabric. "Not if you talk dirty to me. Plus, I have a thing for slightly-red-headed mermaids." Her brunette head pops up in front of me before she wraps her long arms around me. "I love you. Don't be pissed at me."

"I'm not," I insist. "I'm sorry. I just didn't want to have to think."

"Clearly. You haven't shut up once since we started hiking."

I pinch her back. "You always try to make me think."

"I *think*," she says, squirming, "that you should go think by yourself. It's getting dark. I'll set up the tent that you've now completely destroyed—twice." She holds me out at arm's length and smiles. "Just go. Unravel two years of unhinged behavior. I don't think you need me for closure. I think you know in your heart."

I exhale on a smirk. "I got this. Ravel and hinge."

"Unravel and ravel mean the same thing."

"Why do you even know that?" I ask, rolling my eyes.

"Words," she says. "Simple and beautiful."

"Irregardless," I say, irking her. She hates when I point out that I can find it online in the dictionary—along with the word 'petfluencer.'

I'm convinced in two thousand years people will discover our ancient texts and wonder: what the fuck? Who were these ridiculous people?

"Didn't I tell you to leave?"

"Yeah. Leaving." I grin and slip out from underneath the tent with quite a lot of effort. I glance back at Sage, who is smiling at me like a lunatic, and deadpan, "You look like an idiot, you know that right?" before I skip off into the woods.

Ha. I don't even watch Grey's head follow me. Much.

Instead, I weave through the trees and the orange sunlight reflecting off the green leaves.

I hadn't been paying attention when we hiked in, but I stray from the path anyway, assuming I'll be able to find my way back. I aim for the summit, the sky I can see just out of reach.

When I reach the top, I won't care if I get stuck up here all night. The orange has turned into a dark purply-blue sky that opens up in a long-range mountain view.

I think I can see the Milky Way. It's like it splits the sky in two, erupting from between the two huge black mountains in the distance.

Maybe our very future descendants won't think we're that crazy after all—because I can see why the ancient Egyptians thought the gods lived in the sky, traveling it by boat. I swear it almost moves like a river.

This is the perfect place to think.

And all I can think about is that I have to let all of this go. Four years is too long, and I might know of the perfect way to do it.

It's my last Hail Mary.

×××

"I WAS ABOUT to send out a search party," Sage says as I zip the flap up behind me. "But I figured I hadn't heard any screaming so it might've been premature."

"I lost track of time because I didn't bring my phone. And I got a *teeny* bit lost on the way back. I was about to scream, but I saw Elliot's bright red tent just in time."

Sage lifts her head to study me as I slip into my sleeping bag, but she bites her tongue about whatever lecture she wants to give me. "Goodnight."

I toss and turn for fifteen minutes. I wanted to make it back before everyone went to sleep, but I'd distracted myself for hours.

I don't know if I'm ready to talk to him. I want to be, but every time I imagine actually doing it, I want to throw up. And who knows if my plan is even a good one.

Certainly not me. My plans never go well when Grey is involved.

He's probably sleeping anyway. It's late. I shouldn't wake him up.

I pull myself into a fetal position and cocoon myself tighter, trying to cuddle with myself. A tag scratches me in the thigh, but when I reach down to grab it, I pull out a small white booklet. It's just a few inches wide, and I recognize Grey's handwriting, even upside down.

Flip Me, it says in bold black lettering.

"Were you going to tell me this was here?" I whisper-hiss into the dark.

"No," Sage replies. "Grey's smile when he put it there definitely told me he would fucking kill me if I touched it or if I mentioned it to you."

"Liar."

"I'm serious. That smile should be banned from existence," she says. "And I would've said something if you'd actually stopped moving for two seconds and fallen asleep, but you clearly still haven't worked out what you want to do."

"He's trying to figure out a way to get to me."

"Open it," she challenges me, "and see if he does."

I don't need to open it to know that whatever Grey's drawn in this thick tiny booklet is going to make me nostalgic.

Fuck that. This entire week has been nostalgic. Actually, has it been two nostalgic years?

I hold it up in front of my face and take a deep breath.

"Is it a note?" Sage asks.

"No. It's a flipbook."

He doodled something for me. I love it so much it hurts, and I haven't even seen it yet. It probably took him all night.

I hate him. I don't know how he does this to me.

And as I let the pages fly out from under my thumb, I love him even more.

There I am in cartoon form, tossing and turning in my sleeping bag until a speech bubble appears. *I wonder if he's awake.* More tossing and turning. Another speech bubble. *He's definitely awake.* More tossing and turning. I sit up on the page. *Okay, fine. I will absolutely go talk to him.*

Sage raises her eyebrows when I look at her. "I'd let him get to me. Just saying."

I toss the flipbook at her face and laugh. "Put it in my bag when you're done." I grab my phone and step back outside of our tent, which I'd bet my life that Grey put up and not Sage. The sound of the little book whirring behind me and Sage whistling softly comes a few seconds later.

"He is good," she chuckles loud enough so she knows I hear. "This is witchcraft."

Don't I know it. Grey draws me a picture and I'm walking over to his tent without a second thought, like I'm a puppet on strings. He and his magical ability have kept me under a spell for four years.

But this is what I decided I wanted to do. This is my plan, just as much as it is his. I have to stay in control.

He wants to talk through my anger. I want to move past it, completely, somehow. So, this might work. Who the fuck knows?

I'll try anything at this point.

Grey just got me here a little quicker, and he must know I'm standing here. My footsteps weren't very stealth. It's silent inside his blue tent, not even a rustling of his sleeping bag.

I'm doubting myself, switching my weight from one leg to the other, until I hear him sigh.

"Ryan," he laughs. "Get in here before a bear eats you."

I unzip the little flap door a little too quickly.

Grey is lying on his side in his sleeping bag, shirtless, with a grin I want to peel off his face.

Heat blooms in every corner of my body as I sit beside him, but I need to focus. I came here for a reason—closure. This is the only option I have left.

"I've had six boyfriends in the last two years," I blurt.

What? So not smooth. Saying that out loud makes me wince. I'm already off the rails.

Grey's smile falls. He closes his eyes, rolls onto his back, then looks up at nothing through his dark eyelashes. I curse to myself when he puts his hands behind his head, flexing his biceps and chest.

"I mean—"

He shakes his head. "I don't want to talk about your exes."

"Grey," I say sternly.

"I'm sorry," he insists, "but I don't want to hear about other men who've made you happy. Who've gotten to spend time with you when I didn't. Who've been able to talk to you when I couldn't. Thanks, but no thanks." He pushes himself up by an elbow and lays his head on my thigh. "I want to talk about us. This. Why are you mad at me?"

"What are you doing?" I ask angrily as he curves his arm around my lap. I nudge him off, trying to keep my voice low. "Fine. I'm mad about this. I can't just be your friend. You're laying your head on my leg, you're straddling me with your huge thighs and putting your Achilles tendons in my face. Then you're not looking at me when I want you to and sitting next to other girls. You gave me a fucking high-five. Now you're letting your hands linger on my skin, and making me feel things, and I *don't* want to be your friend."

He blinks. "I don't want to be your friend either."

"Then *what* are you doing?"

"I'm trying to give you what I thought you wanted. Closure." His jaw tenses when he looks away. "Isn't that what you want?"

Fuck. My brain is muddled, and my body is betraying me. That's why I came to talk to him, but nothing can go right after he opens his mouth. I want it and don't want it at the same time—and I kind of want to sink my teeth into his hardened jaw right now— because I wish things could be different.

"I've had six boyfriends in two years," I repeat and ignore his face when he looks back at me painfully. I don't stop to take a breath. "Trust me, I know it's a lot. Sage even nicknamed me the serial dater and I kind of hate it. And my six boyfriends have all sucked because they aren't you. No one is you. But you blocked me. I couldn't talk to you. I couldn't find you online. I guess I could have written you a letter but this isn't 1850 and I'd have to shamefully send it to your parents' house anyway because I have no clue where you live. Are you in the same apartment? No, don't an- swer that. I tried to move on. Trust me. Just let me show you something. Don't talk—because you're messing up my brain."

My voice sounds winded, so I stop to place my fingers over his lips with one hand, because he's definitely going to try to squeeze some words out, and unlock my phone with the other.

"I've broken up with every one of them *because* of you. You didn't even mean to, but you've made every guy out there for me not good enough. You've destroyed every possible man, without even trying, so you're going to read these crazy text messages that I've been sending you for the past two years, and you're going to deal with it. I need it off my chest. I need to move past this stage in my life. This is what I worked out on top of the mountain, and this is why I walked over here."

He smiles under my fingertips, and I'm going to have to file a restraining order against his lips.

"And don't smile."

I shove my phone in front of his face. His brown eyes deepen as he continues to look at me in surprised humor instead of at my phone screen.

"Read it," I say, narrowing my eyes.

"Fine," he murmurs against my fingers.

I slowly let my hand fall, giving the pads of my fingers a millisecond to appreciate his pretty lips.

He sits up, takes my phone, and starts to read.

His eyes scan back and forth quickly.

Vulnerability is a bitch.

After a second, he laughs under his breath. A swallow comes another second later when I think he is reading about his stomach bug. Then a smirk follows as I know we are both thinking about having sex on top of his washing machine. That smirk quickly fades to serious as he switches to reading about how much he loved me.

"This is a lot of fuck yous," he mutters under his breath.

I'm sure he's putting two and two together on why I would be texting these specific moments in our relationship out of the thousands. On what I assume is number five, he chews on his lips as he thinks about Lily. And when he's done reading the last one, after I just told him there was no air conditioner in the woods, he looks up at me with such piercing eyes that I shudder.

There. It's done. Finished. I'm never going to add another X to this ridiculous list. Two years wasted. I've outed myself, in a good way, I think, because I'm never going to pick up my phone and exhibit this nonsensical behavior again.

And then Grey takes a breath and surprises the shit out of me.

"Do you still love me?"

Tears well instantaneously at the tone of his voice. Husky, deep, and shocked. I try to look away, but he takes his thumb and presses it against my lower jaw, drawing my face back toward his.

I was so incredibly wrong—I've outed myself in a terrible way. Of all the things I thought about earlier tonight, I never thought that *that* was what he was going to take away from this. As always, I wasn't thinking two steps ahead with him. How could I have been so stupid?

"Ryan, I—" His voice catches. "I thought you didn't..." His thumb traces my jawline. "Are you still in love with me?"

My heart is hammering in my chest as I stare at him. That was vulnerable enough, letting him peer into my therapy sessions.

"Answer the question," he demands.

I don't need to say yes and wedge myself deeper, so I continue on being a wide-eyed mute girl who lies to herself and everyone around her.

"I thought I couldn't handle it, that you didn't anymore. You tried to have casual sex with me, for fuck's sake. I didn't know what to think, and I have been freaking out. But now... *fuck*, if you are still in love with me Ryan, tell me."

He is going to hold me in and mesmerize me by that slice of blue in his right eye until I answer.

It doesn't matter how many tears are spilling out of my eyes.

"I shouldn't be," I manage to say after what feels like minutes and drop my eyelids heavily.

"Look at me." Grey wiggles my phone between us when I do. "I am these assholes to every other woman in the world. I'm not special. I'm not the best boyfriend in the world. I am the man you know only because of you." Then he tosses it down beside him with a dull thunk. "I wouldn't order a stupid drink or take care of anyone else while they were sick before I met you. I won't doodle for other girls or ever love anyone else like I love you. You're the only person I've ever met that can compete for Lily's time, and you're for damn sure the only woman that I want to wrap myself up in a blanket with when she's angry. I've known that for six years. There is no one else for me. If I had an ex list, it would be infinite."

My tears are soaking his hand that is still pressed against the side of my face. "You wouldn't have an ex list in the first place. That's the point. You loved someone else after me and I never could. You'd still be with her if she didn't break up with you."

"You're right, Ryan. You went one way when we broke up, and I went another. But it's not what you think. I was resigned to settling from the start. I knew I could never find what I had with you again. So, I settled. I was going to settle for the rest of my life. The whole point was that trying was pointless. God, I used to lie in bed staring at my phone, staring at the unblock button, and just wondering if you'd answer me after all these years. The fucking picture of you and that beached seal is burned into my memory from staring at it for so long."

"Stop being annoyingly you, please," I blubber out a laugh through my tears. "My heart can't take anymore."

Grey doesn't smile back. His face is so serious it makes me abruptly stop trying to lighten the mood.

"Can you ever trust me again?" he asks.

My eyebrows dip, meeting closely together. "Trust you how?"

"Trust me, please. Trust me not to repeat my mistakes."

"Grey..."

"I won't screw it up this time. I can wait years, decades, my whole life even, for you. I should have years ago. I was too young, dumb, and scared you wouldn't come back for me."

"But…" I whisper.

I can't remember what I am trying to say and do; what my end goal is anymore.

"I told myself I was going to be alone. I'm tired of fighting with a non-existent Grey. All this time, I thought you didn't want me. You made the choice. Not me. I didn't have that luxury. I was committed to you and long distance. You never tried to get in touch with me."

"I know," he whispers. "I heard about you through Patrick. He said you seemed happy, and I didn't think you'd ever want to talk to me again."

"And now what? What's different, Grey? You're going to be thousands of miles away. You can handle seeing me every few months? There's so many logistics. It's just not that easy." I scoff. "I told myself no more dating, and you've already shown me that you can't do it. I'm not going to let you trick me again."

That was my decision while I was looking at the stars. I was going to lay my stupid list out to Grey. Then I would go back to San Diego and work on myself. Maybe fix the crazy in me. I don't need any more boyfriends right now.

My decision was to break the serial dating pattern, but five days ago, I never thought I'd see Grey again, and now he's asking me for a second chance.

I glance at his lips uncontrollably. A second chance. I could kiss him and see.

"No more dating," he parrots me slowly. "Then we can be non-friends. We will figure it out together. Lily might be moving out. She's becoming more independent. Patrick says he has a spot in the office in Los Angeles if I want when the funding is complete. I'm here until you're ready."

"That's a lot of information."

"I know," he whispers.

"It doesn't change anything. I tried to sleep with you for funsies so I could move on. And now it's okay? You're flying back to Austin in three days. Am I going to be the bitch that succeeds at make-up sex at your expense? At both our expenses? Because I don't want to be."

Grey is closing the gap between our lips so quickly and painfully slowly at the same time.

He shakes his head a millimeter so close to my lips I can feel the vibration of them moving against mine. "I know it won't be at our expense because I know that I'm not going to do anything to screw this up this time."

My body is so disloyal. The blue wedge in his eye is an inch away from mine and making me wish it was mine. Neither one of us weirdly wants to close our eyes, because otherwise, we won't be able to see and stamp it into our memory.

"I can't go through this again. It would break me, I think. Even more than I'm already broken."

"You aren't broken," he whispers. "You are everything."

This is how I don't turn into Kathleen Copeland and exactly how I turn into her at the same time. Quite the mind fuck trying to work that out in my brain—one door, two outcomes, and I can only figure it out if I open it.

"Ryan?" The side of his nose nudges mine and glides up and down once. "Give me the chance to prove to you that I can do long distance this time. Please."

I can't say yes, but I can't say no. He is so sure of himself. Just like he always is. That doesn't mean anything, but there is no stopping the fact that we're going to kiss.

"I haven't showered in two days," I say stupidly.

But seriously, ew. My brain is doing the math in double time. I cannot have sex with him when I've been hiking in the woods for forty-eight hours and wiping my armpits and girl parts with wipes. That is not how I am going to let this play out after he hasn't been with me in four years.

"Fuck. I love you." Grey chuckles, eyes locked to mine. "As a non-friend. That I'm not dating."

My vision goes black. "I love you, Grey."

His kiss takes what little breath I have away. Perfect lips moving against mine with mind-numbing pressure. His hands catch my hips as I start to puddle and lift me onto his lap.

He tastes like cinnamon, sweet and spicy like always, with a hint of expensive barrel-aged whiskey.

My fingers finally lace through his hair, and I sigh into his mouth. My body folds into his, every notch fitting where it should, where it always used to.

"One, I love the face you make when you do math in your head," he says, biting my bottom lip.

His hand slips underneath my T-shirt and rests against the side of my rib cage. All four of his fingers trace the deep grooves in between my bones.

"Two, I love the sound you make when I kiss you right here." He lifts my shirt and presses his lips against the edge of my cleavage. His tongue traces the outline of my boob and like all the other times his face was between my breasts, which will always remain one of my favorite feelings, I let out a girly coo that never sounds like me.

He peels my shirt off over my head before his mouth travels up my chest and reaches my collarbone. He skates his teeth across it, and my thighs close tightly around his hips. A spark is bouncing down my torso leaving little burnt black specks in its path.

"Shit," I exhale into his hair. One, two, and we're both already topless. *Shit*, it feels good. And too easy.

He pulls back to roam his eyes over every part of me. I feel like I'm glowing. "I've missed you," he murmurs. "Every inch of you, I've drawn you in my mind a million times from memorization." He traces a finger down the bridge of my nose, over my lips and chin, before he drops it to circle his thumb around my belly button.

A picture of me being Grey's nude model uncontrollably pops into my head. I repress my giggle and bring myself back to this moment.

His large hands curve around the creases of my upper thighs and drag me back and forth across his lap. It takes little effort on his part because my hips are shamelessly begging for it.

Grey sucks his way up my neck, stopping just below my ear where he knows he'll make me wet when he nibbles at my skin. "Three, I love when you try to tell a joke and can't stop yourself from giggling at your own humor."

I smile to myself as I look up at the ceiling of the tent. I'm in a blissful trance, rubbing myself over his erection and having his shirtless body pressed against mine, because I know he's going to give me another three reasons why he loves me, and I'm loving every second of it.

His face tilts and his teeth nip my earlobe. "Four, I love how much you enjoy difficult crap like escape rooms and one-color puzzles that drive me to the edge of insanity."

I laugh breathlessly, but Grey sits up straighter and covers my mouth with his. I've missed these kisses deep in my soul based on the disturbing amount of energy coursing through my nerves. I could light up all of San Diego in the event of a downed power grid.

Grey's fingers find the clasp of my bra and unhook it in a quick motion.

As he slides the straps down my arms, he pulls back slightly, sensing my hesitation, and assures me, "I know no sex." I relax as he plants a line of kisses across my jaw and down my neck. When my bra comes fully off, he drops it next to us. "I'm going to keep my dick in my pants, I promise, but fuck, Ryan, I have to have your nipples in my mouth."

I should probably be embarrassed by how harshly I push his face toward my tits, but I'm not. They're probably sweaty too, but at this point, I'm giving in a little.

He chuckles and wraps his lips around my left nipple. "Five, I love how sexy you are when you get demanding."

The suction he applies makes me whimper in satisfaction before he takes my nipple between his teeth and hums deeply. He flicks with his tongue and switches sides, squeezing palmfuls of my boobs. "Perfect," he says, swirling his tongue over me. His eyes meet mine. "I wish I could feel how wet you are right now. How easily I could slide into you."

"Fuck, Grey." I lay my hands over the backs of his and momentarily think I'm going to lead one of them under my shorts to show him. I overthink and stop myself, licking my lips in a daydream. We're going a little too far already, but I have zero fucks in me to care. "My underwear is soaking wet."

He smiles wickedly. "I could get off just thinking about it."

My legs tremble. He's probably right.

"And six, I love how much you overthink because I don't think enough." He pauses to push his tongue roughly in my mouth, making me gasp. It's taking all of my strength not to pin him down and ride his face. My thoughts are *dirty*—along with my body—which Grey knows, so he wraps his hand around the base of my throat and presses me for them. "And how much harder you come when you say your dirty thoughts out loud."

"Shit," I breathe. "I'm going to wrap my thighs around your head and come on your face tomorrow. After I take a shower. No, while I take a shower. I can't even wait the extra fifteen minutes."

"Fuck," he mumbles gruffly, lying down on his back and taking me with him. He grabs my ass hard before he slips both of us into his sleeping bag. "I want to taste you so badly. Hear you moan my name. I really don't give a shit how sweaty you are right now."

"Good," I whisper and kiss him. My two alter-egos—unhinged ex-girlfriend and porn star—have taken over my body because all I can think about is Grey's face wet with *me* and how possessively good that feels. "You're mine."

"I'm yours," he whispers back and smiles. "Now go to sleep before I sit you on my face myself."

I try to slip off to lie next to him, but he holds me steady against his body. "No, stay here." Both of his arms bear hug me down against his torso. "I want to feel your weight on top of me all night."

I nestle my head into his neck and breathe him in. I don't care that neither one of us has taken a shower in days. I'm going to get the best night of sleep I've had in six years.

Grey is mine. I am his. Pipe dream or not.

We were never anyone else's.

No matter what happens.

<u>20</u>

Friday's Alternate Reality

SAGE HASN'T WIPED her smirk off her face since we woke up—her alone in our tent, me in the same spot on top of Grey that I fell asleep in.

She smirks as we hike back to our van and Grey and I flirt. She smirks while we drive the couple of hours back to the hotel and Grey can't take his hands off of me. She smirks as Grey and I make eyes at each other when we step off the elevator from the parking garage.

"Is this what you look like after you get laid properly?" she asks with raised eyebrows when he's out of ear shot. "You must have had a rough four years."

I watch him turn the corner before I smack her arm. "We didn't have sex."

She exhales. "Thank god. I didn't want to say anything, but you stink."

"That's you," I say defiantly, scrunching my nose. "I cleaned myself with a wipe this morning."

I grin as we meander down the stone path to our house. Sage does have a point. I can't stop grinning.

"What now?" she asks.

"I'm going to grab some clothes. Then I'll see *you* at the rehearsal."

"Where I'll finally get to see your post-coital glow." Sage rolls her eyes sarcastically. "Fantastic. And about time."

When she unlocks the door to our house, I shoot past her and stuff everything I need into my tote bag.

"I'm proud of you," Sage says, when I come back into the living room. She looks up from the magazine she's flipping through. "For never settling. I know I'm not the relationship expert, and that you've been stuck with mostly me and my advice on Evie's wedding week. *But* you're you when you're with him, and I've never seen another man look at you the way Grey looks at you."

My smile hurts my cheeks. "Thanks, Sage."

Her eyes widen, and she waves a hand at the door. "Don't get all emotional. I don't have Evie here to buffer."

"I love you, Sage," I sing, as I open the door.

Deep down she's got a slice of something—that hopeless romantic in all of us.

Just before it latches closed, I catch her affectionate tone. "I love you more, you little love nut."

I sing *I'm A Nut* to myself on the walk to Grey's door. She's right—love makes us all a little nuts. We're all part of the unspoken club.

After a few soft knocks, Grey opens his door in a white hotel towel. I have a fraction of a second to watch beads of water dripping down in the paths between the grooves of his abs, which nearly knocks the wind out of me. Before I can take a breath, he pulls me into a kiss.

"What if I was housekeeping?" I gasp into his mouth.

"I could smell you through the door."

I laugh and try to squirm away, but he picks me up under my butt and bites my neck.

"You smell good," he murmurs, nuzzling his nose into my disgusting, dirt-caked skin as he carries me into the bathroom.

He opens the glass shower door, removes my shoes for me, and places me down barefoot on the white hexagon tile.

I attempt to push him out, but he won't budge. He shakes his head playfully and drops his towel.

My heartbeat drops to my stomach and continues downward. I'm half-tempted to just give in because I want him inside of me so badly.

He smirks. "You can look at my junk all you want. It's yours too."

I force my eyes to his and lose focus momentarily when he pulls my shirt over my head and bends to kiss me. His jaw clenches as his eyes travel the length of my half-clothed body. "Let's get you out of these leggings."

"Out," I insist. "Out! I have to *do* things."

"I wouldn't give a shit if you hadn't shaved in years," Grey laughs. He certainly wouldn't based on how hard he is.

I roll my eyes. "Give me five minutes."

He narrows his. "Four," he says before he backs out of the room and leaves me to finally put myself together for an all-day love affair.

Two and a half minutes later, Grey impatiently opens the bathroom door. "That was enough time," he huffs.

The shower walls have steamed over, so I rub a circle over the glass and smile at him through my new window.

"I see you still take the hottest showers known to man," he says.

He opens the door and reaches to turn the water colder when

someone knocks loudly and frantically at his door.

Grey whips his head back toward the sound, then looks back at me wide-eyed and frozen in place.

"Shit," he mutters, stepping into the shower. "Let's ignore that."

"Did you put a do not disturb sign on the door?"

"No," he admits, "but they already cleaned my room this morning."

He kisses me forcefully and pushes his full body against mine to wedge me against the wall.

The same knock crashes through the room again louder, more frantic, like they need something desperately.

We both stand here, water spraying against Grey's back and misting around us, naked. Our eyes cascade down each other's bodies again. We're so close. Four long years, pining, yearning, wishing for him, and he's right in front of me—seconds away from fucking my brains out.

I can see it all written on Grey's face. Neither one of us actually wants to acknowledge that there is an outside world right now.

But of course, we have to.

This isn't our wedding week. It's not about us, and whoever is behind the door needs something.

"Fuck me," Grey sighs.

"I'm trying," I joke.

He steps out of the shower and dries himself off before he angrily grabs a pair of shorts off the bathroom floor and adjusts his erection (half-successfully) inside of them.

I shut off the water and stand there quietly, freezing.

"Grey!" Elliot says as soon as I hear Grey open the door. It's not often that Elliot sounds distressed.

"What's wrong?" Grey asks.

"I need your help. All the groomsmen and I are about to head to this ridiculous yoga relaxation class that Evie signed us up for. Don't even ask. And my parents are at lunch with Evie's parents. I'm sorry to ask you, but the florist van with all of the flowers and decorations for the rehearsal dinner tonight got fucking stolen. Someone just made off with it as they were finishing loading it. I think they saved like one thing."

"Jesus, I'm sorry," Grey says. "What can we—I do?"

I smile to myself. He thinks of us as a *we*.

"The hotel has a van they'll lend us. Would you mind driving it over there and loading up whatever they have that they can replace it all with? Just use your judgment—and do not tell Evelyn, whatever you do. She doesn't need more stress."

"Sure, man. Anything you need. Sounds like you could use a yoga class right about now."

Elliot laughs. "I'll text you the address." I hear a clap on the back. "Thanks."

Grey stalks back into the bathroom.

"Yaaaayyy," I say half-heartedly, waving my arms.

He pulls a towel off the rack and holds his face away from me when I open the shower door. "I can't even look at you or I'll get turned on again."

I motion for him to give it to me. "I'm shivering."

Grey gives in and slowly lets his eyes fall on me. His heavy gaze sweeps over every inch of my now clean and freshly shaven skin. Hardened, angry lines crease in his forehead.

He curses under his breath and tosses me the towel. "That fucking thief stole more than just flowers."

×××

I HOLD UP my arms to show off a large pink and green bouquet like I'm a *The Price is Right* model. "What about this one?"

"They all look the same," Grey whines.

"They do not. This one is objectively pinker and greener and bigger."

He rolls his eyes. We've been in this enormous cooler, freezing our asses off, for an hour.

We picked out some short, smaller arrangements for each dining table, and two larger ones for the terrace. I've come close to what Evie had picked before—well, close enough for having to pick from premade flower bouquets the same day. Now, we need the entrance table, the show stopper.

"Does it go with the other ones we've picked out?"

"Mmhmm," he says absentmindedly, tucking my hair behind my ear. "Your hair is objectively longer and redder and sexier." Grey brushes his lips against my temple. "It's cold in here, isn't it?"

My breath hitches. "Subjectively, yes. Focus."

"Let me warm you up," he says, letting his fingers crawl across my waist and then kissing me like we're not in a florist shop. "Remember the cooler at Nacho Mama's?"

"No, remind me."

Grey's eyes blacken as he pushes me up against the table. His knee forces my legs wider before he steps up against me.

"Not ringing any bells," I tease through my unexplainable panting.

"How hard do I have to remind you?"

"Hard," I repeat as he winds his fingers into my hair and tugs at my roots.

He kisses me forcefully, pushing his tongue into my mouth to taste me. "You taste better than I remember," he groans when he pulls back. He runs his palm between my legs. "How much better I know you taste here."

Two of his fingers play with the button of my shorts. Then his eyes flicker over my shoulder. "Shit. Why are there cameras in here?"

Bummer. I take a deep breath to try to return to baseline.

"In case someone steals something. Obviously."

A skeptical smile draws his lips out and he scoffs. "So soon-to-be newlyweds don't have sex. Show me a bouquet I can fit underneath my shirt. They'd be better served in their delivery vans."

"We should crash every rehearsal dinner and wedding in the city and find Evelyn's flowers," I joke.

"I assume they've driven to Denver and sold them on the black market already."

I hop off the table and turn to weave through some pink tulips. "Is there a black flower market?"

"There's a black market for everything," Grey answers.

I stop in front of the only flowers in here not suitable for a wedding.

"What about this one?" I ask over my shoulder.

His eyes don't leave my ass. "Beautiful."

"Yes, Grey, these black velvet petunias are perfect for the rehearsal dinner," I tease. "They remind me of death. Focus."

He shrugs. "I'll focus when it's our wedding."

A cough gets stuck in my throat.

"No, I'm lying," he says. My throat muscles relax, thinking I must have misread his serious tone, but no. "I'll be too busy looking at you then too."

"Non-boyfriend to husband in less than a day? That's ambitious," I say. She pops into my head. I'm not sorry. "You had a girlfriend who outlasted me. Three years is a long time. You never thought about proposing?"

"Never. Not once," he says. His tone is matter-of-fact, and Grey doesn't miss a beat. "I knew in my heart the entire time that you are the love of my life and the only person I want to call my wife. I know you don't believe me right now, and that's my own damn fault, but I'd marry you today if you'd say yes. I get that you don't trust me enough yet, but I'm going to earn every ounce of it back because I'll never let you go again. I promise you, as long as you'll have me, I am going to marry you one day, Ryan Walker, and your last name is going to be Beckett."

I refuse to blink and miss a nanosecond of this parallel universe. Everything about the moment I want to sear into my brain. Because even if Grey can't fulfill his promise, I know he truly feels this way. The sincerity in his voice is like a blanket, covering me.

I think he felt the same way four years ago too. He thought he could do it, and I don't blame him. It's enough for right now. Just having him with me is enough.

I wonder if there is another Ryan standing in this same spot with Sage instead, because Grey never came to this wedding. Or I'm standing with Evie. Or Mitchell. Or a completely random guy that I hooked up.

Maybe there's already a Ryan Beckett out there.

This is the version I want to be though. The universe I want to be living in. This Ryan has it the best—she has Hawaii, she has two best friends, and she has Grey—and she's just herself, not settling.

I smile back at him innocently. "I love you, but when you do propose, make sure it's not in a florist shop called Kiss These Tulips."

He laughs. "Weirdly sexual, right?"

"I know I'm thinking about different lips."

"I bet you are." Grey takes two large steps into me. His hand wraps around my cheek. I think he's going to kiss me, but at the last second, he diverts his path, smirking and leaving me looking like an idiot, and hovers his lips over my ear. "I'm serious, Ryan."

My entire body fizzles. "I know," I whisper.

"Good," he says back, husky and deep. Grey looms over me, twirling my hair through his fingers, as I place my forehead on his chest and listen to his heartbeat. He kisses the top of my head and lifts me onto the freezing plastic table. "Play a game with me."

I narrow my eyes at him playfully. "What're the rules?"

"You have to say the first thing that pops into your head," he replies, nestling between my legs.

"I can't focus with you standing so close," I argue.

"Hm," he murmurs noncommittally in my ear and makes no attempt to move. "Where are we going to get married?"

Immediately, I say, "On a beach in Hawaii."

He rewards me with a kiss on my neck. "That's going to be my once in a lifetime trip."

"Who's going to be there?" I ask.

"Family and best friends. Ten max." He pinches my thigh. "What will our wedding flower be?"

"Calla lilies." It's the only thing in this room my eyes keep roaming back to and wishing I could take home because the vase is taller than me and stuffed with them.

"I like those." Grey smiles against my skin. "Am I going to wear a tux?"

"Of course. You look sexy in one. Are you going to agree to do a first look?"

"Where I see you before? Absolutely not. Are you going to let me come visit you in a couple months?"

"Yes," I say. "Are you going to let me come visit you?"

"You can come home with me on Sunday if you want."

"I wish I had a day of vacation time left or I would."

"Hmm," Grey hums disappointedly into my temple before he pulls back and smirks. "Are you going to pick out the last flower thingy so we can get this over with? I have better things to do."

I laugh breathlessly as his fingers find one of the notches in my lower back and he continues to press his tongue against my throat.

"This week isn't supposed to be about us," I say.

Us echoes in my head.

He chuckles. "Then I'm selfish. I own it." His hands suddenly feel greedy, urgency shooting out from the end of his fingertips.

This. I've missed this feeling—charging Grey like I'm his electrical outlet.

I'm reaching a new level of deprivation. We both are. Starved, wild, sexually frustrated depravity.

A small, nervous sound of a throat clearing jerks Grey's head back.

The thirtysomething florist stands in the sliding doorway of the cooler, trying to look professional with her shoulders pulled back. She's tinier than me in a black dress which matches her black, silky bob.

"I'm sorry to… interrupt." Her eyes dart to everything but us. She must think we're the engaged couple instead of two people who've been deprived of each other for four years. "Have you decided on the last floral arrangement?"

Grey smiles at her. I don't miss the fact that she now can't tear her eyes away from him. I wonder if that's what my eyes look like when I can't stop staring—cartoonish spirals like I'm hypnotized. Her black eyebrows crease slightly. Maybe she's doing the math in her head and wondering if she's too old to date him.

"We'll take the pinker and greener and bigger one over there," he says, cocking his head toward the enormous glass vase on the table behind him.

"Of course," she replies. "I'll get someone to load it up for you."

Grey bites my earlobe when she turns around. "They better do it quickly and leave enough room back there."

21

Rapture

IT'S ONLY FITTING that we pick up exactly where we left off. Besides, this is me and Grey; neither one of us can keep it in our pants very long when we're alone together.

Four years ago in the front seat of his black SUV, Grey leaned over and kissed me before I told him there was enough room in the back seat and enough time before my flight.

Fast forward to right now, and he is looking at the back, filled with flowers up to the top, then looking at his watch.

He can't wait another second.

Neither can I.

"There's enough room and enough time," I say.

Déjà vu.

"Are you sure?" he asks, catching me off guard. "I forgot I don't have a condom."

I don't think twice when I say, "I'm still on birth control," but it hits me that he might not be comfortable with that; with *me*. We're not together like we used to be. He's the only person I've ever had unprotected sex with, but he doesn't know that he still is. "I've never… you're the only one. It's okay."

My mind wanders to the fact that I didn't even think about him doing that with someone else.

"Ryan," he says, tipping my chin to force me to look at him. "I trust you. I just didn't want to push you. I wasn't sure if *you* would be okay with it." He pauses and gives me an intense look. "And you're still the only one too."

I smile and try to push the other girl from my mind, though I silently give her a quick thank you for not being on birth control apparently. "Then I'm sure."

I crawl over the center console. Grey starts to laugh but cuts it short to slip his hand up my jean shorts and kiss the bottom of my butt poking out.

There is a space the florist left in the middle like an aisle, just big enough for both of us to lie down and only be a tiny bit squished. She probably read the room and sensed we were about to rip each other's clothes off.

As I lie down on my back, Grey slowly and methodically maneuvers himself between the front seats and down to the floor of the trunk.

I can draw a lot of parallels between then and now, but there are also a lot of differences.

Grey seems to float over me. "Hi," he whispers.

This isn't his usual M.O.

In the past, he'd have me naked, shaking, and clenching my thighs around his head before I could manage to catch my breath, and as soon as I did, he'd be fucking me against anything solid he could leverage.

Now he seems content, luxuriating in me, and determined to drag out every second of time that ticks between us.

I grip him around his biceps and run my thumbs up the hardened lines of his muscles.

He watches me, letting out a shallow breath. "Is it weird I don't want this moment to start, because if it starts, that means it has to end?"

Nothing has ever sounded less weird.

I shake my head. "Fuck me slowly."

Grey's eyes flare brightly before he dips his head and his lips are on mine. Everything could be summed up with this one kiss. It's love and heartache wrapped in one.

His tongue tastes mine as I wrap my arms around his back, pressing him against me.

Grey trails his mouth down my neck. He sits me up and lifts my shirt over my head. I unhook my bra and let him slip the straps down my arms before he lays me back down and kisses his way up my stomach and over my chest. Every place he sucks, my skin tingles, melting like cotton candy on his tongue.

"I've missed having you underneath me," he says against my sternum, letting his body weight drop heavier on me.

No one else feels like this. I've been seeking each and every part of Grey, hoping I'll find anything that compares to this. But nothing ever will. Nothing will ever come close.

I lace my fingers through his hair and guide him to every spot he can sink his teeth into. He starts at my collarbone, nibbling his way across, then goes to the side of my rib cage, and ends at my hip bone. His movements feel soft but possessive, like he's staking claim to every square inch of me. He doesn't know it but I've been his all along.

Grey switches to my breasts, taking one of my nipples between his teeth. I suck in sharply when his lips curl up around it in a smile and his eyes plaster themselves to mine.

He unfastens the little gold button of my shorts, and the sound of the short zipper breaks the silence.

"Why are you so quiet?" he asks.

I'd been so intensely inside my own head, taking in every possible feeling and movement, I hadn't even noticed.

"I'm focusing."

Grey smirks. "Focus less." He grips the waist of my jeans, shimmying them off back and forth along with my underwear down my legs, which he then pushes wide open.

"I don't want to miss something," I whisper, but Grey can't take his eyes off from between my legs like I'm a piece of artwork.

He pauses, lost in thought. "You're never quiet," he says eventually.

Which *was* true, but not anymore. I used to need a pillow to muffle the embarrassing sounds I'd make so one of our roommates didn't hear me. But four years of lackluster orgasms changed me. The blood is rushing down, pulsing, at the thought of what Grey used to do to me and how I am going to finally get it back.

Smugness creeps across his lips. His eyes meet mine as it clicks. "No one can make you come like I do, can they?"

"I don't want to think about that right now," I say airily.

"I do," Grey chuckles. "I want to think about how I am the only man that fucks you into a moaning mess." He kisses the inside of my left knee, and I'm already trembling from the anticipation. "I want to think about how much you've been dying for this for years." He bites halfway up my inner thigh. "I want to think about how your orgasms are mine." He gives me one last soft kiss so close to me, I vibrate in response.

"So perfect," he whispers. "And it's all mine."

When his tongue finally licks up me fully—feeling how wet I am, tasting me—he gets straight to the point.

He remembers what I like like he did it this morning, not four years ago. The thought that he's been dreaming about me while he's been with *her*, sends me into overdrive.

Short bursts shoot up to my belly button with each swirl of Grey's tongue until my hips are rocking uncontrollably.

My alter ego is a bitch, but she likes to come like this—unfocused, black-out euphoria.

I'm about to pull Grey's hair out by the roots, when he suddenly stops completely.

"Fuck," I breathe out harshly. "Grey."

"There you are," he replies and licks his lips.

I didn't even realize how loud of a moaning heap I was being until my head isn't buzzing anymore.

I prop myself up on my elbows to glare at him for depriving me of finishing.

He laughs. Grey has turned on his cocky side. I didn't get it often, but he would let it out occasionally. He worked hard to learn every little thing I liked. He's good, he earned it, and it's not the worst thing in the world for him to know it, so I'll allow it.

"You thought I was going to give it to you that easy?" Grey slides two of his fingers into me slowly, showing me he remembers exactly where my G-spot is, before pulling them out and sucking them into his mouth. If he's not careful, he's going to give me a braingasm, because that affects me more than it should. He raises his eyebrows. "Come on, Ryan. Play with me. It can feel better than that."

This non-asshole likes having his face between my legs just as much as he likes being inside me.

"You're such an asshole," I tease him.

"An asshole who makes you feel good—the best," he counters, smirking, as I push his head down. He resists. "So pushy."

"I want to play," I exhale.

He rewards me with his tongue. "Good girl."

Grey picks up where he left off, slower this time. He adds his middle finger and circles the pad of it against the front wall of me.

I don't know how much more of this I can actually take. It's one thing when I regularly had sex with him, but now… it's like a four-year edge. Torture in the best fathomable way. He builds it perfectly and I'm so fucking close, I almost don't want to tug on his hair.

But I do anyway, because Grey has his other hand fanned out across my inner thigh, and the moment he felt my muscles quiver, he'd pull back anyway.

"Shit." My breathing is stilted, my heart is galloping.

Grey brushes his tongue everywhere, except where I desperately want it, as I come back down from the wave of pleasure he controlled.

"Ready?" he asks when my chest stops heaving.

I nod and prop my weight up again. Grey goes half-speed this time until I'm on the brink of losing my mind. His eye contact combined with the white-hot, raging fire he's stoking is blinding me. My blood pressure has dropped so drastically, I'm seeing stars across my vision. I'm ignoring the fact that I sound like a deranged troll.

Just as it's about to crash down around me, I yank his hair, and Grey loses contact with me completely.

"Fuck," he smiles. "You are the sexiest thing I've ever seen and heard."

I groan. It sounds absolutely mental, but it's all I can manage to say in reply. I was so. Fucking. Close. Seconds from the point of no return.

I'm completely naked, Grey is completely clothed, and we're edging in the back of a windowless van surrounded by my best friend's wedding flowers—and it's the hottest fucking thing I've ever done.

I'll chalk that up to the four years of having missionary-positioned sex.

Life is weird.

"I don't know how many more I can take," I say, breathing heavily.

Grey rubs over me with his palm, challenging me with my eyes. "But this is my favorite game."

I whimper at the warmth that cascades over me, but he just smiles, pleased with himself that he's about to make me come with the mere breeze of his words.

"Did someone stupidly tell you as a child that you'd get whatever you want with that smile?" I ask him like that's a totally normal question to ask in this moment.

He smiles bigger and climbs up my body to kiss me. Then he presses both of his huge hands against the backs of my thighs, and pulls my legs open so far, my groin stretches just to the point of pain. "Hold your legs," he instructs me. I obey (because, of course, he's smiling), and nod when he says, "One more time."

I sound embarrassingly feral when he licks me. He uses two fingers this time. I should have rethought the fact that there is no pillow here to scream into. But I also don't care quite enough because I know how fucking good, how much better, it's going to be when he lets me feel the release.

Grey is the only person who can do this to me. He watches my face, taking in every cue, as he guides me to the edge.

That edge that I have a toe over, that I'm about to fling myself off of—if he wasn't in charge.

He pulls back and kisses the inside of both of my thighs as soon as they twitch. "So fucking wet," he mutters happily.

From the look of his face, I would have to agree.

I haven't been this wet in... ever.

"Jesus Christ," I pant, throwing my head back and releasing my legs. Everything below my belly button feels like a blow torch that is now slowly dying.

I arch my hips up to his face, and he lets me rub myself against his smirk. He won't give me his tongue or his fingers until I say something.

"Fuck, Grey," I plead. "Please."

He lets me ride his tongue for a second. "No one else fucks you like I do."

"No one," I repeat.

"I own these orgasms, Ryan. You're mine. No matter how many miles are in between us. No one can make you feel as good as I do. No one knows you like I do, and no one loves you like I do."

"I know," I whisper, weaving both of my hands into his hair. "No one is you."

Finally, he gives in. Perfectly.

The roller coaster hits its ascent as soon as he touches me. And it's the world's fastest and most violent roller coaster ever built.

The drop is like nothing I've ever experienced. My heart is beating out of my ears. I'm moaning his name like I'm deranged—well, I am, but that's beside the point. I'm convulsing from my head to my toes. I will probably pull out some of Grey's hair.

This is rapture.

And he just straps me in and doesn't let me budge as he holds me down with his strength and makes sure I come (pun intended) to a complete and full stop.

Grey slides up my exhausted body and lies next to me as much as he can, which is technically on top of me.

I have vertigo, but Grey's hard-on is digging into me, keeping me grounded.

Everything is still, but my brain keeps spinning.

Grey chuckles into my ear. "Round two?"

"Shit," I say breathlessly. "I need a minute, but I want you inside me so fucking badly."

Grey sits up and slips his T-shirt off by the back of the neck before he rolls on top of me. I push his athletic shorts and boxers down his hips. I use my feet to get them off the rest of the way.

He holds his weight up by his arms and lowers his head to kiss me. Tasting myself on his tongue makes me jolt back to the starting line.

I reach down between my legs, and we just hang out for a second. The tip of him resting against me. Anticipation is sky high and we're just staring into each other's eyes, daring the other person to start because neither one of us wants to be blamed for it ending.

Then I guide Grey into me—I'll take the blame. His forehead falls on mine as he slides into me so slowly, he's creating a new definition of the word. He sucks in a sharp breath, and our eyes have turned on a closed-circuit electrical current.

He makes missionary position out to be some goddamn other worldly experience compared to any other man.

His words come back into my head. He's an asshole to every other woman. Maybe when he had sex with Kennedy, it was so-so. It was lame vanilla missionary position for her because he wasn't meant for her; he wasn't her soulmate.

Maybe Chase, Brendan, Ian, Preston, Austin, and Joey are out there right now blowing some girl's mind with things I found lackluster. I only feel that way because I am meant for someone else.

This is how it should feel when you're with the one.

And I shouldn't be thinking about all of this right now, but I am, because it's sort of simple.

Like $1 + 1 = 2$.

"Why are you doing math right now?"

I lift my eyes to Grey's just as he fills me completely, and I suck in a breath. "Because I love you."

Grey smiles and kisses me. "I love you," he says softly into my mouth. Then he bites my bottom lip and lowers his voice gruffly.

"But if you can do math right now, I'm not fucking you hard enough."

He pulls back until it's just the tip of him stretching me and slams back into me.

Everything inside me ignites, stealing all of the oxygen from my lungs. I gasp for air and dig my nails into his shoulder blades as he does it again.

Finally, I find my voice enough to let out a strangled sound that resembles his name while I bite down on his collarbone.

"God, I've really, *really* missed your cock."

Grey exits me completely, and I whimper in response. "So desperate," he smirks, playing with himself against me. He slips back inside me, repeating his leisurely, delectable, slow-paced punishment multiple times. "And to think I've spent the last four years thinking you didn't want me anymore."

My hands drop to his ass, feeling the rhythm of his hips as they roll. I smile at how good the motion feels and claw into him. I can't take the drawn-out pace any longer, and I'm desperate for him to fill me completely and hit me where I'm going to come the hardest.

But Grey shakes his head and slips his thumb into my mouth. I circle my tongue around it, then slide it up and down. "This fucking perfect mouth." He presses himself all the way into me so quickly, I gasp in surprise. Then he just holds himself there as far as he can. "Moan for me. I want to hear how desperate you are."

I moan around Grey's thumb before he switches to two fingers inside my mouth and holds my jaw. Sliding slowly out of me, I groan in frustration until he drives himself back into me so deep that my legs start to shake.

Then his speed comes back with a vengeance.

I moan into his chest. Into his neck. Into his jaw.

He grunts and huffs my name into my hair. Into my ear. Into my mouth.

We're sweaty and slick. Nothing we're mumbling is coherent anymore. Our tongues are just a dirty mess, tangling themselves together.

Grey pinches my nipples and hitches my legs tighter around his waist. His mouth drops to my chest to claim everything he can with his tongue and his teeth.

My hands roam his back, my fingers sink into his ass. My eyes are rolling into the back of my head as I start to climb again.

We're turning sloppy in a coma of pleasure.

I have no idea what a math equation is anymore.

But I can tell that Grey is close.

"Fuck." He sounds delirious. "This is so fucking good… you're so fucking good… feel so fucking good." He's a regular wordsmith when he can't think straight. One of his hands reaches up and wraps around my throat. The other reaches down and rubs over me quickly. His weight bears down on me, pinning me in place. "Come for me again, Ryan."

There's nothing for me to grab on to except Grey's skin. I've probably drawn blood by now, but it's nothing compared to how hard I'm clenching around his dick.

I'm coming, going, up, down, and sideways, into oblivion.

Grey's entire body shudders. He whispers into my hair how much he loves me until he collapses down on top of me.

We both lie in silence after, waiting until the absolute last second possible. We still have to set up the flowers and get ready for the rehearsal, but our minds aren't back to any type of capacity where we should be driving.

Grey sits up first and finds me a towel to clean up with. When I'm done, we both climb back into the front seat clothed. It rumbles to life when he puts the key in the ignition and pulls out into traffic, but neither one of us can focus.

"Eyes on the road," I tell him after the fourth time I've caught him staring at me lovingly. But I get it because my entire body is still trembling from exhaustion and endorphins. I'm still so incredibly turned on that I'm uncomfortable sitting in my seat.

Maybe three minutes goes by in complete silence before I just can't take it anymore. I know it's his favorite and Grey brings out a little something extra in me.

I lean down across the console and rub one hand over his crotch.

He breathes out harshly, and he's already hard. "Shit, I don't deserve you."

I smile up at him sweetly as I pull back his athletic shorts and take him in my hand.

Road head might be Grey's favorite but sometimes it's my favorite too. The thrill of all the people driving next to us who have no clue what's going on. And now we're higher than most cars in this van so whatever. And I've been thinking about having his dick in my mouth for six days because my mind is *much* dirtier than I let on.

My thumb runs over the tip as I admire him. I mean dicks aren't that pretty, but Grey could at least compete in a contest for Mr. Least Ugly Dick. I trace the same path with my tongue.

Grey shifts in his seat and takes the wheel with one hand. His right hand gathers my hair and twists it around his palm. His voice comes out commanding, low and gruff. "You like tasting yourself on my dick, don't you?"

He's not really asking me because he knows, but I nod anyway—because yes, I'm a possessive and submissive woman who likes it and missed it *a lot*. I let the saliva drop from my mouth before I wrap my lips around him and glide up and down.

"That's it," Grey says, his hips coming off of the seat an inch like he just can't wait. He guides my head by my hair to set the speed while he turns on his blinker and switches lanes. "Fuck," he whispers when he hits the back of my throat. "Stick out that tongue. Take it all." I obey, opening my throat and taking him deeper. All the way. Grey presses down on the back of my head until I gag around him and his legs twitch. "Such a good fucking girl," he praises me.

Inside my stomach, a brush paints smug pride from top to bottom and across from side to side. Sometimes Grey just wants an incredibly sloppy and enthusiastic blow job, and I am here to please.

It's not for everyone, but there's something about turning a nice guy completely animalistic that makes me feel sexy as hell.

Grey is whispering under his breath, lost in his thoughts. "You're so good at sucking my dick. God. You've missed that cock in your mouth. Fuck, just like that."

I hum back in appreciation. It's hard to say anything with my mouth so full, so I let him continue praising my blow job skills.

He runs his free hand down my back and under my shorts to squeeze my ass. "I've missed this view," he moans as I work my tongue over him. The one thing I hate about road head is zero eye contact.

The van slows and stops at what I assume is a red light.

I pull his shorts down further, switching to stroking him with my hand and focusing on his balls with my tongue. He moans like I've sent him to heaven. "I'm going to have to pull over and strip you naked again. Fit both of them in your mouth."

I open wide and suck both of them in. My tongue works its way back just behind them, and Grey loses it.

"Fuck, you're so naughty, Ryan," he groans happily, weaving his hand back through my hair and running his fingers over the nape of my neck when I lick back up his shaft. "I'm close."

I let him guide me to the speed he wants until he's moaning and shuddering and I'm swallowing everything he's giving me.

I'm only a good fucking girl for Grey.

Don't judge me.

<u>22</u>

Friday Evening

'LL TAKE COMFORT in knowing I can always fall back on floral design if I lose the ability to figure out a math equation.

The room looks surprisingly beautiful for a few hours' notice. White, light pink, light green roses and peonies grace all of the tables. Our centerpiece is beautifully displayed on the round table in the middle of the restaurant.

My whole business model will be hiring someone to steal brides' wedding flowers, and then I swoop in to save the day, making double the money when I sell their stolen flowers on the black market.

Win-win.

"The flowers look great," Elliot gushes, clapping Grey on the shoulder.

"That has nothing to do with me," Grey jokes. "They'd be black if it had been my decision."

Elliot laughs and picks me up off my feet into a hug. "Thank you, Ryan."

"Anything for you and Evie." I nuzzle my cheek against his. "I love you. You know that."

"And now you also owe me forever," he chuckles softly into my ear, "because I technically set you back up with the love of your life."

"It's not like that," I say awkwardly.

Out of the corner of my eye, I see Grey quietly assess me.

"Sure, sure," Elliot replies, putting me back down. "You'll have a closet and a nightstand in his new fancy big-boy house pretty soon."

I slide my eyes curiously to Grey while Elliot turns toward the room full of people. My body feels heavy under the weight of Grey's eye contact.

"Fourteen of us to thirty-four of us," Elliot says, oblivious to whatever just slipped from his mouth. "Plus all of our parents' friends. I'm going to be happy when this is over so I can stop talking."

Everyone is tightly packed around the food and bar like typical humans—stuffing their face and soaking up the alcohol. By the looks of it, Sage should have a better pool of candidates than Mitchell and the bizarro H twins.

"Have fun," I tease.

Elliot waves to an old man by the hors d'oeuvres. "Uncle Bill!" he calls before he walks off.

Grey pivots into me, his body flush with mine. He wraps an arm around my shoulders and angles his face down into my temple.

"What do you want to drink? Blueberry lemon drop? Dirty Shirley?"

He doesn't sound mad. Am I allowed to be mad?

Grey has left something out—a part of the equation—and it feels like it might be kind of a teeny big deal.

"You mean a Dirty *Evie*. I'd love one," I say into his scratchy gray suit. "Are you buying a house?"

"I haven't closed on it yet. Nothing's signed," he replies non-committally.

Grey curves his hand around my jawbone and kisses me intently, gazes at me intently. He's saying nothing and everything at the same time. Then he walks away before I can discern it.

I watch his ass for a little too long—I can't help it since my hands were just on it *again* in his room as we were putting our clothes on twenty minutes ago—before I scan the room for Sage.

After I find her sitting at a table and mulling over an Elliotini, I plop down in the gold velvet seat beside her.

She takes a short sip of her yellow concoction. "I've counted six hot guys I don't recognize. Four of which I haven't seen with a woman."

"Good odds," I say.

She smiles softly as her eyes track a familiar looking handsome blond in a navy suit. "I've got my eye on him."

Mystery Man does a double take at Sage, who takes another sip behind her smirk, before he turns on the blue-eyed smolder.

"Even better odds," I quip.

"Where's Evie when you need her?" Sage asks.

I spot her and Nell chatting with Elliot and Uncle Bill. Nell throws her head back in the most elegant way to laugh at something Uncle Bill is saying with dramatic hand gestures.

"Uncle Bill must be a riot," I comment, cocking my head toward them.

Evie crosses her eyes when she sees us. I watch her force some lie of an excuse out, and she breaks away from the laughter.

"Uncle Bill is single," Evie deadpans as she sits. "And funny."

I give his too-tight suit a once over. "So cheugy."

Sage blinks at me. "I swear you are the reason these words make it into the dictionary."

I turn my nose up at her. "Don't be cheugy."

"I don't even want to know what that means," she replies.

"Gotta keep up with the kids," I laugh and snap my fingers back and forth. "Because, you know, I'm not *old.*"

Evie scoffs sarcastically. "Coincidentally, when you look up the word cheugy in a future version of the dictionary, you'll see Ryan's picture."

Evie and I dissolve into a fit of giggles at her sick burn, because, fuck, she's so right. I only know what this is because my "much" younger intern called me it affectionately when I wore skinny jeans to happy hour.

Awesome.

Little does she know, the next generation will come up with a name for her when she's old, out of touch, and trying too hard. So, whatever, I'm not giving up my skinny jeans, and she'll realize one day her youth is fleeting.

Sage continues to drink her martini as she waits for us to stop being idiots.

"Finished?" Sage asks, bored.

"Okay, okay," I laugh, "no more cheuging. Please, let's talk about Sexy Smolder."

Sage rolls her eyes at me and focuses back on Evie. "I need a brief rundown…" She scans the room. "Of *him.*"

Him is standing at the bar with two other guys. He's broad shouldered and tan, and he runs a hand through his blond curls as he steals a glance at Sage again.

Evie smiles. "J.P.? He's sweet. Sage, you would like him. He's pretty witty."

Grey appears from behind J.P. and crosses the room toward us, holding his whiskey and my Dirty Evie.

He places my drink down on the table in front of me and steps behind my chair. Evie and Sage stare at him as he brushes my hair to the side and bends to kiss my neck like he doesn't give a fuck who is gawking at us.

When he breaks away, he changes his mind and hums just loud enough for me to hear, coming back to kiss my skin open mouthed with tongue.

"I'll be outside," he whispers against the cartilage of my ear. "I need to call Lily."

The sound of her name clenches my heart into a hardened spasm. I stuff down the guilt and nod. My fingers brush over his as he pulls back. I focus on what Sage and Evie are talking about and try to ignore my stomach caving.

"…not many serious girlfriends, I don't think," Evie says.

"Hm," Sage says intrigued. She sits back and waits for J.P. to look at her again.

"Evie," I comment with the little black straw between my teeth, "you're so good and *dirty.*"

"I'm going to punish Elliot for naming it that."

I laugh. "Don't be too hard on him. He helped save the day today…"

I swear J.P. just gave me a small wave. I glance at Sage, who glances back at me. Both of us couldn't be mistaken.

"He's not on your list, is he?" Sage asks.

"No," I laugh, racking my brain for why he looks so familiar. "Have we met him?"

"Maybe. He surfs." Evie furrows her eyebrows for a quick second then pops her eyes open. "Oh. He's friends with—"

It hits me at the same time.

"Shit," I hiss. "*Shit.* How could I forget Joey was going to be here?"

I look around as unfrantically as I can, but I don't see him. "Is he here yet?" I ask Evie.

"I haven't seen him, but he RSVP'd for tonight," she replies.

Her sympathetic face draws inward as she helps me search for him.

I groan. "I need a drink."

"There's one in front of you," Evie says dryly.

Right. Of course. I pick it up and finish it in three big slurps.

"Who cares about Joey?" Sage offers before she drops her voice. "You've been busy."

I don't care about Joey. Far from it.

Grey is everything I want. The man who convinced me no other men out there exist for me, and we love each other deeply. We want to be together.

Why do I feel like I'm on the verge of tears?

"I'm going to get another drink." I push my chair back and make a beeline for the bar. I will not let Evie see me about to cry, and I'm not about to make this even more about me.

Boo hoo. Grey lives in Texas and I live in San Diego. I have an amazing job and amazing friends. Grey has an amazing family, and apparently he's about to buy a freaking house. Nothing is different than it was four years ago, but the world has bigger problems than my sob fest of relationship drama.

So, I'm going to hold it all in.

I take deep breaths as I wait for my drink.

A hand slides down my back and settles against my hip.

I inhale and smile. "Hey," I start, turning my head up. "Say the first thing that—"

But instead of Grey, it's Joey in my face.

His blond hair and tan features tower over me. His sharp jaw and nose, which look surprisingly a lot like J.P.'s, are so close to me, it makes me feel uncomfortable.

"Hey," he smiles back.

"Hi," I stammer, grabbing his hand and shoving it back into his side. "Sorry. I thought you were someone else."

"Funny," he laughs like what I said is very unfunny. "Why haven't you texted me back?"

"I forgot," I say. "I'm sorry. I've been busy."

Understatement of the year.

It's buried in my text messages beneath Grey and Evie and Sage and Elliot and my Hawaii group text and my parents—I can't wait to see you—and I forgot.

Joey leans down toward my ear. "Let's go talk somewhere quieter."

I thank the bartender and pick up my drink. "I don't think that's a good idea."

I need fresh air. Joey smells like the beach. I take a step back—away from the ocean and sun filling my nostrils.

Homesickness is hitting around my heart like hammer denting metal.

He reaches out to take my hand, but Grey's arm finds me first. Joey's eyes follow it as Grey slides it around my shoulders and down my arm. He rests the palm of his hand exactly where Joey's hand had been a minute ago.

Joey locks his eyes to mine as Grey kisses the top of my head.

"Hey, I'm Grey," Grey says, putting his glass on the bar and extending his hand toward Joey.

Grey's smile is genuine, no threat, no anxiety. He's completely unaware that he's talking to my ex-boyfriend as of three weeks ago.

Joey reels back his surprise and shakes Grey's outstretched hand. "Joey."

We're all stuck in a silent triangle for half a second, just long enough for it to be recognized, before Elliot's mother announces that it's time to take our seats.

Fuck my life.

And thank god for Mrs. Sharpe.

I'm getting saved by so many people who may be ex-beauty queens this week—well, two, but that seems like a lot.

×××

RATIONAL PEOPLE HIDE in hidden sofa nooks like this one. The blue floral Victorian settee (I only use this word because it looks like the hotel won it when they auctioned off the set of *Pride and Prejudice*) has no cushion left under the curve of my butt, and there's a matching pillow that's unraveling because everyone who hides here strokes the threads nervously.

I wonder how many people have chosen avoidance in this cranny. It's down the hallway, way past the bathrooms, and you'd only ever see it if you turned around at the dead end. I also wonder how many people have made out here—or worse.

I try to keep my bare skin from touching the fabric when Grey breezes right past me with his phone to his ear.

I shrink back into the shadow of the corner and hold my breath. He'll see me if he turns around, and I'm supposed to be using the bathroom, not hiding from him and Joey.

Both of them keep trying to hold my eye contact, and I can't help but drop mine to the floor. I need space. No, I need miles, but there's nowhere to go.

Grey huffs into the phone, "I love you," and thankfully as he hangs up, he spins in the opposite direction to walk out the way he came.

His left foot is the last thing I can see, and just when I think I'm in the clear, it stops and backpedals.

One step, two steps, and he's staring straight at me like his sixth sense is to know I'm there.

I try my best to hitch only one eyebrow for dramatic effect. "Your realtor?"

"No, my dad," he sighs. "Why are you hiding back here?"

"You're buying a house," I say.

He blinks. "So?"

"You're buying a *house*," I repeat. "That's… roots. Deep roots. Like digging into the ground, then digging some more, and clamping down into the soil with claw hands."

"People sell houses every day, Ryan," he says, sitting beside me.

"Why didn't you tell me?" I accuse him.

Grey puts his elbows on his knees and clasps his hands in front of him. "Because it has nothing to do with us. It doesn't change anything." He hangs his head. "And I knew you were going to freak out."

"I'm not freaking out."

I'm freaking out.

Grey is burrowing further into Austin, and he didn't tell me. He looks up at me skeptically.

"That feels like a little bit of a big deal," I add. "You know, when I live halfway across the country. It seems like something you should have *mentioned*."

Grey looks away so quickly, I instantly know there's more to his omission. I only have our familiarity to thank for that.

"What else aren't you telling me?" My voice comes out an octave too high, and I sound like I'm biting back tears no matter how hard I'm trying to hide it.

"It doesn't change anything," Grey insists again, wrapping a hand around my thigh.

I shove him off. "I don't know what *it* is."

Grey bites his lip and sighs, fidgeting with his cuticles. I'll sit here all night until he answers me.

"I've been interviewing for a job," he finally says in a hushed tone.

"A job?" I ask, confused. "You've always worked for yourself. You mean like a real job?"

And then the magnitude of what that means hits me. It must be a job he desperately wants. A job that's important and pays a lot of money and has some sort of reputation. Because those are the only types of jobs he would ever entertain, let alone interview for. That's the only thing that makes sense if he's willing to give up the freedom he has as his own boss.

I rack my brain for the numerous huge companies that are headquartered in Austin, but there's too many to even pick one.

I widen my eyes. "What company?"

"Ryan, you mean more to me than any job." He grabs my hand and refuses to let go. "This is more important."

"Tell me the position and the company, Grey," I stress.

He knows as soon as he says it, there's a real possibility I change my mind. We both know it.

He closes his eyes and groans out, "VP of UX at LodgeIn."

"LodgeIn?!" My laugh sounds like I'm happy he stabbed me. Of course—only a hundred-million-dollar company that's publicly traded could sway Grey to ever take a corporate job. "Great. You will be renting me short-term vacation rentals for forever on top of setting me up on dates into my old age. Any other apps I should avoid in the future?"

"They reached out to me," he says. "I'm happy. I didn't go looking for this job, but I made a name for myself after Fuse, people knew who I was."

"For someone who creates apps, it's weird you don't actually *use* any of them," I joke to avoid crying. "Are you going to be one of those Silicon Valley tech moguls who sends their kids to technology-free schools?"

"Ryan," he says, "no jokes. And I don't live in Silicon Valley."

"You have to take it," I say.

"They haven't offered it to me yet," he replies.

"Well, they will," I whisper. "And you're going to take it. Otherwise, you're going to resent me."

"I could never resent you."

We've come full circle. Grey and I have switched places, done a complete one-eighty. Tears are welling, and I'm not going to be able to blink them back. It's too fast of a rush when I comprehend exactly how Grey felt four years ago.

I am so damn proud of him. This means so much, to be recognized for all of his hard work and natural intuition and talent. That huge companies want him to lead a team and make important decisions. He needs this for himself, and I can hear it in his voice how much he wants it. Just like I wanted the University of Hawaii.

"I'd rather you hate me than regret me," I manage to say as they spill down my cheeks.

"Don't turn my words around on me." Grey kisses me softly. "I already told you what I did was a mistake. Don't do this."

I shake my head against his forehead. "Let's just be with each other for the next few days."

What's done is done.

"That's not what I want," he says firmly. "I'm not going to give up."

"Then I have to do it for both of us."

There's nothing I can do except let him go—just like he did for me—and he sees it in my eyes.

23

Later Friday Evening

THROUGHOUT DINNER, MY face looks like the epitome of happiness and excitement for my best friend. Inside this skull, my brain can only play my and Grey's conversation on repeat.

I've composed myself enough to not let my emotions surface. I choose not to sit by Grey so he can't put his hands on my body or his lips on my skin. He can't gain the upper hand over me.

Sage unknowingly buffers, repeatedly distracting me with her narration on her and J.P.'s witty exchange at the bar.

But Grey just continues being Grey. He doesn't let his eyes drift off of me for longer than a minute. Each time he holds my gaze, it seems to get more purposeful, his eyes softer, like he knows I'm drowning in my thoughts.

I listen intensely to how much everyone is obsessed with two of my best friends because they are easy to love.

Finally, when the toasts are over, Grey gets up to use the bathroom.

Fourteen friends to thirty-four friends allows me to slip out of the room unnoticed.

After maneuvering the hotel maze of hallways, I find the bar where we kicked off the wedding festivities this past Sunday.

"Lots of vodka," I tell the bartender when I sit on a high brown leather stool.

After he places an overflowing vodka martini down in front of me, I carefully try to sip from it without spilling all over myself.

"Who is that?" a deep voice asks seriously in my ear.

I startle just enough for vodka to dribble down my chin. "Joeyyy," I whine.

His scent catches my nose, like his fruity surfing wax. I'm only three sips in, and it's so strong, it may have already gone to my head.

What a loaded question.

Grey is certainly not no one. I can't even bring myself to say that, so I don't answer his question and take another giant sip.

"Are you going to give me a chance to talk?" he asks.

"Sure." I pat the seat next to me. "Sit down."

Joey listens and slinks down onto the barstool. "I'm sorry about that whole fight we got into. I'm sorry I forgot about the wedding. It slipped my mind when I made the plans, but I didn't want to end our relationship over it. I miss you."

As I stare at him with a half-drunken smirk, he drags his chair a few inches closer to mine.

Something like a slurred snort comes out of my nose. "*I* slipped your mind. You don't seem to understand that part. And you just don't really get me. It wasn't just that. It was everything; on top of forgetting about me. That wasn't the first time. It was just the first time I was pissed enough to get in a fight with you about it."

"It won't happen again," he insists. "I promise."

I squeeze my eyes shut. It will. I don't believe him.

"I've been thinking a lot this week," he continues, "and I understand now what you meant about your mind. Mine is a jumbled mess and you straighten that out. I'm not proud that I walked out after that first fight, but I won't do that again. I get it now that you need me to talk."

But here I am believing Grey. Why? He lied by omission. Isn't that still a lie? We're conditioned to expect history to repeat itself. Nothing has changed. Everything is the same. No, it's harder. Why do I miraculously think this time it's going to work out? Because Grey can surprise me every time he opens his mouth? Even the bad things surprise me in a horrifyingly good way—on top of feeling like I'm crushing under Grey's weight, I want him to have everything he deserves. Why do I let him back in so easily?

Maybe I should try to let Joey back in, like I can recreate the same feeling. Maybe if you pretend long enough, it becomes reality. I could give him a second chance to win my heart. I can't expect to love anyone else if I don't give them a chance to love me back.

Even though Joey has never surprised me—not once—my morbid destiny is to settle anyway.

When you really love someone, sometimes you know it's better for them if you leave them alone. This is me embracing it.

You win, Universe. Just call me Kathleen Copeland, because I'm not myself, I'm my mother.

"You smell like home," I say, smiling.

He chuckles. "I've missed surfing with you. The beach isn't the same without your math side-commentary."

"I've missed surfing… too," I trail off, unable to add 'with you.'

Joey lifts a hand to my face and tucks a strand of hair behind my ear. "Who was that?" he asks again, softer this time.

The man whose hand I will always wish yours was, I think automatically, but I'll never let on.

"Someone from my past," I say. "It doesn't matter. He lives in Texas."

Joey decides not to press it and takes my hand in his instead. "How's your week been?"

I stare down at our intertwined hands. I wonder if this is what happened to my mom. Maybe there's someone out there who isn't my dad, who she loves and can never stop, but she can't have.

"It's been fun," I say. "You know how lethargic Elliot is—fishing, mountain biking, camping, ropes courses. I'm exhausted."

Emotionally, I don't add.

I have to switch it off. I'm so fucking tired, and I need my logical and rational side on. No more emotions. I close my eyes, and when I open them, I feel numb. The vodka doesn't hurt.

Joey laughs. "What was your favorite?"

"I can't pick just one thing," I joke.

But maybe it's welcome drinks on the terrace? Before.

Pins and needles travel across my skin. I take another sip of my martini. Fuck numb. My heart needs to be dead.

"You showing up," I lie.

Joey leans into me and lowers his voice. "Are you three doing anything tonight?"

"Of course, it's the eve of the wedding."

"Maybe you can get away, and we can go sit by the fire and tal—" He stops mid-word when his eyes bounce over my shoulder and sits back. "Certainly doesn't seem like no one."

I roll my eyes, since I know I never said that, and look back to where Joey is still staring.

Grey is leaning against the doorway, hands in his pockets, watching us stoically. He pushes himself off the frame, crosses the bar confidently, and slides his arm across my shoulders when he stands beside me.

"I'm sorry to interrupt," he tells Joey. "Would you mind giving us a minute?"

Joey searches for my answer in my eyes. "Is that what you want?"

I nod. "It's fine."

Grey moves out of Joey's way as he slides past both of us.

"We can talk later?" Joey asks.

"Yeah," I smile.

He gives Grey one more hesitant look before he walks off.

Instead of sitting, Grey stalks off to the terrace through the French doors and lets them close heavily behind him.

I wish I wouldn't follow him. My brain knows not to. My body has other ideas.

I pull my sweater tighter around myself when I step out onto the balcony.

Grey is standing, gripping the glass edge of the railing just like I was a few days ago.

He turns when he hears me. "What are you doing?"

"Exactly what you did," I say, crossing my arms over my chest. "Settling."

"Ryan," he whispers angrily before he raises his voice. "You're not even giving me a chance. You'd rather turn into your mother, keep going with your list, settle like I did? You're making a mistake."

I raise my voice back. "Say the first thing that pops into your head."

Grey pinches his eyebrows tightly and waits with his back against the railing.

"Where do you want to live?"

"Wherever you live," he replies.

"Grey…"

"That's the first thing that popped into my head," he insists.

"It doesn't work like that."

"It can, Ryan," he says.

"When are you going to move?"

"I don't have a timeline written down."

"How is it going to work?"

"However it works out is fine with me."

"Those aren't answers to any of my questions. You don't have any real answers. I have to ask you to move to California? I become the bad guy. That's selfish. I can't be selfish. You are about to buy your dream house and have a dream job. You cannot give up those things for me. Lily will miss you too much. You cannot give up your family for me. I'm not going to ask you to. What happens when I'm not there for you to touch or kiss? You haven't taken your hands off of me for longer than a minute in the last twenty-four hours. What happens when you think, 'I can't do this' again?"

"Don't do this, *please*," he breathes into the chilly air.

"Nothing has changed," I hiss. "You expect me to think that we're going to go back home and everything is suddenly different? Absolutely nothing is different. I'd say everything is even harder. Adulthood has made it way more complicated. We have real things that we'd have to sacrifice. You said so yourself; people don't change. That's what's so beautiful about math. You get the same answer every time. You can even solve an equation in different ways, but you always come to the same conclusion no matter what because there's only one answer."

"We're not math. People aren't x and y. I'd say I'm even more complicated than differential equations, and you're the only person in the world who likes that shit and understands it, but you don't get to compare me to some predetermined solution. So what if I buy this house and take this job. That doesn't change a damn thing. People sell houses and quit jobs all the time. Circumstances can change. You are my only circumstance."

"I know you feel that way, Grey. I feel that way too, but in real life, it doesn't always work out how you want it to. Real life plus real people equals the harsh reality that we settle, we get complacent."

"I know you don't trust me right now, but I *am* different. I *want* to change. I've already changed for you, and only you, since the moment I made my first bad decision. However long it takes for you to realize I'm serious, that's how long I'll wait. I'm not going to fuck it up this time."

"You're going to go back to Austin, and I'm going to go back to San Diego, and what are we going to do exactly?"

"I'm going to go back home and see my family. I'm going to go to work. I'm going to interview for this job. I'm going to close on my house. And I'm going to miss you every fucking second. You're going to go back home and do the job you love. You're going to hang out with your best friends. And I hope you miss me every fucking second. But this time, we're going to call each other, FaceTime, text each other. I'm going to fly to see you, you're going to fly to see me. And we're going to love each other, Ryan. It's pretty simple really."

"And later?" I question him. "Later is hard."

"Good," he says, smiling. "You wouldn't like it if it was easy."

"Can you stop being annoyingly you for like two seconds?" I ask. "And stop tricking me into loving you while you're at it. This is history repeating itself."

"You are repeating history if you are seriously entertaining the idea of dating Joey again," he accuses me.

"What?"

"Joey. Was that the ex-boyfriend who doesn't fight with you correctly?"

I narrow my eyes. Grey widens his.

He knew the whole time and didn't even react. He's *such* a non-asshole.

"It doesn't matter which one he was," I say. "I've accepted it. I'm making this choice for you because I love you. This is what I want."

"I know you love me, and I know I can't make you do anything, so fine. I'm not sure anyone really gets to choose who they love, but we do get to choose how we love. All I can do right now is make you see that this time I'm choosing differently. So have your doubts. Walk away tonight and think we're not together. I don't care about being your boyfriend right now. It doesn't have to 'be like that'. I'll just show you how much I mean it when I say that as long as you want me around, I'm here. Where I live and what I do for a living will not change that. No matter how much you think it will."

"I want to believe you," I say, "but I think you forgot how hard it was for you."

"Trust me," Grey scoffs. "I haven't forgotten. I've lived it every day for four years."

I sigh, and my warm breath creates a cloud in front of my face.

"Maybe I shouldn't date either one of you," I argue. "Maybe I should stay single, like I decided before."

"Come here," Grey says, dropping his arms.

I float like I'm a dandelion seed in the wind, like I have no say in the matter.

"You think you have an answer for everything," I mutter into his chest when he bear hugs me.

"I really don't," he replies into my hair. "That's you."

"Maybe that's my problem. Grey plus Ryan times love equals failure. Math equations don't change, Grey."

"It's cold out here. Do I need to grab a blanket?"

Somehow, he's already wrapped me up with his body. How did he even get me close enough to touch him? I don't remember.

"God, when you say it out loud…" I scrunch up my nose and shrug. "Am I crazy? I'm crazy."

He chuckles. "Knowing how to fight with someone—that's everything. Fighting can be healthy, but you have to do it correctly, figure out what makes the other person tick. I know you like the back of my hand, Ryan. Nothing I say is going to convince you. You're going to have to actively watch me in the process of loving you from Austin, even when I have a new house and even if I have a new job, so I'm not worried about it because I'll prove it to you over time. Go have fun with your best friends tonight and stop worrying. There's not going to be another ex on your crazy list as long as you don't choose him. I know that."

"Definitely crazy," I repeat, shaking my head. "You shouldn't do any of that for me. Why do you even love me so much?"

"I don't just love you. I *like* you," he insists, pulling me into the world's slowest and sensual kiss. He holds me up as I start to puddle, even though I try my best to act like it has no effect on me, and whispers into my ear, "For instance, I'll fight with you over the fact that your formula isn't even correct. It's Grey plus Ryan times love to the like equals forever. You can't argue with math."

He's numbed my mind long enough for me forget how to think, but my heart is on fire as I take a step back.

I blink up into his face.

Is it just my deranged brain or am I the only one who sometimes thinks "like" sounds even better?

24

Even Later Friday Evening

GIRLS' NIGHT.

You can't help but say it with that twang—high-pitched and nasally with that touch of valley girl—because it's fun.

I don't care how annoyed every guy gets or how hard they roll their eyes when they hear it.

It's the little things.

I've got my *Grease* DVD, perler beads, a friendship bracelet kit, and I even snagged the '90s game Dream Phone in mint condition off the internet.

Sage has the wine.

I step off the elevator when it stops on the top floor and run straight into a body that reminds me of everything I hate about myself.

The little things are always ruined by that one guy who just won't leave you alone. Joey and Grey have that in common, but they elicit very different reactions from me. Grey uses mind control, but I've already ignored Joey's **What room are you in?** text.

Joey grunts as my precious cargo crashes to the floor. I sigh because *Ryan made a scene* will never be words uttered by anyone, and he *is* scrambling on his knees to pick it all up.

He laughs and picks up my game. "Dream Phone?"

"Giiiiiirls' night," I twang uncontrollably. "You know…" I wave my hand over my ridiculous items. "Seventh grade girls' night."

He looks down at the board game in his hands and shakes it gently. "Right. Have to find out who has a crush on you." Then he stands slowly but takes a step back when I reach for my stuff. "I've been looking for you. Are you going to tell me who that was now?"

I look down the hallway, which is stretching out into infinity like a horror movie, to Evie's door, wondering if he knocked on it.

"Joey," I say sternly.

He screws up his face. "He definitely wasn't no one."

"I never said he was no one," I counter.

Joey's eyes simmer. "It's been three weeks, Ryan, and you're already sleeping with someone else?"

"That's none of your business," I say. "We're not together. I'm not just sleeping with him. I…" I make zero sense. I don't even know what I'm trying to say.

I like you, but I like him more doesn't have a good ring to it.

Joey draws his lips inwards and hesitates. "Can we go back to my room and talk?"

I want to scream an obscenity, anything, but instead I sigh. "Can we talk when we get back to San Diego?"

San Diego, where I'm in a completely different state than Grey so he can't mess with my mind. Far enough away where he isn't going to come back around with his trickery.

The plan had been to work on myself, and now I'm stuck between these two awful places where neither of my choices is good.

"Here is fine," he challenges me.

"Fine!" I huff. "Joey, I don't think I want to get back together with you. Unless you want to settle with me, then I'm all yours. Who knows? Maybe it could turn out great, but I don't have high hopes. This week I realized it's even more than that. I am someone else's. I always have been. I'm sorry. I told you I needed to be single, and I meant it."

Joey runs a hand through his hair. "So, you're saying you're in love with this other guy, who you broke up with me over, but you're going to be single anyway?"

"Yes, exactly," I sigh-smile since he finally gets it—gets me. Maybe we really would've worked in another life.

He laughs darkly. "You really do just serial date."

"W—what?" I stutter.

Never mind. I hate him. Joey has *never* surprised me. Except for this moment. I kind of wish I had Sage's stiletto shaped nails to run down his face right now.

"I thought people were just kidding when they said that, but no, it looks like your reputation precedes you. I thought you were different."

"I wasn't serial dating," I yell—softly. "I was trying to find someone who I like more than that *no one* guy. Turns out, I can't. The whole problem is that I met him first. If I had met you first, it might be a completely different story. Now, no one else stands a chance anymore. It's not that simple. I broke up with you because you aren't him. Not even close."

It's really me that doesn't stand a chance anymore. I hate the words that are coming out of my mouth, and I'm angry with myself. Grey is not my identity.

Joey can only keep looking at me, bemused.

I grab my board game from one of his hands. "Besides, I don't need anyone. I don't need a man to tell me I look beautiful or that

I'm smart or that he loves me. I don't know why I'm chasing this ideal. I've spent years tied to it, mounting the pressure on myself as time ticks by, with each new guy I meet. So, no I don't miss you, and no, I don't want to get back together. I do fine by myself, and it's about time I was single for a change. You wouldn't want to *serial* date me anyway."

I'd been so caught up in my hissy rant, I didn't notice Sage poking her head out the hotel door. I catch her wide, round green eyes before she disappears back through the doorway.

I relax my shoulders. I unclench my jaw. I pull back from the edge of *Ryan made a scene.*

"I'm sorry," I say, reaching for my things. That's all I can say. I want this conversation over.

Joey relents and carefully places everything else into my outstretched arms. He rests my precious perler bead bucket on top.

"Yeah, me too," he says.

"It's not you." I attempt a half-hearted laugh to try to salvage any semblance of a friendship we have left. You know—mutual friends and all. "It's him. And sometimes I'm not even happy about it. Obviously."

Joey presses the elevator button and makes sure I completely understand that I am a psychotic lunatic with the look he shoots me.

Trust me, I know.

And I don't even know what this means for myself.

When I open the door to Evelyn's suite, she and Sage are waiting patiently for me on the couch.

"My life is a shit show," I sigh. "Who's ready to belt out *Summer Nights?*"

Sage rummages through the pile when I dump everything on the coffee table and pouts. "No *Grease 2?*"

"You're the only person in the world who thinks that movie is better," I argue, flopping down between them on the couch.

"False," Sage shoots back. "I can find hundreds of people on Reddit or a few BuzzFeed articles that agree with me right now."

"That's the beauty of the internet," Evie says. "You can find another like-minded person no matter what."

"Did you find a cross-stitching support group for twentysomethings?" I tease her. "Or are you still the only one?"

"I'll take back everything I've ever made you," she warns me.

"No," I laugh. "I love the look I get every time someone walks into my room and sees my eggplant and taco emoji pillow. It's the centerpiece of my bed." I jokingly widen my eyes and smirk. "Did you cross-stitch Elliot a peach?"

She hits me. "What was that in the hallway?"

"Nothing," I say too quickly.

"Ryan, you can't avoid it," Evie replies. "Talk."

"It's not a big deal."

I send Sage, who shrugs, a murderous glance. I imagine her exact words to Evelyn were 'Joey's trying to get himself back into Ryan's pants.'

"It was nothing," I repeat. I turn to Sage. "I am already tired. And thanks for telling me I have a reputation by the way."

"What?" Sage asks, confused.

"Your nickname must have caught on. Joey accused me of being a serial dater."

Her jaw drops. "What an asshole. He can't call you that."

"*You* call me that," I joke.

"But I love you," she explains. "And I've never called you that in front of anyone. He isn't allowed to say that. You can date whoever the hell you want for however the hell long you feel like it."

"Yeah, well, I won't be dating anyone anymore."

Sage narrows her eyes, assessing my aura.

But Evie gasps under her breath. "What? Why?" she exclaims.

"I'm tired."

"Of what?" she forces out.

I stare at her.

She stares back harder.

I swallow the bubble about to pop out of my mouth. "Of everything. Dating. Men. Myself."

I don't even know why she's mad, but Evie cuts me with her eyes. "He's your soulmate."

I shrug. "I guess Joey's okay."

"Ryan," she says, unamused.

"What is a soulmate anyway?" I say. It's too late. The words have slipped, and I can't reel it back in. "We have this idea that we're supposed to find our soulmate, but I don't even know what that means."

I should leave it here. I should shut my mouth.

"Whatever," I add.

Evie looks *worried* for me. "I'm not going to drop it."

So, I stupidly don't either. "No wonder so many people settle. This shit sucks sometimes. A single person cannot be everything for someone else. It's like we expect them to like the same things we do, read our minds, be the best travel partner, be the best co-parent, be the best shoulder to cry on, fight with us correctly. Literally everything. No one can be that for someone else. There are seven billion people in the world. Statistically, there is more than one person out there for me. Grey might be one of thousands."

You know when you can feel yourself talking too much? You know you should shut up, but then you get the bright idea that you can talk yourself out of it, that more words will somehow fix the issue, but they never really do?

That's me right now.

"Don't drag math into this," Evie says. "Love defies physics."

I roll my eyes hard. "Nothing defies physics. That's, like, the law; the definition—how nature behaves. We behave like shitty people to each other. And what have I even been doing? Trying to prove to myself that I'm not my mother? That I won't have to settle? Well, I will. The universe is fucking cruel, and because, according to you, my *soulmate* lives across the country. We aren't going to make it work unless one of us gives up something. I'm in his four-year-old shoes, and I completely get it. I cannot ask him to sacrifice anything for me because I love him too much. He deserves everything and more." My mind spins like it's catching up. "Did you know?"

"Know what?" Evie asks, innocently.

I laugh haughtily. "You knew."

She sighs. "He wanted to tell you himself."

"Thank god for Elliot's innocence," I mutter.

"*I* don't know," Sage says.

I turn toward her. "Don't worry. I only found out an hour ago that Grey is closing on a house in Austin in a couple of weeks, and he's going to be rivaling your VP job within a month."

Sage whistles when I confirm that she did hear me correctly and it is indeed the giant company LodgeIn, where he will probably make twice what Sage makes.

"So, I force him to give all of that up and leave his sister, who adores him, behind? He forces me to leave both of you behind? You're my family. Doesn't work. One of us has to be selfish when neither of us wants to be."

"Don't drag us into this," Sage retorts, "just because you're scared."

I throw up my hands. "Why are you not on my side?!"

Now Evie just looks sorry for me.

"I feel personally attacked," I laugh.

"It's not funny!" Evie exclaims. "Quit joking for two seconds."

I open my mouth to make yet another joke but clamp it shut

and cross my arms defiantly. "Y'all are no fun."

Sage is right. I'm terrified.

But I refuse to admit it out loud.

So what if I'm scared? I'm allowed to be. It's a normal human emotion. Maybe that's the reason my deranged side comes out. I'm crazy to cover up how afraid I really am.

"You're going to have to work for it," Evie says. "That's what love is. It's not a feeling."

"It's a feeling," I counter.

We both swivel our heads to Sage, looking for backup.

"You're both wrong," she says. "It's both."

"What do you know?" I mumble. "You don't fall in love."

"Because I have never *felt* that way, and I *choose* not to," she laughs. "You *feel* that way, but you're stupidly *electing* to ignore it."

"What about being independent? I can channel my inner Sage. I don't need another thing to complicate my life, complicate his life. We're both going to end up as the bad guy." I throw my hands up. "Let's not forget that it was both of you egging me on. *Talk to him.* Sure. *Oh, he loves you.* Sure. *You love him.* Sure. I told you this shit would happen. He's like a huge mind fuck. Just sucking you in and gaining control because all he does is say the very last thing you ever expect him to say. He messes up the equation I'm using to get through life. I can't help it. I'm like the goddamn sand in an hourglass. Eventually he'll claim all of me, and then turn my entire life upside down. And when it happens, I'll remind you that it is all your fault."

"Why are we turning on each other?" Evie whines.

"I'm not mad," I say matter-of-factly. "It's called sarcasm."

Evie scoffs. "You're being a pain in the ass. A truthful, sarcastic pain in the ass." She sinks back into the couch and looks away. "What if I don't feel like being the serial monogamist? I've been dating Elliot for four years. Before that, it was Grant for five years.

Before that, it was Drew for three. What if I think I missed my opportunity to date? To throw all caution to the wind? Maybe I want to sleep around and break some hearts."

The mountain range out our window must be making her seriously upset because I catch a glimpse of a tear before she blinks it back.

How could I have let it get this far?

I'm a bitch with a *Grease* DVD and a smart mouth.

It's also *all* Evelyn's fiancé's fault for never mentioning his elusive friendship with my ex-boyfriend, who he calls Beck, and then bringing him here to torture me—but I'm not going to point *that* out.

"Evelyn, this week isn't about me," I say softly. "This is about you and Elliot and your eternal love for each other. My relationship drama is eternal and dumb. But you and Elliot are going to have an amazing wedding and my stupid shit isn't going to fuck it up. End of story."

Evie continues to stare out the window. "Yeah, okay."

I pick up the movie and pop it in the DVD player.

Singing along to *Grease* at the top of your lungs makes everything better.

End. Of. Story.

25

Not My Wedding Day

"SHE'S GONE."

Half-asleep me has no idea who is talking.

"Who's gone?" I mumble into my warm pillow. I roll over, away from the voice. "Who are you? Close the curtains."

My covers are yanked down, letting the cold air rush in. I groan and grab for them.

"I am Sage. And Evelyn isn't here."

"What time is it?" I ask groggily.

I open my eyes in a hazy dark room. The sun looks like it's just about to peek over the skyline.

"Five forty-two," Sage shouts.

I bolt upright.

The tremble starts in my hands. "Maybe she just went for a walk."

Yeah. A walk to revel in her last hours of singleness.

"You don't think…" I trail off. The tremble rises up my arms, so I grip the bed sheets to control myself. "Maybe she's with Elliot."

That seems more likely. A secret lovers' rendezvous before the nerves kick in.

Who the hell am I kidding? This is Evelyn we're talking about. She would never allow Elliot to see her on her wedding day.

"Fuck," I mutter, wide-eyed. "Sage. She couldn't have gotten cold feet, could she?"

"Oh, no, of course not," she hisses, mocking me. "Soulmates don't exist. I'm going to be alone because love is a mind fuck. Monogamy is for losers."

"I didn't say monogamy was for losers."

Sage levels me with her gaze. "No? What would you call it?"

"Girl power?" I whisper.

"Fix it," Sage demands, throwing my clothes at me. If she could kill with this one look, I'd be on my way to hell right now. "And start by being honest with yourself."

I'm dressed and out the door in less than a minute because Sage, in her red eye mask pushed up high on her forehead and a *There's no such thing as bad publicity* T-shirt, terrifies me and might be Satan in disguise hiding behind a stellar PR team.

The problem is I'm still standing in the hallway six minutes later.

I don't know where to start. If I should call anyone. What I should do.

Evelyn knows not to take anything I say seriously. But I *was* serious, which is another problem.

I pull out my phone and try to sound casual.

Want to watch the sun rise with me? Where'd you go?

I let three unresponsive minutes pass before I text Grey.

Any chance you're awake at 5:56 a.m.?

My phone buzzes within ten seconds. **I haven't been able to sleep** past five all week because I've been so eager to see you every day, so yes, wide awake.

Stomach clench.

If one wanted to find Elliot, would you say he is still sleeping wherever y'all ended up last night?

Grey replies with an unamused emoji face and, I thought this was a booty call, and no, he's walking out of the gym with me right now. Tell Evie he's sweaty and gross and it's their wedding day, so no peeking. I'm sweaty and gross too but happy to take a shower with you.

Sex isn't going to solve all of our problems, I text back. For one, you're going to have to learn how hard it is when you can't have me.

That's what video calls are for. I like to watch too. Want to practice?

God, that sounds fun. Back to the issue at hand, I'm busy looking for Evie. Text me if you see her and don't mention ANYTHING to Elliot!

Well, fuck, Ryan. Shouldn't you have started with that? How do I help?

Find her? K thanks.

Don't 'K' me. I want to help you. Give me fifteen minutes.

All I can do is start looking.

I hurry to the end of the hallway and push open the door to the stairs. When I reach the bottom, I throw open the second heavy door. I'm not appropriately dressed for the brisk air that hits me, but I rush out into the dark anyway.

At least I know she's not at the gym.

I try the bar first because maybe I drove her to drink her best friend sorrows away, but it's locked and there are no lights on.

I don't know what I expected. This isn't Bourbon Street where the bars never close. It's freaking Telluride, Colorado—population 2,500.

The spa isn't open. The restaurant isn't open.

She's not in the pool. She's not by the fire pits.

I see exactly one staff person, who informs me I am the only person he's seen and confirms that nothing is open before the sun comes up.

I look up at the glass balcony, where I stood on Sunday, defeated. This week could have gone so differently.

I could have looked out over the golf course and been happy, not crawling anxiously out of my skin because Grey popped up into my life out of nowhere like the haunted jack in the box of my past.

My week would have been fun. Sage and I could have been silly and carefree girls all week, instead of trying to put together failing PR campaigns.

I tried. I tried to make this not about me. I tried to own up to my ridiculous past and move on from it.

And I definitely wouldn't have fucked shit up with my drama.

I just stand there imagining that version of myself, living in that parallel universe for a second, and honesty is like a punch in the gut. It hurts like a bitch (the bitch that I am), and Sage is right—I'm lying to anyone who will listen, including myself.

I turn around to look out over the golf course to envision how it all would've gone. It certainly wouldn't have ended with me standing here, being the biggest asshole in all the world who told her best friend love doesn't work out on the eve of her wedding.

My heart burns, and it's possible I've induced a heart attack when I realize I wouldn't go back if I could. I still wouldn't reverse back to Sunday and not have Grey here. I don't want to be the Ryan who lived a blissful Grey-free week. I'd still choose this fucked up ending if it was the only alternate reality that ended with Grey in my life.

That's life. We do get to choose. We get to choose who we surround ourselves with, who we spend our day with. And I hope we all choose the people we *like*, because life is too short to spread misery.

There will always be someone who thinks I'm old, but there will also always be someone who thinks I'm young; that if they had the time I had left, if they could time travel back to my age, that they'd choose something different.

And mostly, I don't ever want to wish I could go back and make a different choice. I don't want to think *what if?* Now, I have a very rare second chance to find out how my *what if?* turns out and I want to give it up.

"Evelyn!" I scream when I see someone in the shadows like Bigfoot, stalking through the trees on the edge of hole sixteen. It's too small to be Grey or actual Bigfoot.

When it emerges from the trees I scream, "Evelyn!" again, louder.

The body stops short, so I take off sprinting toward it. Her shocked face comes into focus when I'm twenty yards away.

"I'm sorry," I pant, closing the gap and throwing my arms around her neck when I reach her. "I'm so sorry."

"What are you doing?" Evie asks, still stunned.

"I fucked up," I say all in one breath, "and I'm fixing it. Your relationship isn't mine, and I never should have said anything even close to that effect. You and Elliot are soulmates. I see it every day. He loves you more than a golden retriever can love his human. You are his person, and I feel how much he loves you and treats us like family. You're going to have a beautiful wedding and a beautiful life together. You're going to make babies with him and be the perfect mother. And I'm so, so sorry for ruining this week for you."

She goes from stiff to lax in my arms and hugs me back. When I let out a strangled sob, she pushes me back by the waist. "Sit."

I listen, dropping to the perfectly manicured lawn right there and pulling my tiny shirt over my knees.

The wind whips around us, so Evie huddles in closely, even though she's bundled in a sweatshirt and thick leggings.

She takes my hands and gives me huge, blue doe-eyes. "I don't know how to…" Her eyes gloss over in tears. "I wish I could…"

"It's okay. I love you," I continue. "Sage is right—don't tell her—I'm the most terrified I've ever been in my life. I never thought I'd get a second chance, and then I come here and get what I've been secretly wishing for for years. So of course I screw it up because it doesn't make sense. I lose something no matter which choice I make. Grey loses something no matter what choice he makes, and all he can tell me is the one thing he chooses emphatically is me. But I know that's not the whole truth. I know it isn't that easy. And I was jealous that you get to marry the love of your life who lives in the same city, and I disguised that as hatred against all love. And I know that makes me selfish. I've been selfish all week. I lied to everyone—you, Elliot, Sage, Grey. I couldn't even admit it to myself. But I played the game, knowing full well it was going to rip my heart open. He is my soulmate, I know. He is the one person who I would jump in front of a freight train for— no offense."

Evie smiles and shrugs.

"I know that if I end up in Austin though, that you aren't going to let me go. I forgot you're the glue. You keep us all friends because you always remember to call, and you always remember the little things. You plan the parties and the birthdays and host everything at your house. And Sage is too hardheaded to let a trip to the Texas wine country ever go to waste, and she'll never have kids so she can always visit. I know things are going to change because you're going to have a husband and eventually children. Our time spent together is going to change whether I stay in San Diego or not, and maybe I'm a little, no, a *lot,* scared of that because I'm going to be left behind, because we're getting old and all of these life events are happening at lightning speed.

"I was looking up at the terrace like ten minutes ago—where I'd contemplated throwing myself off of it earlier this week just to escape this hell hole I knew was splitting wide open—and I realized emphatically that I *can* live without Grey. I've been doing it for four years. I've made a home for myself and have best friends who I love like family. I could live without him for the rest of my life. It wouldn't be so bad, right? I've been doing it this long, four years is like forever, and I could go back and be happy enough. My life doesn't revolve around him because I've got other great things in my life that make me happy and living without true love or marriage or a man isn't the worst thing in the world. So yeah, I could live without Grey—the thing is I just plain don't want to. I want to be with him every step of the way, in the same city or not, because he's part of my family too. He makes my life better, even when I'm ruining your wedding week. I don't even know how to explain how deeply I love him because I can't make an equation out of him in my mind."

Evie sniffles and crushes me in a hug. "I know," she slobbers into my shirt. "Everyone could see it except you. Grey is your better half"—I pinch her until she squirms—"I mean he *makes* you better, like he's your complement, and I've never seen someone else understand you more than he does. I love you so much, but sometimes you just piss me off. All I wanted was for you to realize what you're giving up, regardless of pointless houses and jobs. Absolutely no one lies on their death bed and reminisces about their C-suite job or their perfect house. It's about the people we love who make our lives have meaning. People that really matter don't come around every day, even when there are billions of people in the world. Love is still rare. I'm sorry we fought. I can't live without my best friend."

"I love you more, and you don't want to live without Elliot either. Please take your own advice and mine," I say, nodding into her shirt. "That was a really long way of telling you that my declaration of 'love is a fallacy' was bullshit. Please don't doubt that you are exactly who you should be with him and that you are perfect together. What you two have is the rarest thing I've seen."

"What?" Evie laughs and holds me back by the shoulders at arm's length.

"No more cold feet?" I ask. "You promise? Because I could never forgive myself for coming between y'all. I low-key want you to adopt me so you can be my parents."

"I'm going to marry Elliot, Ryan." Her eyebrows deepen for a split second before they spring back up within normal range. "But only because of your love-declaring speech. How could I not after hearing that?"

"I kind of wish Grey had heard it," I joke. "It was better than anything else that I spew out of my mouth around him."

The sound of a subtle cough behind me makes me whip my head around.

Elliot and Grey are standing there staring at me blank-faced and motionless.

I don't know what to address first. "We—I—we weren't, aren't talking—did you hear that?"

Elliot and Grey glance at each other before Elliot turns back to me. "Which part? That Evie was having second thoughts or that you are finally admitting that you want to love Grey from halfway across the country?"

Dammit to all hell, shit, and fuck. I can do absolutely nothing right.

My chest tightens, panic is clenching around my lungs so tightly I can't breathe. "Who has an inhaler?"

Grey laughs at me in my time of need. "You don't have asthma."

I glare at him. "This is all your fault."

"I think I just heard you say it was yours," he says, raising his eyebrows in surprise.

I ignore him, but later I might get a full set of stiletto nails just so I can scratch his eyes out.

"Evelyn?" Elliot's eyes widen. He's frowning. I've never seen this man frown in my life. Is he going to burst into tears? It actually sounds like he's going to burst into tears, and now I'll need to move into a monastery and repent for the rest of my life.

The altitude has stolen all of my oxygen, so I sound like a struggling parrot. "Elliot. I was joking. Evie isn't having cold feet. In fact, she has the hottest feet ever. So hot that she could make millions on OnlyFans."

Evelyn bursts out laughing. "Ryan, relax. You two are cruel."

I turn back to her, and my lungs thank me when I suck in a deep breath.

"I wasn't having second thoughts because of you," she says. "I wasn't having second thoughts at all. Elliot and I were coming out here to do yoga and watch the sunrise."

"And eat ass," Elliot adds.

My brain is still catching up. I look back at Elliot and Grey grinning like fucking childish teenagers.

"I texted you," Grey defends himself.

I glance at my phone laying face down in the dark grass. Dammit.

"You!" I stress, twisting back to Evie. "You let me sit here and word vomit my entire sob story."

"I thought you needed me!" she insists. "I don't know. I thought you were emotional because it was the wedding day and you finally realized how much you need Grey in your life. You know, until you said that last part."

"And you just let them walk up behind me and eavesdrop?"

She shrugs and stands, joining in on the group of people I want to peel grins off their faces. "I didn't see them until it was too late, and you were on a roll. I was not about to interrupt your revelation and ruin it—like you almost ruined my wedding day."

Elliot crosses in front of me and picks Evie up over his shoulder, then slaps her ass. "I'm taking Evelyn with me before you ruin the sunrise too."

"All of you will pay for this," I call to them as they disappear down the sloping fairway. "On a day in the near future when you're not getting married."

"I love you, Ryan!" Evie yells. "You're welcome for fixing your life. And don't tell anyone Elliot and I saw each other today."

"Seriously!" Elliot screams. "You are indebted to me forever. Both of you."

"Watch your backs," I yell back louder. "I play the long game."

"Four years?" Grey teases.

"Longer," I say, getting to my feet without his help as I mumble under my breath. "You think you know someone, and then they do the very opposite of what you think they'll do—seeing the groom on her wedding day. That is *not* Evelyn Lawrence. What the hell?"

"Well, she is about to become Evelyn Sharpe." Grey roams his eyes over my chest. "Also another example of people being weird—why are you wearing that tiny see-through spaghetti strap thing and no bra in thirty-degree weather?"

"No time. I had a wedding to save," I say sarcastically.

He pulls his sweatshirt off by the back of his neck and slips it over my head. It feels like it just got out of the dryer and smells like Grey's soap.

"How much of that did you hear?" I ask, jumping into his arms.

He wraps my legs around his waist and cradles my butt. "I came in somewhere between 'I'd die by train for him' and 'I could take him or leave him.'"

"So poetic."

Grey's face turns serious. "It's okay to be scared. I'm scared too, but we're going to take it one day at a time. Tomorrow I'm going to love you and then the day after that I'm going to do it again. Because right now, that's all I can do."

"You know what it feels like when you don't know how to finish an equation? Like there is no right answer?"

"No," he chuckles. "I hate math."

"I know," I smile. "Well, I don't like it."

It makes me feel lost, like I don't have control. I want to put people in a nice little row and be satisfied when I watch everything play out as expected.

But Grey always does the last thing I expect and he screws it all up. Maybe everyone does.

"I know," he says softly, placing his forehead against mine.

"I don't want to exist without you in my life," I say into his face. "I'm going to figure it out, okay? I promise."

"I have no doubt that you would," Grey smiles back, "but we're going to figure it out together."

"Don't let me turn into my mother," I whisper. "Please."

It's the one outcome in life that I've been trying to break, trying to blow up, solving repeatedly and hoping for a different answer. And for a minute, I thought it was going to break me—that it was a law of the universe that would never be disproven—no matter how hard I tried.

They'd even name it after me—Copeland's law of becoming your parents. At least if it happens, I'll go down in history.

"You won't. I promise," he says and kisses me hard. "I will always order you girly drinks, sacrifice my esophagus for you, play any sex game you're down for, tell you how much I love you every single day, be part of your family, and wrap you up in a blanket when we fight."

"You turned me into a crazy person," I tease.

"I like you a little crazy. Will you serial date me, Ryan?"

"I love you," I reply, nodding against his lips, "and I don't have any more Xs in me."

"I have one," Grey laughs and pinches my waist. "Fuck you. I cannot love a woman who isn't Ryan Walker Copeland."

I kiss him hard back and try to rack my brain for some statistics. "How many Ryan Walker Copelands do you think are out there?"

"No one else is you, so exactly one. And she loves me," he says, playing my ass like drums. "Now, let's go take a shower and get ready for this wedding. Did you know this week isn't about us?"

I hug his neck tight.

"But the week after?" Grey laughs and starts walking back toward the hotel. "And the week after that? And the week after that one? Fair game."

Life is beautiful.

One day at a time.

One week at a time.

One month. One year.

All of them are filled with the people and things that I like and love, and that's all I can really ask for.

<u>26</u>

Grey, One Sunday Nine Months Later

I KNOCK ON Lily's door.

The sound echoes into the empty hallway. It's a dull white, but the walls have been decorated with colorful artwork that I stop to look at every time they put up something new—which is often, because people who aren't Lily enjoy art class.

The piece I drew last week of the five of us—me, Lily, my parents, and Ryan—sitting on Lily's brand-new sofa is hanging to the left of her blue door. I recreated it from a photo we took after we moved Lily into her apartment last month.

When the door swings open, her roommate, Hannah, doesn't recognize me.

"Hey," I start. "Is—"

"Grey!" Lily cries from somewhere in the living room. When she steps into view, she tells Hannah, "That's my brother."

Hannah smiles. "Sorry. Come in."

"It's nice to see you again," I say, stepping past her.

I hold up the pizza I brought. Lily hugs me tight, but her face falls when she realizes I'm alone. I've been demoted to second-best for at least six months now, and I'm not even mad about it. I know Ryan's the better half. "Where's Ryan?"

"I'm going to see her this time in San Diego. I was coming to see you before I leave early tomorrow morning." I cross her living room and sit down on her sofa. I put the pizza box down to pick up the remote and scroll through Netflix.

Lily's recently watched movies are definitely not her usual taste. I see action, action, horror, action.

I raise an eyebrow at Lily, who catches what I'm looking at. Her cheeks and the tips of her ears turn the slightest pink.

Surprising myself, I hold back a smile. No wonder she and Ryan were whispering with their heads together last time while they were hanging clothes in the closet.

After years of worrying about this moment, it's here, but all I feel is happiness for Lily. She won't sell herself short, and she can tell me when she's ready.

I let the moment pass. "What movie are we watching?"

"Will she come see me next time?" she asks, ignoring me and curling up into my side. "I wanted to show her how I decorated my room."

"Of course. She wouldn't miss seeing you while she was here. Besides, we saw her last month when we moved you in."

Lily pouts. "I want to see her all the time though."

I stress out a laugh under my breath. "Me and you both, Lily."

The past nine months have been incredible.

Ryan and I haven't gone more than eight weeks without seeing each other. Sometimes I fly to San Diego, sometimes she flies here. It's going exactly like I told her it would, how I knew it would.

And the past nine months have been incredibly hard. I can't talk to her when I want to, or put my hands on her waist when I need to, or kiss her whenever I feel like it.

But that doesn't mean I'm quitting.

In fact, it's the opposite. I've started the motions: talking to my realtor about selling or renting out my house, feeling out how Patrick feels if I work from San Diego and not Los Angeles most days—though he should feel grateful I'm going to quit the new, serious corporate job I enjoy and only has Ryan to profusely thank.

But then there's Lily. I don't know how to feel about that yet. I tell myself nothing will happen tomorrow. But maybe it will happen one day soon. Maybe one day soon I'll feel better about it.

I'm going to talk to Ryan about it this week. After I talk to Lily about it right now.

I put the remote down next to me.

"Lily, how would you feel if you saw me as often as you see Ryan?"

"Sad," she says matter-of-factly.

I slide the pizza box across the coffee table toward me and flip it open. I need something to do with my hands before I peel off my cuticles.

"Do you think you'd be less sad now that you have a new house and friends?" I ask, offering her the largest pepperoni slice. "You're busy with your classes and your job now. Would that make it easier?"

"Maybe." She chews on her bite quietly. "I'll miss you like I miss Ryan. Where are you going?"

I stuff my face and mumble through the cheese to hide my emotions. "Maybe San Diego, where Ryan lives. You could come visit whenever you want, and I would come see you every couple of months. San Diego is fun. It's always sunny in California, and there's the ocean and the beach."

"I love the beach," she says. "But you're going to San Diego tomorrow, and then you're coming back."

"I'll always come back. It might just be longer in between."

"Ryan can come here and live with you, so then I have both of you."

I shake my head. "It's not that easy. She just got a big promotion at work, and there aren't many jobs for her here."

"She can work at the coffee shop," Lily offers.

"Maybe so," I say. "She doesn't want you to be sad."

"I don't want you to be sad either."

"I'm not sad."

"You look sad sometimes when we watch movies."

"I just miss her." I look out the window behind Lily's head to hold back tears.

"I know," she replies, hugging me. "You love her and she's far away."

That's my whole problem.

San Diego. Austin. California. Texas. Thirteen hundred miles separate them. Ryan's in one. Lily's in the other.

When I get there, it's the same thing, different city.

× × ×

I ZIP MY suitcase closed and make sure I have my wallet and driver's license for the tenth time.

Then my nerves redirect themselves to cleaning as a way to distract myself because I'll never be able to go to sleep.

I start in the kitchen and pick up the dried flower petals lingering on the counter. I haven't been able to bring myself to throw away the dead bouquet that Ryan put in my one vase a month ago.

Next I scrub the stove raw.

This might be the first time I've ever been nervous to talk to Ryan, because I think she's going to tell me no. She's going to tell me that it's not the right time, that Lily needs more time, that I like my new job and team too much to quit, that Patrick's not even ready, that I'm rushing it. And then I'm scared she's going to think she was right, that this isn't going to work, that I can't do long distance, because she thinks I can't even last a year.

I give myself a little credit though since I've lasted nine times longer than the first time, but I don't really care how long it takes. One day at a time is what I'll keep doing for the rest of my life, because the few days I have with her in person every other month are worth more than having any other woman here with me every day.

After I dump out all of the old containers of food stacked in my fridge, I cinch the garbage bag closed and yank it from my trash can.

It's dark and chilly when I step outside. A U-Haul truck swings around the corner too tight and clips the stop sign. I wince at the scraping of metal on metal but pretend I didn't see it as I walk around the side of my house.

I'm not getting involved in that shit, and I have better things to worry about. I let the outside trash can slap shut and pull out my phone to text my next door neighbor.

Hey, man. I'll be out of town tomorrow through Sunday. Can you please put my trash out on Wednesday so the HOA doesn't flip their shit about it being on the curb for multiple days?

Nothing screams *I'm an adult* quite like that.

I text Ryan, **Are you still going to love me when I'm yelling at kids to get off my lawn?**

I wait a few seconds to see if she responds immediately, but I don't get that lucky. This is why I need her near me at all times, so I can tell her every jewel that pops into my head as soon as it happens and then kiss her.

Also, it's too cold here for March, just so you know, I add, wondering why I'm still standing here freezing my ass off.

When I round the corner back to my front yard, there she is

standing at the bottom of my steps and staring at my front door like I conjured her out of thin air with my wishful thinking.

I can't believe that's worked twice for me now.

There's no mistaking her from the way her reddish curls fall over her shoulders, from the curve of her perfect ass, from the slight scowl she has while she's trying to figure out something in her mind.

It takes everything in me not to jump her, but I choose restraint so I don't scare the shit out of her.

"Ryan."

She snaps her head toward me, wide-eyed. Her smile starts slowly, hesitant, like she's unsure if she's about to make me mad.

"I'm homeless," she says.

I think I teleported in front of her face. I'm kissing her lips, her neck. I'm wrapping my arms around her tiny frame, picking her up, suffocating her from how tight I'm holding her.

"What?" I say, dropping her back to her feet when I realize what she said. "I'm supposed to fly to San Diego in the morning."

"Are you going to yell at me to get off your lawn?" She motions to the moving truck that she just hit a stop sign with. "Because my entire life is in that truck."

I narrow my eyes. I have every reason to be mad. I'd be angrier if she wasn't so goddamn sexy and not here in the flesh, but I try my best. "What about San Diego? Your apartment? Your job? Your friends? I didn't ask you to give up all of that for me. You should have talked to me. And now I have to fix a stop sign tomorrow. Otherwise, the HOA will send out an email asking for Ring camera footage."

Ryan waves me off. "When I got off the plane last time, I realized I didn't want to be there. I think it happened slowly, piece by piece, visit by visit, but it isn't home anymore. When I realized, the first thing I did was break my lease, and it turns out, my boss didn't want to lose me. I'm pretty persuasive when Sage puts together a *successful* PR campaign." She bats her eyelashes up into my face. "You're looking at the new consultant for my firm, so I get to do math at my computer in my pajamas. And my friends understand. They're the kind that help you move. Basically family."

"But—"

"Grey," she cuts me off and wraps her little arms around my waist. I stay firm and stand there awkwardly with my arms down stick straight. "I love you because you laugh off most things, because you are selfless, because you always challenge and surprise me, you always talk to me, because your family is important to you, and because I love fighting with you. I love you because you gave me Hawaii, and I'm not going to take Austin from you."

"But…" I can't remember what argument I'm trying to make because Ryan's hair smells like her citrus shampoo, and it's been too long since she was this close. "You shouldn't have done all of that for me. Why didn't you talk to me? That's one of the things on your 'reasons to love me' list."

She lets out an annoyed breath, along with, "Stop being so damn annoyingly you," and stands on her tiptoes as high as she can reach to press her lips against mine.

"Dammit, Ryan," I mutter into her mouth, giving in and pulling her into me as close as I can manage. "I can't stay mad at you for longer than two minutes."

She shrugs. "That's what I was counting on. Obviously."

"Sounds like you figured it all out," I say against her cheek.

She shakes her head. "I still have one problem."

"What?" I sigh.

"I'm homeless."

This is the point where I realize I never stray more than five feet from the ring I bought nine months ago.

I don't know what I expected. I don't have an elaborate plan. I have no planned speech. It's these little slices of time that are my favorite. It's been chilling in my pocket because I knew one day this moment would come out of nowhere, the feeling Ryan always gives me—sudden longing and desperation, like she sustains life in me—and I'd have to propose that very second.

It's slow motion watching Ryan's face change as I bend down on one knee and open the little black velvet box. Her blue eyes, welling with tears, bounce back and forth between mine and the diamond ring that she described to me over five years ago.

"God, Ryan, have you even rung the doorbell yet? He's not going to be pissed, and I have to pee."

I close my eyes for a second before I crane my neck to see Sage, who must have materialized from the back of the truck, staring at us with her mouth agape.

"Holy fuck," she says. "I'll pee in the street."

I look back at Ryan who is about to dissolve into a fit of teary giggles.

"Ryan Copeland," I power on, "you wouldn't be you if you weren't laughing right now, and I wouldn't be me if I wasn't loving you. There is no one else I'd ever want to call me their husband, and I promise that I will love you to the absolute best of my ability for the rest of my life. Will you marry me and do me the honor of becoming my wife?"

She nods frantically. "Yes." Then she leans down to kiss me and rub my face with her tears. "Yes. I've never wanted anything as badly in my life than to become Ryan Beckett. I'm no one else but myself with you, and I love you more than I can comprehend, Grey."

I slide the ring on her finger as slowly as I can, but honestly, I'm so eager, I'd toss it over my shoulder and carry her to the courthouse right now. I do kind of want to go to Hawaii though.

I scoop her up under her butt as I stand.

She places her head against my shoulder and admires the solitaire emerald cut. She's studying the lines she once told me she likes because they are geometric.

"It's beautiful," she whispers. "When did you get this ring?"

"The week I got back from Colorado," I laugh.

"You remembered," she whispers.

"Of course. I remember everything you tell me. Everyone else, not so much." I kiss her on the head. "Come on, Sage," I call over my shoulder.

"You ruined our engagement," Ryan laughs happily at her. "I'm never going to let you live that down."

"Is Evie here too?" I ask Ryan.

"No, her doctor wouldn't let her drive cross-country nine months pregnant, and I didn't want to have to deliver my goddaughter in the back of a moving truck. I'm going back in a couple weeks anyway because I'm not missing that little girl's appearance."

"*We're* not missing it," I correct her. "I'm the favorite godfather."

"You're the only godfather," Ryan jokes before she lowers her voice. "And I'm already the favorite godmother."

"I heard that!" The night air carries Sage's voice across the dead silent street behind us as I carry Ryan up the stairs, and Sage follows behind. "You know what? I'm not even upset I ruined that. You can't be mad at me, Grey. I missed out on the whole Ryan thinking she ruined Evie's wedding thing, and then I missed Elliot carrying Evie off for a secret mistaken-baby-making romp, and *then* I missed you two making up. I'm just happy I get to finally be a part of something, and you have to include me now every time you tell the engagement story. I'm crucial."

"It's only fitting though that you interrupted it with your commentary, Sage," I tease her. "I wouldn't have wanted it to go any other way."

I hold Ryan up with one arm and swing open my door with the other.

The kiss she gives me sucks my heart right out of my chest like she's claiming it. It's hers though. It always has been. And as soon as I asked her her middle name almost seven years ago, I knew I'd never get it back.

She smiles up at me when I cross the threshold.

"I love you, Ryan Walker. Welcome home."

Acknowledgments

I didn't write one of these in my first book.

If you can believe it, three people read that book before I edited and published it myself. I'm very proud of it, but secretly. I can still count on two hands the number of people in my real life who know I write books.

Maybe the fact that I have now written two makes me feel less like a fraud—or maybe not.

This time though, I want to thank all of those people who put up with me through all of this.

My sister-in-law, who is the first to read anything I write, even though she doesn't do romance and still tells/lies to me that she likes mine anyway. I'm sorry I send you an updated version whenever I change a comma. Go enjoy a murder mystery now.

My best friend, who reads non-fiction over fiction but still insists that I can keep her attention and my books are good. (Obviously, I never trust anyone who knows me to tell me the truth with this writing business.) Thank you for giving me the idea for this book, and I wish that you didn't live eight hours away.

Rachel LaBerge for being the best author-to-real-life friend, who reads my drafts and puts up with my idiotic questions *and* has held my hand as I try to actually "market" a book. You gave me invaluable voice texts and ideas that I will forever be grateful for.

Laura Parker, who takes my rambling texts and turns them into beautiful artwork. You always happily change the slightest thing so I can visually see it, and I am so appreciative that I know you. I couldn't have asked for someone better to walk through every step of this with me. And you can officially say you've fulfilled your college dream, because you've now designed not one but two book covers.

My early readers Mariah, Jo, Colleen, Meagan, and Caroline for your attention to detail and your honest thoughts on what works and what doesn't. I couldn't have shaped this story without you.

To my husband, who lets it slip that I'm an author and is the reason I can count on two hands and not one the amount of people who know. You put up with these fictional worlds consuming my life sometimes, and I always, *always* choose you to spend my real days, weeks, months, and years with.

To my children who are my world and are too young to know I write—but maybe that's a good thing because you'll probably be embarrassed one day that I write sex scenes when Daddy lets it slip.

And lastly to my readers. Thank you for picking this book up and taking a chance on me, on an unknown author, on an indie author. This is hard, and if even just one of you liked this book, it made it all worth it.

Titles by Grace Pearce

× × ×

Leigh Makes Three
The Ex List